# Mary Balogh

# The Double Wager

A SIGNET BOOK

## NEW AMERICAN LIBRARY

SIGNET, SIGNET CLASSIC, MENTOR, PLUME, MERIDIAN AND NAL BOOKS
are published by New American Library,
1633 Broadway, New York, New York 10019

First Printing, June, 1985

1  2  3  4  5  6  7  8  9

PRINTED IN THE UNITED STATES OF AMERICA

# SIGNET Regency Romances You'll Enjoy

# THE DISCONCERTING DUKE

*Miss Henrietta Tallant met the Duke of Eversleigh for the first time at a ball—when she tripped over her own feet in a waltz and stumbled over her own words in conversation.*

*Then he appeared again—in her drawing room.*

*"Miss Tallant," he said, in a languid tone that belied his clear strength of person and authority of bearing, "I can see it is useless to try to make polite small talk with you. I shall get immediately to the point. Will you do me the honor of becoming my wife?"*

*Henry's jaw dropped. "Your wife?" she said faintly.*

*"I have taken you by surprise, I see," said the Duke. "Should I have paved the way more carefully by falling on my knees and declaring undying love and devotion? I can still do so if you wish."*

*Henry stood frozen. She had only to say yes to possess everything any young lady could want . . . any young lady but her. . . .*

# ❧ THE DOUBLE WAGER ❧

# CHAPTER

————————◦◦◦————————

# 1

"It's a melancholy fact," philosophized the young dandy Viscount Darnley, squinting through the brandy in his raised glass, "life ain't what it used to be." He turned his whole body and eyed the faces of his companions. His head would not move without taking his torso with it, imprisoned as it was between the high points of his starched collar.

"Darnley's right for once!" The haughty voice belonged to Sir Wilfred Denning, a satin-clad exquisite, who threw down his cards on the table and yawned delicately behind a white, well-manicured hand. The same hand patted his fair curls to make sure that no hair had strayed from the careful coiffure during the exertions of the game he had just played, and lost. "One wonders if any of us will be left at the end of another five years."

Rufus Smythe, at the other side of the card table, checked the folds of his neckcloth, smoothed white lace over the backs of his hands, and gathered together the guineas and vouchers he had just won. He tried to feign indifference, as if the winnings would not be the first hard cash to line his pockets for several weeks.

"Poor Hanley," he commented. "One wonders which one of us will be the next to go."

"Poor" Hanley was slumped in the depths of a leather chair drawn close to a dying log fire. He sighed pitifully, not removing his eyes from the blaze. "Mama insisted," he said plaintively.

"A life sentence, Hanley," Sir Wilfred reminded him.

"She wouldn't take no for an answer," Hanley explained. "Then Papa took her part. Ganged up on me."

"I say, old fellow, that wasn't too sporting, you know. Gad, it's too bad when a fellow's father throws in the chips with his mama on a subject like this." The speaker, Lord Rowland Horton, a small, vivacious man, made his way from a sideboard, where he had been replenishing some empty glasses, and handed one to his luckless friend.

"He never could withstand her," Hanley bleated. "Nobody can. My brother-in-law tried when he married Fanny. He ended up getting a post in India and taking my sister with him. Said he would rather risk the fever there than have to pay duty calls on Mama at least once a month."

Having finished this long speech, Hanley lapsed into his former semicomatose state, the now-almost-empty glass of port dangling from his limp fingers.

Lord Horton stood in the middle of the floor and let his glance stray around the room to take in the other ten occupants. All were in a state of dejection induced by hours of drinking and playing cards, and by the melancholy of the occasion. He smiled.

"Well, gentlemen," he began, "our number is now down to ten, not counting Hanley, who is, to all intents and purposes, a goner. What is to happen to the Knights of Freedom Club? Are we to renew our vows and continue, or have we all changed our convictions since we began with such high ideals eight years ago? There were seventeen of us then."

"It was all very well eight years ago to pledge our allegiance to the single state," Smythe said hesitantly, playing with the lace at his wrist. "It seemed a noble idea then to swear to uphold one another in our resolve never to marry. But, dash it all," he said, looking defiantly at several of his companions, "what's a fellow to do when his pockets are to let? The dice cannot always be relied upon to bring one around. I have to eye the market, I have to admit. Not a happy prospect, but there it is. Almack's! Ugh!" He shuddered delicately.

"Poor Hanley's problem is that his mama wants him connected to a title," Darnley said in a hushed voice, as if he were talking about someone already deceased. "An earl's daughter was too much for her to resist."

"Why do earls' daughters always have pimples or big noses or flat chests?" Denning wanted to know, testing his curls again with a light touch.

"You're very quiet, Eversleigh," Lord Horton commented, turning everyone's attention to the man who was lounging elegantly against the mantel. He was a tall man, dressed all in black, with the exception of his white shirt points, which were not as high as those of the dandified Darnley, and the white neckcloth, which was not as intricately tied as that of Rufus Smythe. Beneath dark hair, brushed forward in a fashionable Brutus style, his face was thin and sharply drawn. He had a strong jawline, lips that were habitually drawn into a thin line, a straight nose, and blue eyes that were usually partly hidden behind half-closed eyelids. His whole stance suggested a lazy boredom. Only a close observer would have noticed that the broad shoulders, slim waist, and muscled calves owed nothing to a tailor's tricks—corsets and padding and such. A close observer might also have noticed that the eyes behind the lazy lids were unusually keen.

"Well, what do you say, Eversleigh?" Horton prompted. "Are you in this to the bitter end? Are you prepared to die a bachelor in your eighty-fifth year or thereabouts?" He grinned.

Marius Devron, Duke of Eversleigh, lifted a quizzing glass, his only ornament, to his eye without hurry and surveyed his friend's grinning face.

"Well, it's like this, Horton," he said at last. "We were young puppies, were we not, and assumed that the realities of life need never catch up to us. A foolish notion, of course." He lowered the quizzing glass and glanced cynically at the almost-unconscious figure of Hanley.

"The realities of life?" Sir Wilfred prompted.

"The need for alliances and such." Eversleigh waved a languid hand in the air, his elbow still resting on the mantel.

"It's all very well for you to talk so scathingly," Smythe complained. "You have no need to marry money, Marius. You're as rich as Croesus. And you don't need to marry position. You can't get much higher than duke. You really do not need to marry at all. You can keep the club going single-handed when the rest of us have been forced to bow out. And you have the delectable Mrs. Broughton as a, er, companion."

Eversleigh raised his quizzing glass again and surveyed an uncomfortable Rufus Smythe in silence for a long moment.

"Ah," he said with amiable languor, "but you forget the craving of every man to perpetuate his dynasty, my dear fellow. Even I, I find, shudder at the prospect of being the last of my line. Wives, alas, become necessary evils when one's thoughts turn in such a direction."

"Marius!" Lord Horton bounced across the room to clap his friend heartily on the shoulder. "You aren't actually contemplating matrimony, are you, old boy? You? You have so perfected the art of totally ignoring each year's crop of debutantes and freezing out their hopeful mamas, that you would not know how to start choosing, would you, old fellow?"

"Do you have someone in mind, Eversleigh?" Darnley asked gloomily.

"My betrothed has a sister," said the sepulchral voice of Hanley, who still had not moved a muscle as he sat on in his chair. "Not quite so spotty, either."

"Choosing is a simple task," Eversleigh said.

"Eh?" asked Sir Wilfred.

Eversleigh made the supreme effort of pushing himself away from the mantel and strolling over to the sideboard to pour himself more brandy.

"Choosing a carriage is a difficult task," he said as he returned to the group. "One has to consider style, height, springs, upholstery, color. Choosing a horse is even more ticklish. It should take days and much sober consideration. Choosing a wife is simple. If she is young and virgin, why look farther?"

"Spots," muttered Hanley.

"There are plenty without," Eversleigh replied, lowering himself languidly into the nearest chair. "And I have never observed that beauty ensures good performance in bed, anyway, my dear chap."

"It certainly helps outside bed, though," Horton said with a laugh.

"Perhaps." Eversleigh shrugged.

"I'll wager that you would not really choose so carelessly if it came to the point, though, Marius," Sir Wilfred Denning said.

Eversleigh considered the words at his leisure. "Ah, but it has come to the point," he said.

Horton threw back his head and laughed. "You can't be serious, old boy," he said. "You really want us to believe that you would go out and grab the first female you see just because you have taken it into your head that you wish to be a papa?"

His laughter became less hearty when the quizzing glass was raised again and his friend's half-closed eye, magnified out of all proportion to the rest of his face, was fixed on him again. "Ah, but it is not so much my paternal instinct that motivates me," he said softly. "I really cannot imagine being fond of any person below the age of five and twenty. It is my dislike of my present heir that disconcerts me."

"Can't say I blame you, Eversleigh," Darnley said sympathetically. "Oliver Cranshawe ain't everyone's cup of tea. The ladies love him, of course. Oozes charm."

"He's a smarmy devil, right enough," Denning agreed.

"Is he giving you a rough time, old boy?" Horton asked.

"Nothing I can't handle," the duke replied. "But I find it does not help one's digestion too much to have the fellow inviting himself to breakfast and making a mental count of every silver fork and spoon on the table and sideboard. Especially when one knows that one is being mentally consigned six feet under at the same time."

"I'll still wager that you are not serious about choosing a wife at random, though, Marius," Denning persisted. "Why, it was you, man, who suggested our forming this club eight years ago, and you have been its staunchest supporter."

Eversleigh drank slowly from his glass. For a while it seemed as if he would not answer. Eventually he looked up at Sir Wilfred, his eyes keen behind the heavy lids, a cynical smile playing about his lips.

"Now what would that wager be, Wilfred?" he asked.

Sir Wilfred leaned back in his chair and steepled his smooth fingers beneath his chin. The light of a new game shone in his eyes. In fact, all the occupants of the room suddenly looked less melancholy and riveted their attention on the two central players.

"If you are serious, Marius," Sir Wilfred said, "I wish to see your betrothal announcement in the *Morning Post* within the month and your marriage vows given within two."

Eversleigh's eyes were steady on his challenger. The smile that was not quite a smile curled one side of his mouth even further. "Ah, but you make things almost too simple, Wilfred," he said quietly.

Sir Wilfred smiled too. "Very well, Marius. If you insist on talking yourself into a quite impossible corner. Shall we say six weeks?"

Eversleigh's expression remained unchanged.

"I say, old boy," Horton said, interrupting the air of interested tension in the room, "aren't you acting rather hastily here? As Wilfred said a while ago, we are talking life sentences here, you know. It's no topic for a light bet, Marius."

Eversleigh showed no sign of having heard him. "And if I win?" he asked Denning.

Sir Wilfred considered for a moment. "I have too much regard for your good sense to believe that you will carry this through, Marius," he said. Then he smiled. "If you win, Eversleigh, my matched grays."

Eversleigh's brows rose. "You must be confident, my dear chap," he said lazily. "I have been trying all winter to get you to sell me those horses. And now you are prepared to give them away?"

"I do not believe I am in any danger," Sir Wilfred replied.

Eversleigh raised his quizzing glass and surveyed the other steadily. "And if I lose, Wilfred?"

Denning did not twitch a facial muscle. He paused for effect, until all attention was focused on his answer. "Mrs. Suzanne Broughton," he said finally.

Eversleigh lowered the quizzing glass unhurriedly. He rose to his feet and sauntered to the sideboard again, where he took his time to refill his glass. He crossed the room again and took up his old position against the mantel.

"I have no intention of losing this wager, Denning," he

said, "but even if I did, how can I give what is not mine to give? Mrs. Broughton is her own person, dear boy. She clearly has a mind of her own. I am not even her, er, protector, you know."

"We all know what you are to Suzanne," Sir Wilfred said. "But let us face facts, Marius. If you would take your title and your wealth and your damned good looks out of the way, I have reason to believe I would stand next in line to her good graces."

"Ha! The modesty of the man!" observed Horton.

"All I ask, Marius," Sir Wilfred continued, directing a quelling look at Horton and patting his curls into place again, "is that you undertake to cut all ties with the lady if you lose this wager."

Eversleigh considered. "You would leave me very womanless, would you not, Wilfred?" he observed dryly.

"A true knight of freedom!" someone remarked.

Eversleigh pulled himself upright and extended his right hand to Sir Wilfred Denning. "I accept the wager," he said.

"Splendid!" Rufus Smythe declared. "Bring us the betting book, Horton, and let us have the matter properly recorded."

It was duly entered into the book that by Friday, May 25, four weeks from the date of the entry, the Duke of Eversleigh's engagement to a lady as yet unknown must be publicly announced, and that his marriage must take place on or before Friday, June 8. If either event did not transpire, the duke was to break off all connections with the widow Mrs. Suzanne Broughton. If both events occurred on or before the dates specified, Sir Wilfred Denning was to relinquish to the duke his pair of matched gray horses. Both men signed their names to the bet. Sir Rowland Horton and another member of the club signed as witnesses.

Soon afterward, Rufus Smythe decided that it was time to see "poor" Hanley home to his bed. A hackney was summoned and the inert form of the unhappily betrothed man was carried out to it. His departure was a signal for the breakup of the whole party, it being little short of three o'clock in the morning.

Sir Rowland Horton walked home with the Duke of

Eversleigh, his own home being close to the duke's residence on Curzon Street.

"You're going to regret this wager in the cold light of day, dear boy," he said, shrugging deeper inside his greatcoat as the chill of the April night penetrated his consciousness.

"I think not, Rowland," the duke replied coolly. "A wife I must have. I cannot imagine ever finding a woman whose companionship I would enjoy for the rest of my life. Taking time to make a choice would be a pointless exercise. Anyone will do."

Horton laughed uneasily. "Why not Suzanne, Marius? She is beautiful, witty, experienced, and I am sure she would have you at the drop of a hat."

Eversleigh cocked one eyebrow and glanced sidelong at his friend. "Are you quite mad, Rowland?" he asked. "Marry my mistress? The situation would be quite intolerable."

"Why so?" Horton persisted. "It would not be like marrying a light-skirt. Suzanne is accepted by all the highest sticklers; she is independently wealthy."

"She also knows our world too well from the inside," Eversleigh reminded him cynically. "One would not be able to live one's own life and forget her existence during the day. She would demand too much. And frankly, Rowland, I would not bet on her fidelity. As things are now, it matters not to me if someone else occasionally occupies my place in her bed. But to be a cuckolded husband, Rowland? It is out of the question."

"Well, never say I did not warn you," his friend concluded sagely.

"You may depend upon it," Eversleigh assured him, slowing his steps as they approached the gate of Horton's house. "Will you be at Jackson's in the morning?"

"Yes, I think I shall need a good workout at the punching balls," Horton said, patting ruefully his liquor-filled stomach.

"I shall see you there, then," Eversleigh said. "Good night."

Later the same day, in a remote corner of the estate belonging to Sir Peter Tallant in Sussex, four youths could be seen walking their horses on one side of a hedge, keeping to the shade. They were avoiding the unexpected heat of the April afternoon sun, having galloped and dared one another over fences for the past hour or more.

George Hyde and Douglas Raeburn were spending the day with their longtime neighbor and friend Giles Tallant. Henry Tallant had tagged along with them, as so often happened. The three friends were reminiscing about their days together at Oxford University, now still in recess for Easter. Henry listened with avid interest.

"Do you remember old Boner's face when Freddie Cox smuggled Bessie Lane into the dorm one night and then took her out the front door the next morning as bold as you please?" Douglas said.

There were three hearty guffaws.

"What happened?" asked Henry.

"They met old Boner, our warden, at the bottom of the stairs," Giles explained. "He turned six shades of purple."

"Old Cox didn't turn a hair," George continued. "He introduced Bessie to old Boner with as much civility as if she had been a lady being presented at court. And old Boner was so taken aback, he bowed as formal as you please, and said, 'How d'ye do, ma'am?' After that, he could not very well do anything to Cox. He just pretended to forget the whole incident."

This time there were four guffaws.

"The funniest part was that, as he bowed, old Bessie curtsied," Douglas chortled. "He got more of an eyeful than he had ever had in his life, I'm willing to bet."

Giles cleared his throat and the three friends suddenly showed signs of discomfort. Douglas glanced furtively at Henry.

Henry stared candidly back. "You mean she had a large bosom?"

Douglas suddenly found it imperative to check his horse's shoes. He muttered something about suspecting that the horse was limping.

Giles and Henry strolled ahead. They were remarkably alike in appearance, both slim and lithe and youthful. Both had short, tumbled auburn curls, healthy suntanned faces, and sparkling eyes. Both were dressed informally in breeches and loose-fitting shirts, open at the neck. The only noticeable difference was that Henry was a head shorter than Giles.

"Well, this is it, then," Giles said, smiling ruefully down at his companion, "our farewell to Roedean Manor. Tomorrow we will be on our way to London. And I suppose life will never be quite the same again."

"When Papa died last year," Henry said seriously, "and Peter inherited, it seemed like a blessing that a year of mourning had to be observed. It seemed like such a reprieve when Peter allowed the twins and me to spend the year here instead of dragging us immediately to London."

"Yes, but time passes so quickly," sighed Giles.

"And it is quite horrid to think of having to move to town," Henry agreed. "I don't think I can live without room in which to move. Papa was such a brick. He let us grow up as we wished and never cared for appearances. And he never ever suggested removing any of us to London."

"The twins will be like monkeys in a cage, too," Giles said. "Before we know it, Peter will have Phil at Eton, and poor Penny will be learning embroidery and pianoforte and such."

"Ugh!" Henry sympathized. "If it weren't Peter, of all people, that we have to live with! Can you believe that he is our own brother, Giles? He is so prosy and starchy. And our sister-in-law, Marian!" Henry rolled bright eyes to the sky.

"Well, there is nothing we can do about it," Giles said philosophically. He snickered suddenly. "Can you see Marian's face when the twins arrive with Brutus? She will not know whether to put the dog into a kennel or a stable."

"Well, he is rather large," Henry conceded. "Let us just hope, Giles, that he does not take a liking to Marian. She may find herself on her back half the time fending off his loving tongue."

They both snorted with mirth.

"What about Oscar?" Giles said, and they both doubled up with loud glee.

"He is rather a naughty parrot," Henry allowed. "The landlord of the Pigeon should never have given Philip leave to bring him home. Goodness knows who abandoned him at the inn."

"Probably someone who could not tolerate his bad language any longer," Giles suggested. "But really, Henry, the one I feel most sorry for is Manny. You know how she can be reduced to a quivering jelly by anyone who says a cross word to her. And I think old Peter and Marian will be blaming her for your lack of behavior, not to mention the twins."

"That would be most unfair," Henry said, temper flaring in defense of their longtime governess, Miss Eugenia Manford. "Manny does her best. Can she be blamed if we have learned to twist her around our little fingers? And I shall tell Peter so, you may be sure."

George Hyde and Douglas Raeburn had caught up with them by this time. "It is certainly going to be different around here without any Tallants living at Roedean," George said.

"It is all very well for you to talk," Henry said, "and for Giles, too. You can be at university and have lots of fun. And Giles will not miss Roedean as I will. Even during the Christmas vacation he stayed in London most of the time, socializing."

"Well, if it's socializing you want, Henry"—Giles grinned—"you will soon have plenty of it."

"You are not going to mention that, are you?" Henry asked with a menacing frown.

"From tomorrow on, my dear Henrietta," her brother taunted, "it is going to be ball dresses and slippers and frizzed curls and bonnets and gloves for you. And balls and breakfasts and routs. Marian has your come-out all planned, you know."

"Don't be horrid!" Henry said, throwing herself in fury at her brother's chest and punching him soundly with flailing fists.

"Hey, watch it, you little termagent," he yelped between laughs. He grabbed for her wrists. "There will be a line of suitors a mile long coming to throw themselves at your feet, and bouquets and posies and proposals by the score," he continued, tempting fate.

"Oh, you!" Henry blustered, aiming a kick at her brother's shin. "I should rather die. I won't do it, so there! And I shall tell Marian so, too. She can't force me into anything so horrid."

"I don't think you need worry, anyway, Henry," Douglas said soothingly, but not too wisely, "I don't think you are in any danger of taking with the *ton*."

"Oh?" Henry had gone very still, her fight with her brother forgotten.

While George coughed warningly and Giles grinned appreciatively, Douglas continued. "Well, look at you, Henry," he said. "Even with girl's clothes on, you look rather like a boy masquerading. You do not do anything as ladies do."

"I do not have a large bosom, either, Douglas," she said, fixing him with a severe eye.

He had the grace to blush. "I was just trying to reassure you that you do not have to worry about attracting the men," he mumbled uneasily.

"Do you want to bet?"

"A wager? You see what I mean, Henry?" he said in exasperation. "Ladies do not make wagers."

"This lady does. This lady will wager that she can find a husband during the Season."

Douglas sneered. "Which Season, though, Henry?"

"This Season," she snapped, her temper rising. "And I shall go one step further, Mr. Raeburn. I am willing to wager that I can win an offer within six weeks from now."

"It would be almost a sin to accept such a wager," Douglas replied.

"Ha, you're afraid of losing," Henry goaded.

"Just a moment, you two," Giles said, holding up his hand for peace, but grinning hugely. "You have made it rather easy for her, y'know, Doug. You don't know Henry. She is quite capable of collaring some poor puppy and forcing him to offer for her. No challenge in that."

"I always play fair!" she cut in indignantly.

"Cool down, Sis," Giles continued. "What you need to do, Doug, is to pin her down to one particular man."

"Good idea," said George. "Who, though?"

The three young men leaned against their horses and thought, while Henry hovered in the background, glowering.

"Cavendish?" suggested Douglas.

"No," said Giles after a moment's consideration, "he

ain't got a chin. I wouldn't want m'nephews and nieces to
be chinless."

They thought again.

"Blaisdale?" George suggested.

"No good," Giles said again. "He has to dangle after an
heiress. Pockets to let all the time. Henry ain't rich. How
about Eversleigh?"

There was a short, stunned silence, and the three friends
burst into laughter.

"No, it would be too cruel," Douglas said. "No wager at
all."

"What is wrong with him?" Henry asked, brows knit.

"The Duke of Eversleigh is about as starchy as they
come, Henry," Giles explained kindly. "He's incredibly
high in the instep. If he notices you at all, he looks at you
through his eyeglass as if you were a toad who has dared
to inhabit the same planet as he. And he never takes any
notice at all of the young girls. Even the most persistent
mamas have given up on him."

"He'll do," Henry decided. "I'll get him to offer for
me."

A roar of unrestrained glee greeted this announcement.

"Within six weeks, Henry?" George asked.

"Of course," she answered. "What is so difficult about
ensnaring a conceited town fop?"

"Town fop? Eversleigh? Oh, Lord," Giles gasped, col-
lapsing into laughter again.

"I don't have to marry him, anyway," Henry decided
crossly. "The wager is only that I receive a proposal. Is it
not, Douglas?"

"Oh, I say," he said, "how will I know that you tell the
truth if you don't marry the man to prove it?"

Both Henry and Giles stiffened. "My sister don't lie,"
Giles said, all laughter wiped from his face.

"It don't signify, anyway," George said practically. "She
ain't going to win."

Henry clucked her tongue in impatience. "Let us get to
the point," she said. "What do I win if you lose this wager,
Douglas?"

He considered for a moment. "A new high-perch phaeton for a wedding present," he said.

"I say!" she replied, surprised. "That is splendid of you. Can you afford it, Douglas?"

He bowed stiffly. "That ain't a ladylike question, Henry."

"What must I forfeit in the unlikely event that I lose?" she asked airily.

He grinned. "Your horse will do," he said, glancing appreciatively at the gleaming black coat of the stallion she held by the reins.

"Jet?" she said uncertainly. "He was Papa's."

"Yes, but he's yours now, Henry. You won't have much use for him in London, anyway. And you would have to learn to ride him sidesaddle."

"Oh, I never would!" she exclaimed in dismay.

"Then it will be just as well to lose him to me," he said smugly.

"He will never be yours, Douglas," she declared. "But the wager is on. Come, shake hands on it. What is six weeks from today?"

They all did quick mental calculations.

"June eight," said George.

"Come. Manny will be fretting if we are late for tea," Henry said, removing her hand from Douglas' and mounting her tall horse without assistance.

"Yes, Your Grace of Eversleigh," Douglas snickered, and they all turned their horses' heads in the direction of the manor.

# CHAPTER

## 2

The Duke of Eversleigh was up quite early and riding in the park on the morning following the farewell party for Hanley. A late night was not likely to keep him in bed. He found a brisk gallop a far more effective cure for a thick head than a morning spent sleeping.

Before noon he had returned home, changed his clothes, and driven himself to Jackson's boxing saloon, where he spent an invigorating couple of hours exercising and sparring with friends. Only the very best of Jackson's clients would accept a challenge from the duke. Lord Horton was not one of that number, but the two friends did sally forth together to White's Club afterward for luncheon.

Eversleigh was back at home again by midafternoon. After changing his clothes yet again, he sauntered down to the office occupied by his secretary, James Ridley. Ridley was a youngish man, about the same age as the duke, in his early thirties. He had been at the university with his Grace when both had been youths. His father was a country gentleman who had fallen on hard times. He had struggled to be able to educate his son, as that son would have to be gainfully employed.

Ridley had been ambitious in those days. He had hoped for a career in government service, or at the very least in the Church. He had accepted temporary employment from Eversleigh, who had befriended him and insisted that he needed a competent secretary, as his title was then new to him and his duties unsure. The temporary employment was now in its thirteenth year.

Ridley sat at his desk surrounded by an ordered confusion of papers and ledgers when Eversleigh strolled in. The latter raised his quizzing glass and let his eyes roam over the desk.

"How revolting, James!" he sighed wearily. "Do I really keep you so busy? And do I insist that you work such long hours? It is a delightful afternoon, my dear boy. You would be much better employed viewing the ladies in Hyde Park."

James Ridley looked up and smiled absently. "Do you realize how often you say that to me, your Grace?" he asked. "I would not feel that I earned my more than generous salary if I did not put in a full day's work. And you know that you already insist that I take off both Saturday and Sunday, and force me to take a two-hour luncheon break each day."

The duke moved into the room and leaned one elbow against a bookshelf. "Do I really, James?" he asked, crossing one booted leg over the other. "And when did you manage to wrest such favorable conditions from me?"

Ridley gave a cluck of exasperation, but did not venture a reply.

"And what letters clamor for my attention today?" Eversleigh asked.

"These, your Grace," Ridley replied, indicating a neat bundle on the top corner of his desk. "And please do not forget the speech that you are scheduled to give in the Upper House next week."

"Am I really? Ah, did I know about this before, James?" asked Eversleigh languidly.

"I have reminded you twice in the last week, your Grace," Ridley replied, pained.

"Have you indeed? You must have spoken at a time when my mind was occupied with more pressing matters," his employer commented.

Ridley locked even more pained.

"The topic, James?"

"The deplorable plight of chimney boys in London, your Grace."

"Ah, yes, now I recall," said Eversleigh, still leaning

indolently against the shelf. "And do you have the speech written for me, James?"

Ridley allowed his exasperation to show. "You know you never allow me to write your speeches on topics about which you feel particularly strongly, your Grace," he said.

Eversleigh raised his eyebrows above lazy eyes. "And this is one of them, James?" he asked. "Quite so. I suppose you are right. You usually are, dear boy. A quite disconcerting habit you have."

Ridley gave him a speaking glance.

"And what invitations arrived today?" Eversleigh continued.

"Invitations, your Grace?" James Ridley looked blankly at his employer. "All the invitations are in the wastebasket, where you have instructed me always to place them."

"Quite so, dear boy," the duke agreed, regarding his secretary keenly from beneath his half-closed lids. "Humor me today, James, by removing them from their resting place and reading them to me."

"Reading them, your Grace?"

Eversleigh lifted his quizzing glass unhurriedly again. "Dear me, is my speech blurred today, James?" he drawled. "I assume that all that crumpled paper in the wastebasket is my invitations. Pull them out, man, and read them to me."

Ridley, convinced that his employer must be in the midst of some kind of seizure, complied with his orders. He pulled out one crumpled card after another and smoothed them on top of the ledger on which he had been laboring when the duke had entered his room.

"The Countess of Raleigh invites you to a musical soiree on May fifth," he began, glancing doubtfully at Eversleigh.

The duke looked back, considering for a moment. "Music?" he asked suspiciously. "What music, James?"

Ridley consulted the card again. "The main artiste is the Italian opera singer Signora Ratelli," he said.

The duke picked up his quizzing glass and began to twirl it slowly by its black riband. "My dear boy, would you show some sense?" he said. "Put that back where it came from."

Ridley did so, the expression on his face and the rigid set of his spine conveying his indignant disapproval.

"Lord and Lady Manning request the pleasure of your presence at a masquerade ball to be held on May eight," Ridley read with stiff formality.

"Hmm." Eversleigh pondered awhile, the quizzing glass still turning in hypnotic circles. "I would not be able to check for pimples," he muttered quietly to himself, though his eyes still rested absently on his disapproving secretary, "and I do draw the line at spots. No, throw it away, dear boy," he said decisively.

"Your aunt, the Countess of Lambert, requests the pleasure of your company at a come-out ball for her daughter, the Honorable Althea Summers," Ridley began, but with a hasty glance at his employer, he moved to throw it in pursuit of the soiree and the masquerade.

The quizzing glass fell still at the end of its riband. "Are my ears failing me, James?" Eversleigh asked. "I missed the date of that one."

Ridley pulled the card toward him again and glanced at it. "May eleven, your Grace."

Eversleigh appeared to be doing some mental calculations. "All the new little girls of the Season will be there on display, I suppose, James?" he asked faintly.

"Undoubtedly, your Grace," Ridley replied. "It *is* a come-out and early in the Season. If you will forgive my saying so, sir, it is not at all your sort of do." He coughed delicately.

"Ah," the duke said, nodding slowly and fixing his employee with a keen eye, "but there is family duty, you see, James. My aunt, you know. Althea, did you say?"

Ridley glanced again at the card and nodded.

"Is she the pasty one with the yellow hair? Or is she the one whose body falls in a straight line from her armpits to her thighs?"

Ridley squirmed in some discomfort. "I believe the Honorable Althea Summers is blond and rather tall and, er, slim," he said.

"Hmm, she is both of those people, then?"

Ridley did not answer.

"Accept the invitation," Eversleigh decided, pushing himself with apparent effort into an upright position again.

"Your Grace?" Ridley stammered.

"James?" The duke's eyebrows rose; his right hand was closing around the handle of his quizzing glass again.

"Yes, your Grace."

Eversleigh walked unhurriedly from the room.

The Tallants had arrived in London, all of them with marked reluctance. Giles was the only favored being who was allowed to ride his horse during the five-hour journey from Roedean. Miss Manford, with a rare display of firmness, had insisted that Henry behave like a lady and ride in the carriage. Her voice had become quite breathless, her hands had flapped in the air as if she were conducting a particularly rebellious orchestra, and her head had nodded until a veritable shower of hairpins had released wayward strands of mouse-colored hair, but she had won her point.

Henry, dressed in an unfashionable muslin dress of faded green, a rather wrinkled gray cloak, and a brown bonnet that looked as if the parrot had been in the habit of using it for a perch, sat sullenly in the carriage for the first few miles until a natural ebullience of spirits restored her to cheerfulness.

In fact, it would have been difficult for anyone to remain sullen and dignified for long in that coach. Miss Manford sat demurely except when, every few minutes, she panicked and imagined that some vital possession had been left behind.

"Oh, children," she cried, slapping her gloved palms against her cheeks, "my workbox. I stood it on my bedside table and forgot to instruct the footman to bring it down. How ever will I mend Philip's stockings when he puts his heels through them?"

"Calm down, Manny," that young gentleman replied. "I think I have a hole in my breeches from where the infernal thing has been rubbing against my hip for the past hour."

"Oh, bless you, dearest boy," she sighed in relief. "And do please watch your language in front of Sir Peter and Lady Marian."

"Damn your impudence!" said a high, cross voice.

"Oh, dear me," wailed Miss Manford. "What are we to do about Oscar?"

Philip and Penelope were rolling around in unholy glee.

Miss Manford's hand suddenly flew to her mouth and her eyes grew round with horror. "Oscar's pink blanket!" she exclaimed. "It was in the schoolroom. You know, children, that he will never fall asleep with any other cover over his cage."

"Oh, Manny darling, will you relax and enjoy the scenery?" Henry chided, laughing lightly. "Brutus has it under him on the floor. And really he is being remarkably quiet when one considers that he has not been exercised today. *Brutus!*" she yelled suddenly, throwing herself forward to wrestle determinedly with the happy canine who was cheerfully chewing away a large corner of the blanket.

For the next few minutes pandemonium broke loose in the narrow confines of the ponderous old carriage. Penelope pounced on the hind quarters of the dog and tried, in vain, to drag him backward. Philip threw himself astride the dog's forepart and attempted, equally in vain, to lift him off the blanket. Henry tugged at the offending article and scolded the dog. Brutus, delirious with happiness over this new game, wagged his tail vigorously, wriggled ecstatically under the combined weight of the twins, and managed to bark loudly in Henry's face while keeping a firm hold on the frayed pink blanket. Miss Manford's hands flapped ineffectually while she chanted, "Bless my soul!" to a God who would have been deafened had he been foolish enough to listen. Oscar stumped up and down the floor of his cage, shrieking "Gosh-a-gorry!" to anyone who cared to take note.

"I say," said Giles, lowering his head from his horse's back and peering cheerfully through a window, "a spot of bother, is there?" It said a lot for the normal behavior of the family that he did not seem unduly alarmed.

It was a flushed, disheveled, and tired family and its entourage that finally disembarked from the carriage in the driveway of Sir Peter's house in Cavendish Square.

Lady Marian Tallant was never afterward to know how she kept her dignified composure under the onslaught. She tried to administer a graceful hug on each of the twins and lay a cool cheek next to theirs, but each of them squirmed away, threw a "Hello there, Marian," in her direction, and proceeded to busy themselves with removing the pets.

"You won't mind having Brutus here, will you, Marian?" yelled Penelope.

Philip's hind quarters were poking out the doorway as he tried to coax his pet out of the warm interior of the coach.

"Brutus?" she asked with a bright smile.

"The twins' dog," Henry explained.

"A dog," she said, clapping her hands with delicate pleasure. "Little Timothy will be so pleased." Then her face paled as what looked like a ragged pony padded out onto the driveway and proceeded to shake himself awake. All five members of the Roedean group tensed for a moment and emitted a collective sigh of relief when it became obvious that Brutus had *not* taken a fancy to Marian, or to Peter, who was hovering in the background asking Giles for details of their journey.

"Bottoms up!" a piercing voice ordered from the depths of the carriage. Marian looked as if she would have swooned if she could have trusted her husband to break her fall.

"Pen, get that infernal blanket over the cage," Philip scolded.

"I did!" she protested loudly. "You must have pulled it off when you went in for Brutus, you clumsy ox!"

"Enough, children," Peter said with chilling command. "If that is the parrot you mentioned in your last letter, you had better teach it manners, or out it goes."

"But, Peter," they both chorused in protest.

"Enough! Miss Manford, the footman will show you and the children to your rooms. Might I suggest an hour's rest and then supper in the schoolroom?"

"Oh, so kind, Sir Peter, Lady Marian. Just what we need. So very thoughtful of you. Oh, please, we will be fine. Come along, Philip. Penelope? Oh, and Brutus. And Oscar? Are they to be allowed upstairs, too? So considerate. The children will be so grateful. Say thank you, Penelope. What's that, my dearest boy? Oh, it is still big enough to cover the cage. Thank you, Sir Peter. So kind." Miss Manford, flushed and embarrassed, fluttered her way out of sight and hearing.

"Darling Henrietta," Marian gushed, turning her attention to her sister-in-law, "how—how *well* you look, my dear. I have been so looking forward to having you here. Since little Timothy was born, you know, I have hardly been out in society. But I have a veritable host of activities lined up for you. I am determined to make you all the rage, you know, though I see that we shall have to get busy to make you acceptable."

Henry glowered but said nothing. She hated to lose a bet, and if winning the one against Douglas Raeburn meant having to be made over into a different person—a simpering miss, no less—then a simpering miss she would become. She smiled grimly as she removed her bonnet and shook out her short curls.

Marian reached for a bell rope in the salon to which she had led Henry. "I shall have Mrs. Lane show you to your room, Henrietta," she said. "You must rest for a while. I shall instruct the cook to set back dinner an hour."

"I would much sooner eat as soon as it is ready," Henry declared candidly, forgetting in the instant her resolve to become a simpering miss. "I'm starved. I could eat a horse."

Marian's smile was strained. "Of course, dear. How thoughtless of me. Traveling does tend to invite an appetite, does it not?"

Mrs. Lane entered the room at that moment, to Marian's almost visible relief, and took Henry to a large, comfortable room and, blessedly, a bathtub full of warm suds.

Marian meanwhile had collapsed gracefully onto a sofa after sending a footman for a tray of tea; she glanced despairingly at her husband, who stood with his back to the empty fireplace, hands clasped behind his back, a grim expression on his face.

"My dear Peter, what are we to do?" she wailed. "They are all so . . . rustic."

"They are Tallants," Peter answered stiffly, "and as I am head of the family, they are my responsibility."

"Oh, yes, of course, my love," Marian added hastily. "It is just such a shame that no one has taken them in hand until now. The twins are quite wild. I really do not feel they should be encouraged to speak until they are spoken to. It appears that their governess has no control whatever over them. And that dog and that bird, Peter! Really, they cannot be allowed to roam the house. Especially when we have the upbringing of little Timothy to consider."

"Under your genteel influence and with my firm hand, they will all come about in no time at all, my dear," Peter reassured her. "Miss Manford has been with them since Giles was quite young. I believe she stands somewhat in the place of a mother to them. She filled a gap after Mama died when the twins were born. If she must be dismissed, of course, then sentiment cannot be allowed to stand in the way. But I shall have a talk with her first."

"And Henrietta!" Lady Marian seemed lost for words for a moment. "Such a fright, my love. I shall have to call a dressmaker and a hairdresser to the house. I cannot take her out looking the way she does now."

"Yes," he agreed dryly, "I knew Henrietta would be the main problem. I reprimanded Papa many times when she was growing up about allowing her to indulge her tomboy ways. But he was a stubborn man. He could never be convinced that she should be properly prepared for the life she must be expected to lead as an adult."

"Her speech, Peter. Does she always speak with such a want of manners?"

Between them they had a comfortable coze over the teapot, pulling apart Henry's character and scheming to put right the terrible wrongs that her upbringing had developed in her.

Henry gradually became aware the next day of the terrible ordeal in store for her. While the twins and their pets were confined to the schoolroom with Miss Manford, and Giles spent the day out of the house somewhere with his brother prior to returning to university the next day, Henry was consigned to the tender mercies of Lady Tallant.

During the morning a hairdresser arrived. Henry was made to sit on a stool in her sister-in-law's bedroom, while Monsieur Pierre (a phony Frenchman, Henry decided as soon as he opened his mouth) walked slowly around her several times, his head tilted at various angles, his eyes narrowed in concentration.

"I know there is not much to be done," Henry told him practically. "The curl is natural, you know, but no one has ever been able to control it. You can brush it and hot-iron it as much as you please, but it will look like a spiky thornbush five minutes later. And you really cannot cut it any shorter. I should be quite bald if you tried it, and Marian would never recover from the vapors."

Monsieur Pierre appeared to ignore this candid advice and proceeded to alarm Henry to no small degree by picking up his scissors, flexing his fingers artistically, as if he were about to play a sonata on the pianoforte, and began to snip.

Henry sat meekly enough through the ordeal, which did not last for very long. When she was finally allowed to examine the results in the mirror, she was astonished. Her hair appeared to be no shorter than it had when she had ruthlessly brushed it for all of ten seconds earlier in the morning, but now it had shape. Soft curls molded her scalp and the nape of her neck. It actually looked tame.

After luncheon, Henry was confronted with her sister-in-law's dressmaker, Madame Céleste (another phony, Henry decided), in the yellow salon. Marian was present, too, having canceled all earlier plans for the afternoon and having instructed the butler to deny her presence to any visitors who chanced to call. Henry had been told quite bluntly that her own clothes just would not do in London, and she was ready to concede that it would be agreeable to have some new clothes. She was prepared for a boring half-hour with the dressmaker in order to accomplish the necessary task of choosing a few clothes—a day dress, a ball gown, and perhaps a riding habit, she thought, though the prospect of riding in London did not possess much charm for her if it meant having to ride sidesaddle.

Henry was horrified to find that the session lasted for almost three and a half hours and that she was to have so many new clothes that it would surely take her all Season to wear each of them just once.

"Why do I need ten ball gowns, for heaven's sake?" she asked, appalled. "Won't one last me for the few months until summer?"

Madame Céleste allowed a superior smile to settle on her sallow features while Marian raised her eyes to the ceiling and struggled to hold on to her ladylike patience.

"My dear Henrietta," she said, "we shall be attending many balls, given by some of the most influential members of the *ton*. Your brother and I move in the highest circles, you know. It would be quite unthinkable to wear the same gown more than twice at the most in one year. Everyone would think you must be a pauper, my dear. And we would never find a gentleman to make an offer for you."

"And is that the purpose of all this fuss and fluster?" Henry asked, one arm indicating the jumbled mass of patterns, bolts of fabric, and cards of ribbons and lace strewn everywhere. "Am I to be put on the market for the highest bidder?"

"Really, Henrietta," Marian replied sternly, "I am trying my best to make you look like a lady. I would ask you to make an effort to speak like one, too. Of course it must be the aim of any young lady of breeding to find herself a suitable husband. What else is there?"

Henry was about to argue the point, but remembering a certain wager that she was determined to win, she shut her mouth with an audible clacking of the teeth.

She endured the seemingly endless spell of standing on a low stool while Madame Céleste measured and pinned, poked and prodded. Then she sat in gloomy silence for the remaining time period while her sister-in-law and the dressmaker discussed styles and fabrics and trimmings ad nauseam. Only once did she express an opinion.

"Not pink," she declared.

Marian looked doubtful. "You are probably right, Henrietta," she agreed. "Pink might clash with your hair."

"I don't care about that," Henry declared, "but pink is for girls!"

Marian wisely refrained from comment.

The tedium of the fitting session over, Henry breathed a sigh of relief and announced her intention of going outside for a walk. A loud argument ensued when Marian forbade her to set so much as a nose out of doors until the first of her clothes should have arrived two days later. Henry lost the argument.

She would, she felt, have gone quite mad at the tedium of the day had one incident not brightened it up. Little

Timothy's nurse could be heard shrieking in near hysteria abovestairs. Henry was sitting in the drawing room at the time busily employed with shaking her foot back and forth and counting how many shakes it took before the slipper flew off. Marian was also there, working some embroidery.

The latter leapt to her feet first and rushed for the nursery whence the sounds were proceeding. Henry followed at a more leisurely pace. Daily crises in the Tallant home had conditioned her not to panic too easily.

The scene that met her eyes when she reached the nursery door delighted her greatly. The twins were busily examining the baby's toys while the toddler himself was on the floor tangled up in the reclining body of Brutus and having his face thoroughly licked. The child was chuckling with merriment. Oscar was perched on the headboard of the gently rocking cradle, viewing the scene before him and repeating benignly, "Bless his boots!"

By the time Henry lost interest in the scene and wandered back to the drawing room, the twins had been sent back to the schoolroom with their pets; Miss Manford, who had nodded asleep over some darning before the twins had made their escape, had been scolded; nurse, who had discovered the scene of horror on her return from a visit to the kitchen, had been left to soothe a howling baby, who had been deprived of his new toy; and Lady Tallant had been helped to her room by her lady's maid and was resting quietly in the hope that she would be recovered in time for dinner.

The outcome of the incident was that Brutus and Oscar were banished to the stable. Sir Peter was quite adamant. There was to be no reprieve. He declared that he was being too softhearted to allow the creatures to be kept at all.

When the first of Henry's clothes were delivered two days later, she discovered that she was still not at liberty to relax and order her own life. Clothed in one of the day dresses, she was whisked off to Bond Street by Marian to shop for bonnets, feathers, gloves, boots, slippers, fans, parasols, and a whole lot of other "useless frippery," as she confided to Miss Manford on her return.

"Really, Manny," she said crossly, "is this the way females snare husbands? It is all a ridiculous game. Does no man choose a woman that he feels he might be comfortable with for the rest of his life rather than a primped-up doll?"

"But some people feel it is delightful to dress up and look pretty, dearest girl," Miss Manford soothed. "And the gentlemen spend no less time in looking their best. Why, I have heard that Mr. Brummell used to spend three and a half hours sometimes merely in tying his neckcloth."

Henry burst into loud laughter. "He must have been a peacock!" was her opinion.

"Perhaps so, dearest girl, but never say so to anyone else. He set the fashion for a long time, I have heard."

"What a lot of fustian!" Henry declared before going out to the stable to join the twins in a mournful visit to Brutus and Oscar.

Lady Tallant finally revealed her social plans to Henry. For the next couple of weeks, there were to be minor social activities, including a few small dinner parties, a musical evening, and a picnic party to Kew Gardens. But Henry's official come-out was to be made with the daughter of Marian's friend, the Countess of Lambert. The Tallants had a ballroom only large enough for a moderately sized affair, but Marian wanted to make a larger splash for her sister-in-law's first official appearance. The countess had been quite insistent that they share the occasion—and the cost. Althea was a shy girl, she declared. It would help her to have another debutante with whom to share the nerves that every girl must endure on such an occasion.

Henry dutifully attended all the pre-come-out activities, listening avidly to the names of all guests that were announced. It seemed that the Duke of Eversleigh attended nothing. How was she supposed to get him to propose to her when she had never even set eyes on the man? She began to appreciate the genius of her brother and his cohorts in naming him as the object of her conquest. They must have known that it was unlikely that she would ever even meet him. But really, she thought, they were playing the game very unfairly. She conveniently forgot that she had insisted on aiming for the duke.

She was beginning to doubt the very existence of the man, when suddenly she heard him mentioned for the first time since she had come to London. Her sister-in-law had introduced her to Althea Summers during a particularly insipid party. There was nothing to do. There was no dancing. Loo tables had been set up, but the older set had occupied the tables and the younger people had drifted into unenthusiastic groups. Althea and Henry sat together, a little removed from the others, not by Henry's choice. She labeled Althea as a twit after one glance at her pasty, anxious face.

"Henrietta, are you not horribly frightened about the ball?" Althea asked, leaning confidentially toward her new friend. "I declare, I do not know how I shall live through it."

"Why?" Henry asked. "What is there to be frightened of?"

"Why, everyone will be looking at us," Althea said, wide-eyed. "And there will be so many gentlemen. What if we do not make a good impression, Henrietta? We will be wallflowers for the rest of the Season. And how dreadful it would be to have to begin another Season next year without any beaux."

"As for me," Henry said unconcernedly, swinging her legs freely, "if the gentlemen do not care to take notice of me, I shan't take any notice of them. There is to be a supper table, is there not?"

Althea darted a frightened, rather doubtful look at her companion. "You are funning, Henrietta," she said. "You really are droll." And she tittered in uncertain amusement. "I am sure I shall forget every dance step I ever learned," she continued.

"Pooh!" said Henry. "Who cares for dancing?"

"Mama says I have to dance with Cousin Marius if she can lure him," Althea continued. "I shall just die, Henrietta. He has such a way of looking down his nose and through his quizzing glass at one. I shall forget even which foot is which. But Mama says it would be a great coup to get Eversleigh to dance with me. It will ensure my success."

Henry's flagging interest perked. "Eversleigh?" she asked. "You mean the duke?"

"He never goes to balls," said Althea. "Mama says he is coming to ours only because I am his cousin. I really wish he would not feel obliged, Henrietta."

"Pooh," said that interested lady. "I should not be afraid to dance with him." And her mind was feverishly trying to calculate dates. Would she have time enough to pull it off?

# CHAPTER

# 3

The Duke of Eversleigh spent the afternoon before his cousin's ball with Suzanne Broughton. There was the usual large gathering of visitors in her drawing room during the afternoon—predominantly male, hangers-on who were attracted by her mature self-assurance, her wealth, and her air of independence. She was a woman who was closer to thirty than she cared to admit.

Eversleigh stayed aloof, not participating to any great extent in the general conversation. His usual air of boredom and cynicism discouraged anyone from trying too hard to engage his attention. His heir and cousin, Oliver Cranshawe, was a particular victim of the duke's chilling manner.

"Why, Marius," he greeted his cousin heartily on first entering the room, "still dangling after the lovely widow? I certainly cannot fault your taste. The competition seems rather stiff, though, eh?" He favored Eversleigh with the full blaze of his very white, very dazzling smile, the same smile with which he had bewitched many women.

Unfortunately, Eversleigh seemed impervious to his charm. He raised his quizzing glass with one languid hand and proceeded to subject his heir to a thorough and unhurried examination. The glass passed over the artful disarray of blond, wavy hair the handsome, smiling face, the skin-tight coat of blue superfine, and the froth of white lace at neck and wrists. It took careful note of the fobs and chains and the numerous rings that adorned Cranshawe's person, and of the jeweled snuffbox clasped in his hand.

"Ah, Oliver," he said chillingly at last, lowering the glass. "Trying to cast all of the other gallants into the shade, dear boy?"

The smile tightened on Cranshawe's face, but before he had a chance to say more or to move away, Eversleigh rose unhurriedly to his feet and sauntered over to stand by the chair of Mrs. Broughton, who was in animated conversation with two very young worshipers.

"Suzanne," Eversleigh said, interrupting as soon as there was a pause in the talk, "shall we begin that drive in the park? If we do not leave soon, the exercise will be quite pointless. There will be no one else there to criticize, and no one to admire us."

The two young men smiled uncertainly, not at all sure whether this speech, delivered with an expression of utter boredom, was meant jokingly or not. Suzanne saved them from further embarrassment by leaping to her feet and clapping her hands to focus all attention her way.

"I do thank you all for calling," she said, smiling with the warm charm that made many men her slaves, "but I have promised to ride out with Marius."

The room cleared like magic. Suzanne went upstairs to change into a carriage dress and outdoor garments. Eversleigh prowled the empty drawing room and stopped to stare frowningly into the unlit fireplace. After a few moments he turned abruptly and left the room. He climbed the second staircase and strode along the corridor to Suzanne's dressing room.

He opened the door without knocking and held it until Suzanne, glancing inquiringly at him, had dismissed her maid, who was in the process of buttoning up the back of her dress.

"Marius," she said with mild reproach after the door had closed, "I have just changed my dress on your instructions and have not had an outing yet today. Are you now to tell me that we are not to drive out, after all? How tiresome you are sometimes."

"Don't be coy, Suzanne," he said, advancing into the room and moving to her back to reverse the process with the buttons that the maid had begun. "Today I need you."

"Do you indeed, your Grace?" she cried, whisking herself around to face him. "And why is need such a one-way process? What about the times when I want you? It seems to me that you come to me only when you feel the need. That is not as often as it could be, Marius."

Eversleigh's gaze was inscrutable. He looked at her for a long time through his half-closed lids. "Do you mean to put leading strings on me, Suzanne?" he asked softly. "I assure you no one has ever succeeded."

Suzanne perceived her error immediately. She laughed seductively and wrapped her arms about her lover's neck. "Marius," she said, "I am merely cross because I am wearing a new dress and was looking forward to bringing every gentleman in the park to his knees, and to turning every other woman green-eyed. And then, in you came, and without even a word of appreciation, you started to remove it." She gazed meltingly into his eyes.

Eversleigh held her at arm's length and let his eyes move slowly and suggestively down the length of her body.

"It is an uncommonly handsome dress," he conceded at last. "But, you see, my dear, I happen to know that what is beneath it is infinitely more handsome."

"Oh, Marius," she breathed softly and with some relief, "you are a shameless flatterer."

Half an hour later, they lay quietly in each other's arms in a large four-poster bed in that warm, drowsy mood that succeeds a session of lovemaking that has been thoroughly satisfactory to both partners.

"Marius," Suzanne murmured, kissing his chin and burrowing closer to his warm, naked body, "I am so glad we forgot about the carriage ride. This has proved much more satisfactory. And the dress can wait for another day."

"My sentiments entirely," he replied, looking down his nose at her. "We certainly have had more exercise than we would have had riding in a carriage." She chuckled throatily. "I do hope that I have not deprived you of all outdoor air for the day, though."

"Oh, no," she replied. "I have a ball to attend tonight."

"Ah. The Lambert one?" he asked.

"Yes, how did you know? You never seem to know what social events are taking place, Marius," she said.

"My aunt, you know," he said evasively. "Cousin's come-out. I have to put in an appearance as head of the family."

She laughed merrily. "Marius! When have you ever worried about family duty? I don't believe it. You are more than likely going just to tease all the mamas and raise their hopes to fever pitch. You are very cruel."

He did not reply or move at all.

"Never fear, my love," she continued, laughter in her voice. "If you need rescuing, I shall be there. And I think you could get away with dancing with me more than the accepted two dances. I am beyond the age of drawing gossip too easily."

"You are too kind, my dear," he said dryly. "I do fully expect to survive the ordeal. I shall certainly dance with you once, however. Shall we say the first waltz?"

"I shall write it on my card," she said, hiding her mortification under a flippant air.

"Now, much as I should like to renew our, er, exercising, I really think it is time we both began to beautify ourselves for the evening's merriment," Eversleigh said, disentangling himself from his mistress's soft body and hauling himself to a sitting position on the edge of the bed.

"I shall see you there, then, Marius," Suzanne said, curling into the warmth left by his body beneath the bedclothes. His silent attention to the task of clothing himself completed her disappointment. He was not, then, going to offer to escort her to the ball.

Henry was ready. She stared glumly at her reflection in a full-length mirror in the dressing room she had been allotted in the home of the Earl of Lambert. She looked like any other empty-headed girl of the *ton*, she decided, with nothing to fill the empty space between her ears except dreams of catching a rich and titled husband. She wore a high-waisted gown of white lace over a pale-peach satin underdress. Peach ribbons were tied in an intricate bow beneath her breasts and fell to the hemline, where they drew attention to the orange satin slippers peeping from beneath the gown. The dress had short, puffed sleeves and dipped into a modestly low, scalloped neckline. She wore a single strand of pearls that Peter had presented her with that afternoon. White elbow-length gloves and an ivory fan completed the outfit. Henry was quite disgusted as the maid, who had been sent to her by the countess, stood behind her and smiled into the mirror.

"Ooh, you do look a picture, miss," she said in admiration.

Henry smiled grimly back and headed for the door. "Time to go down to the drawing room. The receiving line will be forming soon, I suppose," she said.

As she reached the door, it opened from the other side and Lady Tallant came in. "Henrietta, my dear," she gushed, the plumes in her hair nodding in approval, "you look remarkably pretty. Do let us hasten downstairs. We must not keep the earl and countess waiting."

Henry hardly admitted to herself as she followed her sister-in-law meekly down the stairs that she felt a little nervous. Not that she cared a fig for dancing, of course, or for the opinions of all the people who would be coming to look her over. But she did wonder if the Duke of Eversleigh really would put in an appearance and what type of man this was that she was supposed to lure into a proposal. She did not feel any doubts about her own success if only the man would not neglect to come.

She was feeling quite anxious an hour and a half later. She had been standing in the receiving line with the Earl and Countess of Lambert, the Honorable Althea, Sir Peter and Lady Marian, shaking hands with and curtsying to so many people that she was convinced that her right hand must be swollen to twice its normal size and that the smile on her face must be frozen there forever. She was thoroughly sick of answering impertinent questions from all the old tabbies and of being ogled by the young bucks and sized up critically by the young ladies. But when she and Althea were told that they could leave the line and begin the dancing, the Duke of Eversleigh had still not arrived.

An hour later, it seemed that Henry was destined to be a moderate success. Although she had not attracted the attention of any important member of the *ton*, she had been partnered for all dances except one, and that one was a waltz. Knowing that this was her first ball, the gentlemen tactfully left her on the sidelines, realizing that she would not yet have been granted permission to waltz by any of the patronesses of Almack's. It would have been death to any girl's social reputation to waltz until such approval had been given. The older ladies and chaperones who lined the walls of the ballroom (those, that is, who had not retired to the card room) looked on her, if not with open friendliness, at least with tolerance. Two of them, it is true, had commented on the deplorable color of her skin.

"Foreign blood, you may be sure," one of them said.

"Or else she has been exposed to the sun," the other suggested.

"Surely not," said the first. "Her brother, Sir Peter Tallant, is a most gentlemanly man."

"I hear she has only recently arrived in town," the second continued. "I do believe she has some freckles, too."

The other drew herself erect and regarded Henry with piercing disapproval. She looked offended that she had been invited to the come-out of a sunburned, freckled girl.

Henry was accepting a glass of lemonade from a very young, pleasant-faced young man, when Althea, who had been standing close by, grabbed her suddenly by the arm and caused her to spill some of the liquid down the front of her gown.

"Oh, I am frightfully sorry, Henrietta!" she apologized, dabbing ineffectively at the lace with her gloved hands. "He's here, Henrietta. What am I to do?" She turned her back to the doorway of the ballroom, trying to appear inconspicuous.

Henry stared with open curiosity at the man who stood in the doorway. She was hardly encouraged by what she saw. The man was tall and gracefully slim, though there was a disturbing suggestion of strength about his shoulders and chest. He had a disconcertingly strong and handsome face. His coat and knee breeches were unrelieved black, his linen a crisp and sparkling white. He looked completely unself-conscious, though his arrival had caused a very noticeable stir among the gathered company. He was surveying the guests unhurriedly through a quizzing glass. The word *impossible* had never been part of Henry's vocabulary, but she had a funny feeling in the pit of her stomach that winning her wager was going to be the biggest challenge of her life.

As she (and the majority of the assembled guests)

watched, the Countess of Lambert swept up to the duke and took his arm in a gesture of deliberate familiarity. He lowered his glass and looked at her from beneath sleepy eyelids.

Henry's stomach became decidedly queasy as the two figures came closer. She could almost understand why Althea was so afraid of this man. The countess was quite unconcerned with the presence of Henry and her young swain. She was intent only on presenting her cousin to her daughter and seeing them partnered for the next dance, a quadrille. For her, this was the coup of the Season. The success of her daughter was now assured.

Eversleigh danced with two more partners, each a young and flustered debutante. The boredom and cynicism of his expression did not change as his partners blushed and fluttered and giggled through the experience of dancing with the most eligible and most elusive bachelor in London.

Oliver Cranshawe, who had emerged from the card room in time to witness this extraordinary behavior of his cousin, moved gradually closer to Suzanne Broughton, who was not dancing, but who was surrounded by her usual court of admirers.

"So, my dear Suzanne," he commented when her attention moved his way, "you are being upstaged tonight?"

"Upstaged?" she queried, viewing him with hauteur. "Whatever do you mean, Oliver?"

"I see that Marius is eyeing all the little girls," he said, smiling charmingly, as if he had just complimented her on her gown.

She laughed airily. "Poor Marius!" she tittered. "He has been afflicted with a case of family duty, Oliver. Althea is his cousin, you know."

"Really?" he drawled. "It is surely the first case of its kind that I have ever known. He could not be dangling after a wife, could he?"

"Don't be ridiculous, Oliver," Suzanne said more sharply than she had intended. "Can you imagine Marius with a young girl? He would die of boredom in a fortnight."

"That sure of yourself, are you, Suzanne?" Cranshawe asked, a glint of something unpleasant in his eyes. "I think we had better keep a close eye on his Grace, my dear. We do have a common interest in the matter after all, do we not?"

She did not pretend to misunderstand him, though she did not reply. She turned her attention back to the group of gentlemen who were still waiting in the vicinity.

Eversleigh returned his second partner to her chaperone and stood alone close to the doorway. He looked as if he would dearly love to escape, Henry thought as she too stood momentarily alone at the other side of the ballroom. In fact, she was very much afraid that he would escape soon and that she would have lost perhaps her only chance to meet him within the time period of her wager. She did not know how to attract his attention. She had considered asking the countess or Althea to introduce them, but that seemed too brazen even for her. But something had to be done fast.

As she pondered the problem, a young gentleman with whom she had already danced once asked her to partner him in the next dance, too. She gave him a brilliant smile.

"It is so kind of you to ask," she said, "but I am afraid I have already promised the next one. Perhaps later? And excuse me, please. I must go to the ladies' room."

While the young man blushed at such plain speaking, Henry determinedly circled the dance floor past groups of chatting people until she was within a few feet of the duke. She took a deep breath, turned her head back over her shoulder as if someone behind her had called her name, and increased her pace. She stopped only when her body came into sharp contact with a very firm chest and when his foot was beneath her slipper, his chin cracking on her skull, and his hands clasping her upper arms.

"Oh!" she cried, blushing and flustered as she stepped back and raised large, hazel eyes to his lazy blue ones. "How clumsy of me. I am *so* sorry, sir. Did I hurt you?"

The Duke of Eversleigh found himself looking down at a mop of auburn hair that looked slightly unruly, with its ivory-colored ribbon somewhat askew, and beneath it a flushed, sunburned face with sparkling eyes and—yes, definitely—a cluster of freckles across the nose. His hand wandered to the handle of his quizzing glass, but he did not raise it.

"My fault entirely, ma'am," he said unsmilingly. "I should not have been standing in the doorway."

"No, really," she insisted brightly, "Papa always did say I was a clumsy ox."

"Indeed!" he said. "I could hardly be expected to corroborate that opinion, now, could I?"

"It is just good for you that I was not wearing boots," she said, smiling impishly into his impassive face.

"Indeed, they would not complement your gown, ma'am," he conceded.

Henry giggled openly. "You do not appear to be enjoying the ball immensely, sir," she said.

He bowed stiffly. "Marius Devron, Duke of Eversleigh, at your service, ma'am," he said. "We appear to be attracting attention. Would you do me the honor of dancing with me?" He grasped her lightly by the elbow and moved her forward to the dance floor.

"Oh, I am pleased to meet you, your Grace," Henry said brightly. "I'm Henry."

He paused for just a moment. "Henry?" he asked faintly, his hand straying again to his quizzing glass.

"Henrietta Wilhelmina Tallant, actually," she said candidly. "Is it not a dreadful mouthful? And only my mortal enemies call me Henrietta. It always makes me think of a fat, big-bosomed lady with pale hair and puffy face, reclining on a sofa with a lapdog and a dish of bonbons."

The blue eyes beneath the half-closed lids took on a distinct gleam. "I believe I had better call you Miss Tallant," Eversleigh said.

Henry had noticed the gleam. "Oh, dear," she said contritely, "my wretched tongue! I should not have mentioned bosoms, should I? Indeed, Giles warned me about it just a few weeks ago, when I embarrassed poor George and Douglas so. But I forgot already."

Eversleigh was saved from the ordeal of having to answer that one when the music began and he realized that it was a waltz tune.

"I am very much afraid we shall have to sit this one out, Miss Tallant," he told Henry. "This is your come-out as well as Althea's, is it not? You are not allowed to waltz until one of the patronesses has granted permission, you know."

"Yes, Marian told me," Henry replied, "but I don't care a fig for that, you know. I always do as I please. Papa gave up on me when I was twelve years old. He said it would take a better man than he to bend me to his will."

"Ah," Eversleigh said, eyes narrowed even more than usual. "But if you do not care for your reputation, Miss Tallant, I live in fear and trembling of losing mine."

He had steered her firmly to the sidelines again. Henry was about to make a cross rejoinder when she noticed that he had his quizzing glass to his eye again and that he was scanning the room with it, rather more purposefully than he had before.

Having found the object of his search, he turned back to Henry again. "Will you take my arm, Miss Tallant?" he asked, holding it out to her.

She laid her own on top of it and was led around the perimeter of the ballroom to the other side, where a superbly proud and handsome lady, with several magnificent plumes waving above her piled hairdo, was at the center of an animated group.

The group fell silent as the Duke of Eversleigh approached, his manner one of utter boredom, Henry noted with interest, stealing a glance up at him.

"Ah, Sally," he said on a sigh, "may I present Miss Henry, er, etta Tallant to you?"

"How are you enjoying your first ball, my dear?" Sally Jersey asked, smiling at Henry. "Yes, Marius, I met her in the receiving line. And if my guess is right, you wish to waltz with her."

Eversleigh bowed stiffly.

Sally Jersey laughed again. "It is most irregular for a girl to be approved so soon, Marius," she said, "but I very much fear that if I refuse, we might not see you at a ball for another five years."

Eversleigh inclined his head, his face expressionless.

"Very well, my dear," the famous patroness said to Henry, "do not miss any more of this delightful music, please."

"Curtsy," a voice said very quietly, and Henry obeyed

it before she realized that it was the duke and that he had no business telling her what to do.

Henry did not talk during the first minute of the dance. At first, she was intent on counting steps. Her brow creased in concentration. Then she became very much aware of the close proximity of her partner, his body heat reaching out to flush her cheeks and interfere with her breathing. She did not like the feeling at all. It made her feel little and fragile and not at all in command of the situation.

She came back to full reality when, during a turn, she got her legs tangled together and Eversleigh had to haul her hard against his chest. She trod hard on one of his feet.

"Oh, dear," she said, thrusting herself away from him with ungainly haste, "I should have told you that I don't waltz very well, shouldn't I? Did I hurt your foot?"

"It was a different one from the last time," he replied gallantly, "so it evens the score."

"I used to hate dancing lessons," Henry confided. "Papa had a dancing master come down to Roedean to teach us. I tried desperately hard to forget the classes and go out riding, but I couldn't always avoid them. I learned the others tolerably well, but I never could learn the waltz. I think it was because Mr. Reese used to eat garlic and he had clammy hands. I could feel them right through my dress. Just like a fish. Although," she added reflectively, "they were always hot, not cold."

The gleam that Henry had noticed earlier had returned to the duke's eyes. "You put me in fear and trembling, ma'am," he said. "I am endeavoring to recall whether my cook served me any garlic tonight. I assure you he will be dismissed tomorrow morning if he did."

"Oh, I can tell you that he could not have," Henry said earnestly, staring wide-eyed into those disturbingly half-closed eyes. She was puzzled to see the gleam deepen.

"Miss Tallant," he said, "shall we converse on safer and more genteel topics? How are you enjoying your first ball? Do you feel all the excitement of being a new debutante?"

"Stuff!" she said. "I think it all a colossal waste of time and money."

"Indeed!" His manner seemed distant. His eyebrows rose arrogantly.

"Yes, is it not utterly foolish for so many supposedly sensible people to mince around a dance floor holding on to complete strangers and talking on topics that neither is really interested in and that do not signify anyway?"

"I am devastated to know that my company bores you so much, ma'am," he said stiffly.

"Oh, I don't mean you, silly. I am convinced you feel the same way I do, only you do not like to say so. I just loved the way you looked everyone over with your quizzing glass when you first came in, as if you could hardly believe the world held so much foolishness. I wish I might have the nerve to do the same."

"I would not advise it, ma'am," he said, a slight quaver in his voice, "not, at least, until you are an elderly dowager and can carry off the eccentricity." Henry could feel his shoulder shaking slightly beneath her hand, but as she looked inquiringly up into his face, the music stopped.

Eversleigh released her and held out his arm for her hand. "Come, Miss Tallant," he said, "I shall return you safely to your sister-in-law. Sir Peter Tallant is your brother, I presume?"

"Oh, yes," she confirmed carelessly, "but really I have no wish to go near Marian. She will surely prose on about something I am doing wrong. I'll wager she noticed me stumble during the waltz and will berate me for my clumsiness."

"Nevertheless, ma'am, I shall return you to your chaperone," Eversleigh said firmly, and Henry indignantly discovered that she had no choice in the matter.

Marian was all aflutter when Eversleigh returned Henry to her side, bowed, and wished her a good evening. She fell into a deep curtsy, so that Henry was fearful that her nose might brush the floor.

The duke walked unhurriedly away. He stopped to talk briefly to a man who was standing close to the doorway.

Sir Wilfred Denning was grinning. "Are you giving up already, Marius?" he asked. "Indeed, it is not much of a crop this year, is it?"

"Ah, but I still have two weeks left, do I not, Wilfred?"

the duke replied softly. "It is not safe to count your winnings before they are in your pocket, dear boy."

And the Duke of Eversleigh continued on his way through the doorway to the intense chagrin of many females who had daughters or other relatives to marry off. The younger ladies, on the whole, breathed a sigh of relief.

Oliver Cranshawe, soliciting the hand of Suzanne Broughton for the next dance, smiled with dazzling charm. "I do believe the danger has been averted for this occasion," he said. "That little fright he just danced with seems to have driven him completely from the field."

Suzanne's smile was somewhat forced. Eversleigh had not deigned even to acknowledge her presence; he had not claimed the promised dance.

Henry's popularity was definitely on the upward swing. She was besieged with prospective partners for the rest of the evening, and was led in to supper by no less a personage than Viscount Marley, a widower, who was known to be on the lookout for a new wife and who did not need to hold out for an heiress.

# CHAPTER

# 4

By four o'clock the following afternoon, Henry's head felt rather as if it were spinning on her shoulders. The lateness of the night before and the eventfulness of this day had been an exhausting combination.

When she was finally in bed the night before, she had not slept immediately. She had gone over and over in her mind the meeting with the Duke of Eversleigh. She had very obviously ruined any slim chance she might have had of bringing him to the point. And she had recognized as soon as she met him that the chance was indeed slim. Henry was a girl of some intelligence. She recognized a superior intellect and a more powerful will when she met them. It was just that she had never met either until she had deliberately run against the hard wall of Eversleigh's body the night before. Even so, she berated herself, she might have charmed him had she sighed and fluttered her eyelashes as she had seen other girls doing, or impressed him with witty but ladylike conversation.

But what had she done? She had prattled in most unladylike fashion, mentioning bosoms and admitting to considering balls a ridiculous pastime. And she had tripped all over him—twice! She remembered that gleam she had noticed in his eyes. It was surely disgust that he had been feeling. After he had returned her to Marian, he had not only refrained from asking her to dance with him again, he had left altogether. He had been about to escape when she first ran into him, she was sure. His meeting with her had not served to change his mind.

Henry admitted to herself that her chances of winning the wager were very remote indeed. From all she had heard, it seemed that Eversleigh did not frequent the social events of the *ton*. It seemed unlikely that she would even see him again in the coming weeks. And even if she did, it was unlikely that he would notice her. And she could not again use the device of "accidentally" colliding with him. The situation seemed hopeless.

But then, Henry admitted, perhaps this was a wager she would not mind losing. She had to confess that she had felt out of her depth with the duke. His reactions were not as open and predictable as were those of other people she knew. She had found it impossible to guess what he was thinking. And those heavy eyelids had hidden any clue that his eyes might have shown. Three times he had forced her to act according to his will: getting permission before she waltzed, curtsying to Sally Jersey, returning to Marian's side after the dance; and all three times he had accomplished his will without any hint of coercion. There had been none of the blustering of Papa or the posturing of Peter. Henry had the uncomfortable feeling that, if this man ever did offer for her, she would be drawn against her will into accepting. She had the niggling suspicion—and it kept her awake for longer than she found comfortable—that she was just a teeny bit afraid of the Duke of Eversleigh.

Henry was normally an early riser. But on the morning after the ball she slept until midmorning. Even then she might not have woken if she had not become gradually aware of a commotion in the house. Doors were being opened and closed along the corridor outside her room. She could hear the voices of her sister-in-law, the housekeeper, and a maid, and—finally—of Peter. Henry hauled herself out of bed and dressed as quickly as she could, not stopping to call a maid. She dragged a brush through her tousled curls and left the room.

The center of the commotion was by this time a downstairs salon. When Henry reached the doorway, she discovered that Peter and Marian were inside, together with Miss Manford, Philip, Penelope, Brutus, the butler, the housekeeper, and a filthy, ragged little urchin, who stood in bewildered isolation in the middle of it all.

"You had no business bringing him into the house at all," Peter was scolding, "and certainly not through the front door. Do you children think we are a charitable institution?"

"But, Peter," Philip begged, "he was being beaten for stealing a roll of bread. And he only stole it because he was hungry. He has no father and his mother drinks gin all the time. We had to bring him with us."

"Poor little Tommy!" Penelope added. "We thought you might keep him here, Peter. He could help in the kitchen or stables, or you might train him to be your tiger."

"Silence, children!" their brother ordered. "Take the little beggar to the kitchen, Mrs. Lane, and give him a meal. And then drive him away, if you please. Do you understand, child? If you come back here, I shall have you taken up for loitering and thrown into jail."

Tommy appeared not to have understood a word that had been said to him. He balanced on one leg and tried to wrap the other leg around it, though his purpose in doing so was not at all clear.

"But, Peter—" Philip began.

"You two children may go to your rooms and remain there for the rest of the day," their brother interrupted. "And you can be very thankful that I do not thrash the pair of you."

"Mrs. Lane, the child!" Marian reminded the housekeeper, who did not appear to know how she was to remove the boy without contaminating herself by touching him.

Henry solved her problem. "Here, allow me!" she said indignantly, and stalked into the room, head high, eyes flashing. She stooped down, took Tommy's grubby paw, and led him from the room. "Let us see what we can find for you to eat belowstairs," she said kindly. "And we shall see if cook can spare a cloth or basket for you to take some food home with you. Do you have brothers and sisters?"

Mrs. Lane and the butler trailed out after her, and the twins ascended disconsolately to their rooms.

"Miss Manford," Sir Peter said, turning his attention to that hapless lady, "I am greatly displeased with the morning's events. Why, pray, did you take the twins walking in a part of London that is quite beneath their station?"

"They have a great curiosity, Sir Peter," she stammered. "They wished to visit a street market. But, indeed, I am very sorry . . ."

"And it is quite beyond my comprehension why you would allow them to associate with such a ragamuffin as that child, and to bring him here!"

"I . . . Indeed, Sir Peter, I did suggest to them that you might not like it," Miss Manford explained helplessly, "but you know, sir, your dear father was always willing to aid the creatures and persons they brought home with them. He thought it good for them to become aware—"

"Miss Manford," he interrupted ruthlessly, "I am not my father, and this is not Roedean. I recognize, ma'am, that you have been of inestimable help to my brothers and sisters in the past. For this reason I shall not dismiss you out of hand. I shall give you two months in which to find yourself a new situation. I shall ask you to remain away from the children for today. Good day, ma'am."

Poor Miss Manford was rendered almost speechless. She stammered her way from the room, hands fluttering ineptly in the air.

By the time Henry came back upstairs from the kitchen, having seen Tommy well fed with cold meat and bread and sent on his way with a well-stocked bundle, the butler was busy carrying some half-dozen bouquets of flowers into the drawing room. They were all for her from admirers of the night before. Henry chuckled with amazement. What an amusing game this was proving to be. The largest bouquet, one of deep-red roses, was from Viscount Marley, she noted. She pulled a face. The man was at least fifty and running to fat, but Marian had been all agog, seeming to feel that Henry would be a fool not to encourage his suit. Strangely enough, Marian had not taken Eversleigh seriously as a possible suitor; she was far too realistic for that. But she had been ecstatic over the favorable attention he had focused on her sister-in-law.

It seemed to Henry that she had hardly had time for breakfast and a secret visit to her brother and sister and their governess before Marian was directing her to return to her room to get properly groomed and dressed for afternoon visitors. There were certain to be some after the ball of the night before, she added.

Henry considered the whole business a frightful bore, though in the event she was amused to find that several of her partners of the previous evening were among the visitors. Viscount Marley was one of them. He even contrived to sit with Henry a little apart from the rest of the company. He entertained her with descriptions of his two young daughters, who missed their mama a great deal and were longing for the day when someone would be found to replace her. Henry succeeded somehow in keeping a polite smile on her face. The viscount had just requested the pleasure of Henry's company on a drive through the park when the visiting hour should be over, when a merciful interruption saved Henry from the embarrassment of either accepting or thinking up some lame excuse.

The butler entered the room and bowed to Marian. "Sir Peter Tallant wishes to see Miss Tallant in the library immediately, ma'am," he announced.

Marian glanced across at Henry in surprise. "You had better not keep him waiting, Henrietta," she said. "But do hurry back to our guests as soon as you are able."

Henry curtsied and made her way down to the library, which was Peter's domain. What had she done wrong now? Was he about to banish her and the twins to Roedean after their behavior of the morning? She could hardly think of a punishment she would enjoy more. She grimly approached the closed door and opened it.

The man who stood with his back to the room, staring out the window, was not Peter. A hasty glance around assured Henry that, in fact, her brother was not in the room at all. Then the man turned and she gaped. She found herself staring into the sleepy eyes of the Duke of Eversleigh!

"Ah, Miss Tallant," he said, hand straying to the handle of his quizzing glass, "good day to you. Pray come inside and close the door."

"Oh, your Grace, it's you," she said foolishly. "Pardon me, my brother is looking for me."

"How provoking of him," Eversleigh replied, "when he just a moment ago granted me permission to speak to you." He walked unhurriedly across the room. Henry stood paralyzed, her hand still on the knob of the open door.

"Please allow me to close the door," he said from beside her. "You seem incapable of doing so yourself."

"Oh, yes, your Grace," Henry said, skipping hastily across to the other side of the room.

"I assure you, ma'am," he said, shutting the door and surveying her through his quizzing glass, "I have not been eating garlic."

Henry giggled nervously. "Would you not like to come to the drawing room, your Grace?" she asked brightly. "There are other visitors there."

"How revolting!" he said, lowering the glass. "Are you so anxious to return to them, Miss Tallant?"

"Oh, no!" she confided. "Actually, I was very thankful to be called away. Lord Marley was pressing me to drive out with him, and I had really rather not. But Marian would have put me on bread and water for a week, had I refused. He is rich, you know, and has a title."

"Marley!" Eversleigh shuddered theatrically. "I suppose he is out shopping for a new mama for his two brats?"

"Well, he did talk about them," she admitted.

"Quite so. Come and sit down over here, Miss Tallant, and stop cowering at the other end of the room. Indeed, if I wished to give chase, ma'am, I should catch you in a moment."

Henry bristled immediately. "I never cower!" she said. "And if you did chase me and catch me, you might be sorry."

The eyebrows rose above the blue eyes.

"I should kick and punch," she declared proudly. "I once gave Giles a black eye."

"Giles has my sympathies," he commented dryly. "Stand there and *cower*, if you must, Miss Tallant. I am going to sit down."

Having made her point, Henry crossed the room and seated herself in the chair he had originally indicated.

"Miss Tallant, I perceive that it is useless to try to make polite small talk with you. I shall get immediately to the point. Will you do me the honor of becoming my wife?"

Henry's jaw dropped.

"Miss Tallant?"

"Your wife?" she asked faintly.

"Yes, my wife. I have taken you by surprise, I see. I mistakenly thought you had more fortitude, ma'am. Should I have paved the way more carefully by falling on my knees in front of you and declaring undying love and devotion? I can still do so, if you wish."

"Pray do not," she said anxiously. "You would look mighty ridiculous and I should be hard put to it not to laugh."

"Then shall we sit here in silence while you consider what I have said?" he suggested with unaccustomed gentleness.

"Are you serious, your Grace?" she asked dubiously.

"About sitting in silence? Oh, yes, I very often contemplate the state of my own soul, ma'am."

"No, silly. I meant about marrying me."

"Oh, certainly. It can be dangerous to propose to a lady in fun, you know. She might just accept. Then the joke would be on me. But I would not be amused."

"But why?" Henry asked.

"Why would I not be amused, ma'am? Why, because—"

"No, stupid. Oh, pardon me, your Grace," Henry said, slapping a hand over her mouth. She noticed with dismay that last night's gleam was back in the duke's eyes.

"You meant, why do I wish to marry you?" he prompted. "I have the notion that it might be amusing, Henry. And it is a long time since I have been amused."

"But you do not know me," she protested. "I am dreadfully stubborn and outspoken, you know. And I hate to have to behave like a lady. And I will not let any man tell me what to do."

"I am in fear and trembling that you will bring my name into disgrace and that you will make of me a human jelly in no time at all, Miss Tallant," he said meekly.

Henry eyed him steadily. "You are funning me, are you not?" she said.

He considered her. "I would not squash your spirit, Henry," he said softly, "but I am a man."

Henry shivered, for what reason she did not know. She jumped hastily to her feet and crossed to the window through which he had been looking when she came into the room. He did not attempt to talk to her while she stood there trying to force her whirling thoughts into some order.

She had won her wager, but the victory had come so easily and so unexpectedly that it seemed unreal. If she refused him now, how would she ever get Douglas—or even Giles—to believe that the Duke of Eversleigh had actually offered for her? Would she even believe it herself the next day? But how could she accept? It was all so sudden as to be ridiculous. They had met only the evening before. They were total strangers. Henry knew very little about the ways of the *ton*, but surely, she thought, courtships usually took a lot longer than this.

There was something very strange about the duke's proposal. He was fabulously wealthy, he was astonishingly handsome, and he held one of the highest ranks in the country. He must be into his thirties already. Why, suddenly, had he decided to offer for a little nobody that he did not know? She could not quite accept his explanation that he found her amusing. There had been nothing amusing about her gauche behavior of the night before. Anyway, she had nothing really to recommend her. She was only passably good-looking; she had no feminine graces; she was not wealthy. She would, in fact, make a quite deplorable duchess. Henry a duchess! She had to stifle a giggle for a moment.

And what of her own feelings? Henry could hardly believe that she was even giving consideration to his proposal. She certainly did not wish to be married. She knew that a married lady became the property of her husband. The idea was totally abhorrent to her. The only type of husband that might be acceptable would be one that she could manipulate at will. And yet, even as she thought it, she realized that it would be intolerable to be married to someone whom she could not respect. And what of Eversleigh? There was something about him that made Henry shiver. She remembered the hardness of his body when she had run against him the night before. But his whole person seemed like that—like a brick wall in which she would not be able to make even the smallest dent. "I am a man," he had just said, and the remembered words made her shiver again. Why, then, did she feel so inclined to accept his proposal? It was just as she had thought last night. He seemed to exert a power over her will without any visible effort.

What was she to do, then? Finally, Henry turned back to the room, an idea in her mind. She would throw the decision back to him. She crossed back to her chair and sat down without looking at him.

"Well, Henry?" Eversleigh prompted. "What is to be my fate? I can see by the jut of your chin that you have made a decision."

"I shall be your wife, your Grace, under one condition," she declared firmly.

"Indeed!" he replied haughtily. "Do I dare ask what that one condition might be?"

"In addition to me, you must take Philip and Penelope, Miss Manford, Brutus, and Oscar," she said in a rush.

Eversleigh had his glass to his eye again. "Dear me," he said, "is that *one* condition? And are these persons all members of your family, Henry?"

"Philip and Penelope are my twin brother and sister," she began. "They are twelve years old. Miss Manford is their governess. She was mine and Giles', too. Giles is my older brother."

"Quite so," he said. "The one of the black eye. And the one who warned you not to talk of bosoms."

"Oh," she said, nonplussed for the moment.

"And Brutus and Oscar?" he prompted.

"The twins' dog and parrot," she explained, watching him warily.

"Why do I get the feeling that there is more to say about the twins' dog and parrot?" he asked softly, his eyes beneath the lowered lids watching her closely.

"Well," Henry said uncertainly, "Brutus looks like a small horse and he likes to eat things he is not supposed to eat. And he is . . . playful. Oscar was taught to speak by his previous owner. His language is rather colorful."

The gleam was back in Eversleigh's eyes. "I see," he said. "And why, Henry, would it be necessary to transfer all these personalities to my household in the event of our marriage? Do you feel that you would need protection against me?"

"Oh, no, it's because Peter is quite horrid to them all,"

she cried. "Brutus and Oscar have been banished to the stables and Miss Manford has been dismissed. And the twins have been sent to their rooms for the whole of today." Henry got to her feet in her agitation and found herself telling Eversleigh all that had taken place that morning.

"You would not have sent the poor child away without doing something to help him, would you, your Grace?" she asked as she finished the account.

"Indeed I would not," he said decisively. "I should first have had the little beggar chained to the gatepost and whipped for his impudence."

Her eyes flashed and then she looked at him. "Oh, no, you would not," she said. "I know you would not."

"No, I would not," he agreed quietly.

"Miss Manford has nowhere to go," she said, turning away from his piercing eyes. "She has been with us forever. We are her family. And she is too old to get another position, I fear. She must be fifty, at least."

"Henry," Eversleigh said softly, also rising to his feet, "you will agree to marry me if I take your family, too?"

"Yes," she whispered, eyes wide with apprehension.

"Then, my dear, I shall have the announcement appear in tomorrow's *Morning Post*." He crossed the room until he was standing in front of her. "Don't be afraid, Henry," he said, taking her cold hand in his. "We shall deal well together, you shall see." And he raised her hand and placed the palm against his warm lips for a long moment, holding her eyes with his the while.

Henry just gaped again.

"Will you go now, please?" he directed. "Ask the butler to send your brother back to me. I shall call on you and your sister-in-law tomorrow afternoon. Perhaps you would drive with me in the park afterward?"

And Henry, in a trance, obediently followed his directions.

The marriage of Marius Devron, Duke of Eversleigh, to Miss Henrietta Tallant was undoubtedly the sensation of the Season. It was amazing enough that Eversleigh had decided to marry, but his choice of bride and the hastiness of the event (the wedding took place only three weeks after the betrothal announcement appeared in the *Morning Post*) had everyone agog.

Eversleigh bore up under the ordeal with his usual fortitude.

"Ah, James," he said to his secretary on the same afternoon as he had proposed to Henry, "still at work? Am I really such a slave driver, dear boy?"

"I am just finishing your speech for the House on Friday, your Grace," James Ridley replied, lifting his head.

"Ah," said Eversleigh, "did I not speak a few weeks ago, James? Did I know I was to speak again?"

Ridley gave his employer a long-suffering stare. "You did, your Grace," he said. "You asked me last week to write this speech for you."

"Quite so," Eversleigh agreed. "Some scintillating topic like the effect of the enclosure system on tenant farmers, was it not?"

"Yes, your Grace."

"I do hope you have not made it an impassioned speech," the duke said doubtfully. "That would not be my style at all, you know."

"I have merely tried to show that you care, your Grace," said Ridley. "And you do care, as I know very well."

"Do I, James?" the duke said, looking steadily at his secretary from below lowered lids. He turned to leave the room, then stopped as if something quite insignificant had crossed his mind. "You might write out a notice for the *Morning Post* for me, James."

"Yes, your Grace?"

"Announce my forthcoming marriage to Miss Henrietta Tallant, daughter of the late Sir Harold Tallant of Sussex, sister of Sir Peter Tallant, will you, dear boy?"

Ridley was speechless.

Eversleigh raised his quizzing glass to his eye. "Are you not going to congratulate me, James?" he asked.

"Y-you are getting m-married, your Grace?" Ridley stammered.

"In three weeks' time," Eversleigh said matter-of-factly. "Draw up a list of people whom I will want to invite, will you, James?"

"Y-yes, your Grace, right away," said Ridley.

"Oh, no, dear boy," the duke said with a sigh. "Tomorrow

morning will be soon enough. I am too tired to see you work longer today. Oh, and, James," he added, "do have breakfast with me tomorrow morning. I expect a visit from my cousin soon after the morning paper is delivered."

"Yes, your Grace," said Ridley.

The duke was quite correct. As he sat over his coffee the next morning conversing amiably with James Ridley, they heard the arrival of a visitor in the main hallway. Moments later, Oliver Cranshawe let himself into the breakfast room, unannounced.

"Good morning, Oliver," Eversleigh greeted him without looking up.

"I fail to see what is so good about it," Cranshawe snapped, slapping a folded copy of the morning paper down on the end of the table.

"Have some breakfast, dear boy," Eversleigh said, waving a languid hand in the direction of the sideboard. "Things never seem so bad on a full stomach, you know."

"I wish to talk to you, Marius," Cranshawe said, not moving toward the food. He looked pointedly at James Ridley, who apparently did not notice the hint.

"I rather gathered you did, Oliver," the duke commented, "or you would not be out of your bed at such an ungodly hour. Sit down, please. It makes me tired to see you stand there."

"Marius, will you stop this game of being weary and bored and show some feeling for once. And put your quizzing glass down, for goodness' sake. I know you can see perfectly well without it." He pulled a chair noisily from under the table and seated himself heavily on it.

There was a short silence as Eversleigh sipped his coffee and Ridley tried to melt into the furniture.

"Marius," Cranshawe exploded at last, "I want to know what is the meaning of this!" He picked up the newspaper and flung it down in front of his cousin.

Eversleigh studied the notice with minute care. "It seems quite correct to me," he said. "The only point that troubled me, I must confess, is that Miss Tallant dislikes being called Henrietta. But I thought people might be confused if I announced my betrothal to Henry Tallant.

Some few might even be scandalized, do you not agree, Oliver?"

Cranshawe appeared to be holding his temper in check with great difficulty. "You cannot be serious, Marius. You have been so confirmed in your bachelorhood that you will make yourself a laughingstock with this announcement."

"Indeed so, Oliver?" the duke asked, eyeing his cousin with raised eyebrows. "I had not realized I was so decrepit with age. I suppose we never see ourselves as we really are, do we?"

"The girl is barely out of the schoolroom," Cranshawe added.

"You think I shall not know what to do with her, Oliver?" Eversleigh asked. "I assure you, dear boy, I am still, er, capable, despite my advanced age. With superhuman effort, I might even beget an heir."

Cranshawe turned an interesting shade of purple. "You are doing this to provoke me, are you not, Marius?" he said, his handsome face contorted with anger. "You have always hated the thought of your title passing to me, have you not?"

"You see, dear boy," the duke replied, "it is not a pleasant thought to think of my title passing to anyone, when I must be dead first. Yes, you are quite right, Oliver. I find the thought abhorrent."

"You make a joke of everything," Cranshawe accused coldly. "It is impossible to talk to you. But believe me, Marius, you are making a mistake. For your own good, I tell you you will be a laughingstock marrying such a little fright. The Duchess of Eversleigh with freckles and untame curls and feet that tie themselves into knots in the middle of a dance floor!"

Eversleigh did not appear to hurry. Yet, by the time the last word had left Cranshawe's mouth, he was being helped none too gently to his feet with the assistance of an iron grip on both lapels of his coat.

"I regret that you are unable to stay longer, Oliver," Eversleigh said urbanely, his lazy blue eyes looking into Cranshawe's brown ones, only inches away. "Just a piece of cousinly advice before you leave, dear fellow. Talking with too loose a tongue can be injurious to the health, you know." He released his hold on his cousin's lapels, dusted his hands off, lowered himself casually into his chair again, and resumed drinking his coffee.

Cranshawe stalked across the room without a word.

"Ah, don't forget your paper, dear boy," the duke said kindly a split second before the door slammed behind his cousin.

"James, remind me to tell the butler about the draft in the hallway," he said to Ridley.

"Yes, your Grace."

During the afternoon, before he took Henry driving as promised, Eversleigh visited Suzanne Broughton. She had summoned him by letter and was for once alone in her drawing room when he arrived. She did not waste time in coming to the point.

"Marius," she said imperiously as her butler closed the double doors behind him, "what is the meaning of this ridiculous announcement in the *Post?*"

"Dear me," Eversleigh replied, a mystified frown drawing his brows together, "I shall really have to consider dismissing James Ridley from my service. He seems incapable of writing a communication that a reader might understand. You are the second person to ask me that question today, Suzanne."

"Oliver Cranshawe being the other, I presume," she snapped.

The duke inclined his head. "You must give me your felicitations, Suzanne," he said. "Miss Henrietta Tallant has consented to be my wife."

"A mere schoolroom chit, Eversleigh!" she retorted. "You will be tired of her in a week. I know you better than you know yourself, it seems."

"Quite likely, my dear," he agreed readily, "but an aging man must be allowed his dreams."

"Aging!" she said scornfully.

"Yes. It seems that my heir has hopes that the, er, exertions of the marriage bed might help me to my grave prematurely. In fact, when his temper cools, I believe he might conclude that this is the best thing that has happened to him in some time."

"Don't be so absurd, Marius," Suzanne retorted. "It seems that you have been merely toying with my affections. Am I no more than a light-skirts to you?"

Eversleigh surveyed her haughtily through his quizzing glass. "Suzanne, could it be that you are jealous?" he asked. "Had you expected an offer?"

She blushed and turned away in annoyance.

"No, no, you would not enjoy the restrictions of marriage, my dear," he continued, "especially to me. I should demand fidelity, you see. I believe the late Mr. Broughton was more liberal?"

"Marius, how positively medieval you are sometimes," she fumed, turning back to face him across the room. "What possible difference can it make, provided the proprieties are maintained? Fidelity went out of fashion a long age ago. You surely have no intention of remaining faithful to that pathetic little thing you are going to marry, have you? It would be a resolution impossible for you to keep." She laughed scornfully.

Eversleigh's lips thinned. "Then you must be grateful that I have not put you in danger of becoming a neglected wife," he remarked coldly.

"And do not think that you can come here and comfort yourself in my bed whenever your wife bores you," Suzanne continued.

Eversleigh bowed. "You make yourself abundantly clear, ma'am," he said.

"Oh, Marius," she cried suddenly, tears filling her eyes. She rushed across the room and threw her arms around his neck. "Indeed you are making a mistake. You are a very demanding man and I know how to please you. And you satisfy me. How can I find another to match you? What can she offer that I cannot?"

Eversleigh looked down at her impassioned face through half-closed lids. He did not accept the invitation of her pouted lips. "Amusement," he replied. "You see, she amuses me, Suzanne."

She stared at him blankly and then laughed uncertainly. "She amuses you?" she repeated. "And that is reason for marriage?"

"An excellent one," he agreed. "I believe I shall not know a moment's dullness with Henry."

"Henry!" she repeated, revolted.

\*     \*     \*

Later that same evening, Suzanne Broughton and Oliver Cranshawe met at a card party. They gravitated toward each other at suppertime.

"So, Suzanne," Cranshawe said, not bothering to charm her with his practiced smile, "my cousin has succeeded in thumbing his nose at both of us, it seems."

Suzanne looked haughtily back at him. "You, perhaps," she agreed. "but how me, pray?"

"Oh, come, Suzanne," he said, one corner of his mouth curling into a parody of a smile, "I am perfectly well aware that you were hoping to be the Duchess of Eversleigh. And he did appear to be leading you on, did he not?"

"I wish him well," she said with a brittle laugh. "His betrothal affects me not at all."

"But, if we could get revenge, my dear, you would not be displeased?" he asked, watching her carefully.

"Revenge?"

"I think it is probably too late to prevent the marriage," Cranshawe admitted. "He would not be persuaded to call it off, and she, little minx, must be over the moon at having ensnared such a catch. But perhaps, Suzanne, we could ensure that it is not a prosperous marriage?" His voice had become soft and insinuating.

"How so?" she asked, trying to keep her piqued interest out of her eyes and voice.

"She looks a perfect ninny of a chit, this, er, Henry of his," Cranshawe said. "Should I get to know her and try what my charm can accomplish?"

Suzanne looked measuringly at him and then allowed herself to smile. "You are a perfect devil, are you not, Oliver?" she said amiably. "But keep in mind that Marius as an enraged husband might be a trifle dangerous. There is no dueling weapon at which he is not adept."

"It might be worth the risk, though," he said, the sneer curling his lip again. "Do you not agree, Suzanne?"

"Why do you tell me this, Oliver?" she asked.

He shrugged. "I thought you might like to know that all is not lost," he said. "And if you could contrive to continue your liaison with Marius, we might make mischief out of it."

She smiled briefly and rose to move away to join a different group. "It would be a pleasure," she said with double meaning.

*    *    *

   And so the wedding took place, three weeks after the
betrothal announcement, in St. George's, Hanover Square.
Three hundred hastily invited guests attended and feasted
at a large and lavish reception.

   Finally, the Duke and Duchess of Eversleigh were alone
in his town house, the pair of wagers won. They were to
spend the wedding night in London and set out for a
two-week wedding trip to Paris the next day.

# CHAPTER

5

Henry was alone in her bedchamber. Until now Betty, the new maid allotted to her in her new home, had been in the room, helping her to undress and bathe, assisting her into a new white silk nightdress, and brushing her curls until they were dry and bouncy. Henry had been too busy talking to Betty and finding out about her family and her young man (his Grace's most junior footman) to really examine her new living quarters. Now she looked around her at the high ceiling, the tapestried walls with their delicate blue floral print, the pale-blue carpet underfoot, the royal-blue velvet hangings at the window and draped around the high four-poster bed, and the magnificent heavy furnishings.

She felt as if she were being royally treated, though she could still not believe that she was now a duchess. She certainly did not feel any different. All the events of the previous three weeks were a blur in her mind. They had been filled with a whirl of visits, shopping expeditions, and fittings. Every day she told herself that the next day she would end the betrothal. She had never really believed that she would allow the ceremony to go forward. But each day she had postponed the embarrassing announcement. Sometimes it was because the twins or Miss Manford or the pets were being poorly treated again; more often, it was because she became paralyzed with a kind of terror when in Eversleigh's presence.

She had seen him almost every day during those weeks.

She had gone driving with him, or he had escorted her to the theater, or he had been a dinner guest. But she felt no closer to knowing him. He held himself aloof and dignified. He never laughed or smiled. There was only that occasional gleam in his eyes that might have been a sign of humor, or that might have signaled contempt. His conversation was intelligent and pleasant, but he never revealed anything of himself. If any talk became too personal, he would turn the topic expertly with a comment that might or might not be a joke. It was so hard to tell.

Henry sighed as she stared at a Chinese screen spread out before the unlit fireplace in her bedchamber. And now Eversleigh was her husband. What would it be like to be his wife? Would she find it impossible ever to be free again? She had an uncomfortable feeling that if he set himself against the activities that she enjoyed—like riding, for instance—she would not be able to win a fight against him. Well, today at least was over, she reflected cheerfully, and tomorrow they would be on their way to the Continent.

The door of the dressing room that adjoined her bedchamber and the duke's opened after a light tap, and Eversleigh entered the room.

Henry's eyes opened wide with surprise and apprehension. "Good evening, your Grace," she said formally. "What do you want?" Her heart was beating uncomfortably fast as she noticed that he was wearing a blue satin dressing gown.

He stopped inside the door and folded his arms across his chest. "I am lost for an answer, Henry," he said calmly after a moment. "It *is* our wedding night, you know."

Henry stood her ground. "But what do you want?" she asked.

That gleam was in his eyes again, she noticed. "The answer is really very simple now that I have had time to think of it," he said. "You, my love."

Henry did not know what to answer; so she just stood and waited. Eversleigh let his arms fall to his sides and walked toward her until he stood only inches away. "You could not possibly be shy, could you, Henry?" he asked quietly. "Come, there is no need. You must trust me."

He slid his hands very gently along the sides of her breasts and under her arms and drew her against him.

Henry looked up into his face in wide-eyed alarm. His lips came down softly on hers. Henry stood rigid. Other people had kissed her on the lips: her father, the twins, several people on this very day after the wedding, and always it had lasted a mere second. It was the sort of ordeal that had to be endured in this world. But this kiss did not end after a second. After several seconds, in fact, she felt one hand slide down her body to hold her behind the hips and bring her full against the length of her husband, while the other hand moved up into her hair and cupped the back of her head. His head tilted to one side, and his mouth opened over hers. She felt his tongue slowly trace the line of her lips from one corner of her mouth to the other.

Henry panicked. She pushed wildly against his chest and darted across the room until the bed was between them. She clung to a bedpost and glared indignantly at him.

"Don't!" she said. "What are you trying to do?"

Eversleigh's eyes had opened wide for one unguarded moment. By now they were hooded again. He crossed his arms once more. "You are playing havoc with my self-esteem, Henry," he said with a sigh. "I was trying to make love to my wife."

"I don't like doing that," she said decisively. "Please go away."

He sighed again and seated himself on the edge of the bed. "Henry," he asked, "has anyone—any woman—explained to you what marriage is all about?"

"There is nothing to know," she said. "I have taken your name and I have promised to honor and obey you. Marian wanted to talk to me this morning, but I told her she really need not bother. She had to go away in the end."

"Your mother died when you were quite young, did she not, my love?" he asked.

"Yes. I was seven when the twins were born."

"And you have lived at Roedean ever since?"

"Until a few weeks ago, yes."

"So really you know nothing of marriage, do you?"

Henry looked doubtful. "I know you will want heirs, your Grace," she said. "And I shall be quite willing to perform that duty."

"Shall you?" He watched her for a long moment. "Do you know how, er, heirs are born, Henry?"

"Oh, yes," she replied eagerly. "I watched Majorca have a foal once. She was one of Papa's horses. I was not supposed to be there, but Giles and I had given Miss Manford the slip. The groom told us that human babies are born the same way. They come out . . ." She flushed and stopped as she made eye contact with her husband. "Well, you know," she finished lamely.

"Yes, I know, my love," he said softly. "But do you know how the heir—or the foal—is created, Henry?"

She flushed a deeper red. She did not know, though the question had bothered her for several years. She found it such a frightening question, in fact, that she had always resolutely blocked it from her consciousness.

"I thought not," he said when she did not answer. He got to his feet and walked around the bed toward her. She shrank against the bedpost. "No, don't be afraid, Henry," he said. "I am not about to start kissing you again, since you seem to find the exercise so unpleasant. But you must learn, my love, that there is a great deal more to marriage and to producing heirs than just kissing."

He took her chin in his hand and lifted it firmly until she looked wide-eyed at him. "We shall be in Paris and London until the end of July," he said. "Mingle with society, my love, and keep your eyes and ears open. At the end of that time we shall go down to Kent. My principal estate and favorite home is there. And there you will become my wife, Henry." His blue eyes lingered on her mouth and he pressed his thumb lightly along her lips. "The strain of being a frustrated husband might ruin my constitution between now and then," he added dryly. "You will never know what a heroic feat I have performed tonight, Henry."

He turned and walked unhurriedly back to the dressing-room door.

"Good night, my love," he said.

"Good night, your Grace."

He turned. "Henry, are you going to be your-Graceing me for the next fifty years?" he asked in a pained voice.

"No, your Grace."

"My name is Marius," he said.

"Yes, your Grace."

*     *     *

The next two weeks were surprisingly happy ones for Henry. The Channel crossing bothered her not at all, although the sea was decidedly choppy on the way across. While other ladies retired to their cabins armed with vinaigrettes, handkerchiefs, basins, and maids, Henry stayed on deck with her husband and watched eagerly for her first glimpse of the French coast. When she took off her bonnet and shook her curls into the wind, Eversleigh looked as if he might say something at first, but he merely closed his lips and resumed his study of the white-capped breakers. Henry noticed the gleam in his eyes before he did so. (At the end of the two weeks, she had decided that it was definitely a sign that he was amused. He never showed any other sign.) But when she twined the ribbons around her hand and twirled the bonnet absently while her hands were extended across the guardrail over the water, he did intervene.

"Henry, my love," he said reproachfully, "it is a remarkably handsome bonnet and I should hate to see it end up in the water. But the worst of it is, you see, that if it did fall overboard, I might feel compelled to be heroic and dive in after it. And I should hate that even more, I assure you."

Henry giggled. "You are absurd sometimes, your Grace," she said, pulling her hand back in over the rail.

"Henry!"

"Oh, I mean Marius, I suppose, though I feel very strange saying so," she said candidly. "You are really a very imposing figure, you know, your Gr—Marius. One would feel much more comfortable using your title." She grinned impishly up at him.

"Hmm," was his only reply as he gave her a sidelong glance.

In France, they traveled to Paris, arriving there on the second day. Eversleigh seemed to derive considerable amusement from showing his wife all the famous sites, accompanying her to various entertainments, and introducing her to many prominent people who lived there.

"Have you noticed, Marius," she asked on one occasion, "that the English tend to feel that if they talk loudly enough, the French will understand them? As if talking

French were an affliction of the deaf? Yet the French seem not to do it to the English."

"Sometimes you are uncomfortably observant, Henry," he said. "I shall have to be sure to whisper the next time I address a Frenchman, if you are close by."

She chuckled. "You have no need to either shout or whisper, Marius," she said. "Your French is quite fluent. At least, it sounds fluent." He inclined his head. "I wish I had paid Manny more mind when she tried to get us to converse in French," she added with a sigh.

Henry grew to feel comfortable with Eversleigh. He appeared to be remarkably open-minded and indulgent. And generous. She soon learned that she had only to admire a dress or a bonnet or piece of jewelry, and it was hers. She found herself clamping her mouth shut on several occasions when she was about to express a liking for something. She did not want her husband to think that she was interested only in his money. Indeed, possessions had never been of much significance to her, unless the possession were a horse, perhaps.

On only one occasion did they come close to quarreling. They were strolling along a fashionable promenade one afternoon, the sun beating down pleasantly on their heads. Henry took off her bonnet and turned up her face to the sun with a sigh of contentment.

"Put your bonnet on, Henry," Eversleigh said immediately, "before this plump matron walking toward us sees you and has a seizure."

"No," she replied, "I wish to feel the sun on my face and my hair."

"I was not offering you a choice, my love," he said quietly, and he stepped in front of her, took the bonnet from her nerveless fingers, and put it back on her head. It was only when his fingers began to tie the bow beneath her chin that she recovered from her momentary shock.

"Marius," she said, grasping his wrists, her eyes flashing dangerously, "I choose to walk bareheaded. Is that so terrible? Are you afraid of what people will say?"

"My wife will behave with propriety in public," he replied calmly. "Now, shall I tie this bow or will you?"

"You said nothing when we were on the ship," she said, still clinging to his wrists.

"There were no other ladies present to be scandalized," he explained, "and no other gentlemen close by. It seemed reasonable to allow you to please yourself."

"Well, I choose to please myself now," she retorted with a toss of her head that was meant to jerk the ribbons free of his hands.

"Very well, my love," he said meekly. He relinquished the ribbons of her bonnet and stepped to her side again. "Allow me to escort you back to our rooms. You will, of course, remain there until I am ready to take you back to England."

Henry stared at him openmouthed. "Well!" she exclaimed at last. When he continued to stand at her side, arm extended to her, she said, "Well!" again, tied the bow under her chin with a flourish, took his arm, and walked with him, chin high in the air, a cold haughtiness in her manner.

She succeeded in maintaining the manner for all of two minutes before something distracted her attention and she was exclaiming in delight. They did not return to their rooms.


The homecoming of the Duke and Duchess of Eversleigh was a hectic event. Henry's "family" had moved in a couple of days before, under the general supervision of James Ridley and Mrs. Dean, the housekeeper. Eversleigh had come to an agreement with Sir Peter Tallant on the matter before the wedding took place. Sir Peter was still to be the legal guardian of the twins, but Eversleigh was to have full responsibility for their day-to-day upbringing. He had refused financial assistance.

The twins had taken a liking to Ridley. They rushed into his office at least a dozen times each day to ask him a million questions. Why was it, he asked himself, that their normal manner of moving was a run and the normal level of their speech was a yell? Miss Manford, who seemed always to be several steps behind her charges, frequently came panting into the office after them, and then proceeded to blush and stammer her way through an apology. Really, Ridley reflected, the poor lady had his full sympathy. He wondered rather grimly what would happen when his employer returned. He had a feeling that the two imps would not be tearing around the house with quite such noisy abandon.

Brutus had also taken a liking to Ridley. In fact, to his everlasting shame, Ridley had been bowled backward right off his feet when he had gone into the hallway to greet the new arrivals. He could not even cover his confusion by rising rapidly. The canine was straddling his body and licking his face with panting enthusiasm. The twins were dancing around, yelling at the dog to "Sit!"; the governess was pawing the air with ineffective hands and calling on the Lord to bless her soul; and the infernal bird was doling out sympathy by calling on someone to bless his boots.

It was into this household of cheerful confusion that the duke and duchess arrived in the middle of one afternoon. While a few footmen stood woodenly in the hallway and others rushed outside to haul in boxes and trunks and valises, and while the butler was bowing over his master and mistress and relieving them of their outdoor garments, Philip and Penelope came shrieking down the staircase, Brutus panting on their heels and Miss Manford rounding the curve at the top of the staircase in a vain attempt to organize her charges into a more discreet welcoming committee.

"Henry," Penelope yelled, hurling herself bodily at her sister, "Phil and I have adjoining rooms. We can go back and forth without having to go into the corridor. And my room is green, not that ghastly pink that I had at Peter's, and . . ."

"I say, Henry," Philip shouted, dancing around in the background, "there are some ripping horses in the stables. The groom let me brush one of them down this morning."

"Philip, Penelope, please let your sister come upstairs and sit down," Miss Manford was commanding in the background, without any visible effect. "She must be tired and Mrs. Dean has some tea all ready."

"Down, boy!" a calm voice commanded, and it seemed to be the only voice of which anyone took any notice. Brutus, who had tried to repeat the performance he had accomplished with James Ridley a few days before, was now lying quietly on the floor, tongue lolling out of his panting mouth, eyes raised adoringly to Eversleigh, who had refused to be bowled over.

The duke turned to Miss Manford and extended his right hand. "Welcome to our home, ma'am," he said warmly. "My wife and I will try to see that you are happy here."

Miss Manford was in such a dither of embarrassment that it took her several moments to realize that she was meant to place her own hand in the one still extended to her. But it was obvious to the observers as she did shake hands with her employer, curtsying and apologizing as she did so, that the Duke of Eversleigh had made his second conquest of the afternoon.

"Now, Penny," he said easily, turning to his sister-in-law and, without apparent effort, herding the whole crowd up the staircase in the direction of the drawing room, "should you like to see the parasol that Henry and I have brought you from Paris? I am vastly relieved to remember that it is not pink."

He stopped in his tracks when they entered the room and he found himself being greeted in the usual colorful language of the remaining member of the family. Eversleigh raised his quizzing glass and viewed Oscar haughtily.

"And as for you, sir," he said severely, "you will kindly keep a civil tongue in your head when ladies are present, or I shall have your mouth cleansed with soap."

"Gosh-a-gorry," said Oscar penitently, and he stood still in the middle of his cage and hung his head.


Life quickly settled into some sort of pattern for the newly married pair. They tended not to see very much of each other during the daytime, except at the breakfast table. Eversleigh spent his days at his clubs, at the House of Lords, with his male friends at various sporting activities, or at home working alone or with his secretary. Henry, who was getting more used to the social life of the capital, was adapting to the change. She still rose earlier in the morning than most ladies of her class. She frequently rode in the park before it became too crowded, a groom always a short distance behind. In the afternoons she shopped, or visited, or traveled around London with the twins.

In the evenings Eversleigh usually dined at home. Sometimes afterward he would withdraw to one of his clubs. More often, he would escort his wife to some entertainment: the opera, a play, or a ball, perhaps.

On the second day after their return from France, a handsome high-perch phaeton was delivered to the duke's mansion, a wedding present for the duchess from her dear friends, the Raeburns.

"Ah," said Eversleigh, eyeing the conveyance through his quizzing glass, Henry at his side, "a very unusual wedding present, Henry."

"Yes," she said, eyes shining, "but is it not magnificent, Marius? I shall be able to drive myself in the park. It will be famous."

He eyed her out of the corner of his eye. "Perhaps, my love, I should have a groom run along ahead of you with a hand bell to warn all unsuspecting souls that you are coming."

"Absurd!" She laughed. "Papa used to say I must have been born in the saddle."

"In the saddle maybe, but perched several feet above the horses' backs, Henry, with only the ribbons and a whip to control them?"

"Pooh!" she said. "I do not anticipate any problems."

"For my peace of mind, Henry, allow me to drive with you for a while?"

"When you speak to me like that, Marius, I know I have no choice," she said practically, "so I might as well say yes."

"Quite so, my dear girl," he replied with a slight bow.

Henry was left feeling very glad that there had been no really awkward questions about the strangeness of the "wedding gift." At least Douglas had had the tact to say that the phaeton was a gift from his family.

On the next day, a pair of perfectly matched grays was delivered to the duke's stables. He was away from home when they arrived, but he was informed of the delivery as soon as he set foot inside the house, first by a hurtling pair of twins, who were down the stairs before the butler had time to close the door behind him, and then by his wife, who descended the staircase with only marginally more dignity.

"Marius!" she shrieked, startling his eyes wide open for a moment by rushing straight at him and throwing her arms around his neck. "You really are too generous. Yesterday you pretended to be so cautious about my phaeton.

I really thought you disapproved and did not want me to drive it. But today you surprised me with a pair of grays. They are perfectly gorgeous, your Grace."

"Henry, my love, I think the hallway of our home is hardly the appropriate scene for such an impassioned embrace. Shall we discuss the matter in the drawing room?" Eversleigh asked, apparently unperturbed by the misunderstanding. "And, Phil, if you keep hopping around in that manner, dear boy, you will surely knock down one of those marble busts and Mrs. Dean will have your head, or mine."

Henry twined her arm through his as they ascended the staircase together. "The grays are perfect for my phaeton, Marius," she said. "I wanted to take them out this afternoon, but I remembered that you wish to be with me until you can be certain that I shall not break my neck. I shan't, you know, but it seemed only fair to wait after you had been so generous. Did you go out first thing this morning to buy them for me?"

"I have been trying to acquire them for several months," Eversleigh answered evasively. "I suppose our marriage finally speeded the matter on."

"Did you have to pay a great deal for them?" she asked, looking anxiously up into his face.

He looked back into her eyes, his own half-hidden behind his eyelids. "I begin to think that the cost was not too high at all," he answered smoothly.

The Duke of Eversleigh spent a few afternoons with his wife, sitting beside her as she drove her new phaeton, pulled by the grays. The conveyance was dangerous and daring for a woman; the grays were high-spirited and difficult animals. The combination should have been beyond Henry's skill and strength, but as she had predicted, she proved to be an excellent whip. She drove her dashing new vehicle with precision and apparent ease. Eversleigh's relaxed and almost-lazy posture beside her suggested that he was not at all surprised by his wife's skills. After a few days, she was to be seen driving in the park alone, with a groom up behind. Some members of the *ton* murmured about the amount of freedom the duke was allowing his young wife.

Although Eversleigh accompanied Henry to several evening functions, he did not always dog her footsteps. Frequently at the theater he would leave their box during the intervals as soon as visitors came to call on her. He would wander into the hallway to converse with acquaintances, or enter other boxes to pay courtesy calls on their occupants. At balls he would frequently disappear into the card room after dancing once with his wife, leaving her to mingle with her growing number of friends.

And so Henry Devron, Duchess of Eversleigh, became something of the rage of London that Season. She was titled, rich, vivacious, and pretty in a thoroughly unfashionable way. Young men flocked to her. She was interesting to be with, with her refreshingly open manners and down-to-earth conversation. She knew nothing of feminine wiles and so, paradoxically, was extremely attractive to men; she was safely married and could be flirted with and dallied with without fear that an overbearing parent would demand a declaration from the man concerned. Soon after her return from her wedding trip, Henry had acquired a fairly large court of followers.

She seemed totally oblivious of her own popularity, seeming not to realize that there was anything unusual about having at least half a dozen men calling each afternoon, vying for the honor of taking her driving or of accompanying her in her own vehicle, crowding her box whenever she appeared at the theater or opera house. Eversleigh seemed well aware, but appeared not the least annoyed or alarmed by the phenomenon. In fact, he left the field clear for her court, though he usually looked over the individual members languidly with his quizzing glass before taking himself away.

And so it happened that, a little more than a week after her return to London, Henry came face to face with Oliver Cranshawe at Lady Emery's ball one evening. She had met him at her wedding and recognized him immediately as her husband's heir.

"Your Grace," he said silkily, bowing over her hand and favoring her with the full force of his dazzling smile, "you look even more lovely and sparkling than you did on your wedding day."

"Goodness," she said, laughing, "what a foolish thing to say. I am by no means lovely, sir, and if I sparkle, it is only because I am wearing the Eversleigh diamonds tonight."

He smiled again. "Cousin, I see you are not to be flattered," he said, gazing with smiling gray eyes into hers. "But, believe me, it is so refreshing to see a lady who neither simpers nor affects boredom. You do enjoy life, do you not?"

Henry found herself warming to his friendly, open personality and to his handsome, youthful presence. "It would be foolish to pretend boredom," she said with some scorn. "Surely soon one would be bored in good earnest."

He laughed. "You are delightful, your Grace. I cannot tell you how I envy my cousin. Will you dance?"

"Certainly," she said. "But I must warn you that I have a nasty habit of treading all over my partner's feet."

He grinned. "They say to be forewarned is to be forearmed, your Grace," he said as he led her onto the floor to join a set that was forming.

"If we are cousins," she said, "I think you must call me Henry."

When the dance was over and Cranshawe led her to the sidelines, Henry was surprised to find Eversleigh standing there, looking relaxed and at his ease. He had disappeared into the card room an hour before.

"Ah, Oliver," he commented languidly, "enjoying the festivities, dear boy?"

"I have been making the acquaintance of your very charming wife, Marius," Cranshawe replied, smiling down at Henry.

"Quite so," Eversleigh said, putting his quizzing glass to his eye and surveying the other occupants of the room in a leisurely manner. "I always consider it such a bore to feel duty-bound to converse and dance with family members. In fact, I make it a practice almost never to do so."

"But who would call dancing with Henry a duty?" Cranshawe replied, bowing to her and smiling warmly into her eyes again.

Eversleigh's glass swept in the direction of his heir. "I certainly do not, Oliver," he said, "but then *her Grace* is my wife."

Cranshawe stood uncomfortably where he was for a few

moments. Then he bowed to Henry. "If you will excuse me, cousin," he said, "I see someone that I must talk to."

"Good night, Oliver," Henry said, smiling a little uncertainly at him.

Eversleigh lowered his glass and looked at his heir. "On your way so soon, dear boy?" he asked.

Cranshawe bowed again and walked away.

"Marius," Henry said, turning to him with indignation in her eyes, "why were you so rude to your cousin?"

"I? Rude?" he said, raising his eyebrows in surprise. "But, Henry, I pride myself on always displaying impeccable manners. Will you waltz, my love, before the five young men converging on this spot arrive to whisk you away from a mere husband?"

"Absurd!" she commented, and laid her hand on his proffered arm.

# CHAPTER

# 6

Henry renewed her acquaintance with Oliver Cranshawe two mornings later in Hyde Park. She was out unfashionably early, riding Jet, who had been brought to London since her marriage. A groom was riding within hailing distance of her. She became aware of Cranshawe cantering up alongside while she was in the midst of resisting the temptation to take off her feathered riding hat so that she could feel the breeze in her hair.

"Good morning, cousin," Cranshawe called, flashing her a smile and sweeping off his hat.

"Oh, good morning, Oliver," Henry returned gaily. "Is it not a beautiful morning?"

"All the more so since I saw you," he said, sweeping admiring eyes over her trim figure clad in moss-green riding attire and over her powerful, gleaming black horse. "That is a splendid mount, if I may say so, your Grace."

"Yes, is he not?" she agreed. "But I thought it was decided that you are to call me Henry."

His face grew serious and he looked earnestly across at her. "I understood that your husband did not approve of such familiarity, ma'am," he said.

Henry hesitated. "He was in a disagreeable mood the other night, was he not?" she said. "Is there some quarrel between you and Marius, Oliver?"

"Perhaps you should ask your husband about that," he replied earnestly. "On my part, there is no cause for bad feeling at all. I try my best to be friendly to my cousin.

But I realize that it must be difficult for him to know that I am his heir. I assure you that it matters not at all to me, but I do believe that Marius feels threatened by my existence."

Henry looked at him sharply. "That is surely nonsense," she said.

He shrugged. "You must judge for yourself, Henry. I certainly do not wish you to see your husband in a bad light. I should prefer that you judged me harshly." He smiled rather sadly into her eyes.

"I shall do no such thing," she replied firmly. "I always judge matters for myself, sir. But I do believe family feuds to be silly nonsense."

He bowed from the saddle. "Can I tempt you to test your horse against mine, Henry?" he asked, seeming to consider it wise to change the subject.

"Oh, do you mean a race?" she asked, eyes sparkling again.

"Shall we say to the southern gate and back on the count of three?" he suggested.

Henry had never been known to resist such a challenge. Soon the few spectators who were privileged (or unfortunate) enough to be in the park at that morning hour were treated to the spectacle of two horses galloping full tilt down the grassy avenue of the park, their riders, one male and one female, bent low over their necks. They were almost abreast of each other at the turn, but Henry won the race with a few lengths to spare.

"Ha!" she cried, laughing breathlessly as Cranshawe drew his mount to a halt beside hers. "You must now admit that Jet is the superior horse, Oliver."

"Not so, not so!" he protested, holding up one hand and displaying a wide array of very white teeth as he smiled back at her. "You see, I stopped to pick up your hat, which blew off back at the gate. Had I not played the gentleman, ma'am, I declare the outcome might have been very different."

"Pooh!" she replied. "I should not have stopped to rescue your hat, sir. You must pay the penalty for your foolishness."

"Henry," he said, suddenly serious again and bringing his horse closer to hers, "you are such marvelous company.

Indeed, it was unkind of you to marry my cousin before you had given me the chance to try my suit."

Henry rapped him sharply on the knuckles with the handle of her whip and looked around until she saw her groom holding his horse at a discreet distance. "Now you are being foolish," she said. "I don't like it when people become silly and untruthful."

He smiled ruefully. "You will not believe in your own attractions, will you, cousin?" he said, still serious. "But may I be your friend, Henry? I think you may need one. I fear your husband can sometimes be a dry old stick."

"You talk a pile of nonsense," Henry replied matter-of-factly, "but of course we are friends. I must return home, Oliver. Jet will be overtired. Good morning, sir."

Late that same afternoon, when Henry was in the drawing room looking over some dress patterns with Miss Manford, Eversleigh strolled in. Henry brightened. The activity had not been of her choosing and was not holding her interest to any great degree. He seated himself and conversed pleasantly with both women for several minutes. Then he turned to his wife.

"Will you come to the library, Henry?" he asked.

"Certainly," she replied, bouncing readily to her feet.

"Will you excuse us, ma'am?" Eversleigh asked, bowing in the direction of Miss Manford.

The governess blushed and stammered and fluttered her hands in an ecstasy of embarrassment at being so courteously noticed by her employer.

"Sit down, Henry," Eversleigh said when they were in the library, the door closed behind them. Henry sat and gazed inquiringly up at him.

Eversleigh moved to the fireplace and leaned one elbow on the mantel. He regarded his wife through half-closed eyelids. "Henry," he asked, "are you happier with your life in London than you were when I first met you?"

She looked at him in surprise. "I don't remember ever being unhappy," she replied, eyebrows knitting in puzzlement. "I have always thought the social life rather silly, but it can be amusing. Yes, Marius, I am happy."

"I have been pleased to see you become fashionable and to observe that you have acquired a circle of friends," he continued.

"Yes, I never lack for company," she agreed, not at all sure where this conversation was headed.

"Have I given you enough freedom?" he asked. "Have I ever made any unreasonable demands?"

"No, Marius," she said emphatically, "you are a most indulgent husband, I believe. Except when it comes to bonnets," she could not resist adding impishly.

"Quite so," he agreed, his eyes gleaming for a moment. He continued to look at her in silence for a while before continuing quietly. "I must now make one demand on you, my love. I do not wish you to associate with Oliver Cranshawe any more than strict courtesy demands."

Henry jerked to her feet. "Did your spies report my meeting with him this morning, your Grace?" she asked tartly.

"I do not spy on you, Henry," he replied quietly, "but news always travels faster in the city than if it had wings. I heard that you met and raced with him, yes."

"But why make such a thing of it, Marius?" she asked crossly. "We were in the park. There could hardly be a more public place. How could it be improper?"

"I did not say your meeting him was improper, my love," he pointed out reasonably.

"Then, why?" she asked. "Give me one good reason why I should not be civil to Oliver."

His blue eyes looked steadily into hers. "Say it is because I wish it," he said.

"That is no reason!" she retorted hotly. "I like Oliver. He is friendly and has easy manners. He is fun to be with. I have no intention of pokering up whenever I see him just because you wish it."

"Do you not, Henry?" he asked mildly. "Why is it that I am not in the least surprised?"

Henry opened her mouth and shut it again. Marius really had a disconcerting knack of saying the unexpected and taking the thrust right out of her attack.

"I do request that you humor me on this one matter, my love," he continued.

"Oh, and am I now dismissed, your Grace?" she asked, tossing her head haughtily.

"I almost fear for my life in having to bring up one more matter," he said meekly. "Henry, for my peace of mind, will you refrain from racing in the park? I know you have a splendid seat, my love"—he looked deliberately down to view it—"but I also know that most of your galloping has been done, er, astride your horse. If you can wait until we are in the country, I shall be quite delighted to see you ride in breeches." He allowed his gaze to wander down to the slim legs that were outlined beneath the fall of her high-waisted gown. "But I cannot help feeling that the sidesaddle was designed for more restrained exercise."

Henry stared unflinchingly into her husband's face. Her eyes were blazing, her lips compressed, her teeth clamped together, her cheeks aglow with color. She was infuriated; he had been quite deliberately and unhurriedly undressing her with his lazy eyes.

"And am I dismissed *now*, your Grace?" she asked through her teeth.

He reached out and took her chin in his hand. Then he smiled slowly—yes, actually smiled, she noted with renewed fury. "Yes, my love, you may take your indignation upstairs to your room," he said, and he leaned forward and kissed her very lightly on the nose.

Henry's stomach did an uncomfortable flip-flop—of anger, of course, at the sheer gall of the man. Must he treat her as a child? Could he not see that her anger was real? She swept from the room with as much icy hauteur as she could muster.

It was on the morning following this altercation with her husband that Henry arrived home from her ride to find that she had a visitor waiting in the downstairs salon. The butler did not identify the guest. Henry entered the room, half-expecting to find Oliver Cranshawe and not quite sure whether she should treat him with some reserve out of respect to her husband, or whether to greet him spontaneously as her own inclination dictated. She reacted with a shriek when she saw the room's occupant.

"Giles!" she yelled, hurtling across the room and throwing herself into her brother's arms. "You did not tell me you were coming to town."

He hugged her and grinned down at her. "I say, Henry," he said, gazing admiringly at the smart moss-green riding habit and the jaunty hat with the curled brown feather that she still wore, "you are becoming the grand lady. I hardly recognize my tomboy sister. And this house is rather splendid, is it not?"

She pulled the hat off her head, tossed it carelessly onto a side table, and shook out her auburn curls. "Is term over, Giles?" she asked eagerly. "You did not write to say. Are you staying in town for a while? With Peter? What fun we shall have! You shall come to all the parties and balls with me and we shall laugh at all the foolishness together."

She stopped suddenly, sensing that her brother was not sharing her mood. "What is it, Giles?" she asked.

He grinned ruefully and seated himself in a chair close to the fireplace. "Term is not over," he said. "I was sent down."

Henry stared at him, openmouthed. "Giles! How simply awful!" she said. "Whatever did you do?"

"Nothing much," he said. "A few of us slipped out of the dormitory after it was locked up, to play cards with a couple of visiting fellows in town. Old Boner got wind of it somehow and had a reception committee waiting for us when we returned."

"You were gambling, Giles!" Henry accused, shocked.

"Nothing to signify," he answered airily. "A fellow has to do something to entertain himself, Henry, believe me. We cannot be expected to *study* all the time."

"But you know how Papa felt about cards, Giles."

"Yes, and don't you start in on me, Sis," he said hastily, jumping to his feet and pacing the room. "I have had Peter prosing on ever since I came home yesterday. Life is not going to be very cheerful in that household, I can tell you."

"But, Giles, what are you going to do?" Henry asked anxiously. "You know there is not enough money for you to live like an idle gentleman."

"Don't fret," he assured her. "I was not expelled outright. I can go back again next term. But really, Henry, I would like to join a cavalry regiment."

"Does Peter know that?" she asked.

"Oh, yes, but it will not do," he said bitterly. "Nothing but the Church will suit Peter."

Henry brightened. "Perhaps I can persuade Marius to buy you a commission," she suggested, clapping her hands and also jumping to her feet. "He is incredibly generous, you know, Giles."

"I am pleased for your sake, Henry," he said. "I was not easy in my mind about your marrying him, y'know. I would not have encouraged that wager if I had thought there was any chance of your bringing him up to scratch. But, Henry, you are not to ask him for any favors on my behalf. Understand? It's bad enough to know that he has taken on Phil and Penny and Manny and the animals. I would be mortally humiliated if I felt I was to be added to the list. I would feel like a worm, Sis. Promise me?"

Henry smiled. "If you insist," she agreed. "I promise. But do come up to the schoolroom and let everyone see you. The twins will be ecstatic." She linked her arm through his and led him up the stairway.

Henry had expected that there would be a certain constraint between her and her husband after their conversation in the library. But the matter appeared to be forgotten. It seemed that she had won the argument. She never did race Jet in the park again, but she did occasionally meet Oliver Cranshawe there and spend short spans of time with him. Sometimes, if it were afternoon and she were driving her phaeton, she took him up and drove with him for ten minutes or so. But she was always careful that their meetings were quite public and of short duration. She was not aware of Eversleigh's spying on her, though on one occasion he rode past the phaeton. He merely doffed his hat and bowed to her. He took no special notice of Cranshawe at all.

It seemed that her husband's heir was at most of the social functions that she attended, a fact that did not strike her as odd in any way. There were numerous other people that she saw almost wherever she went. He usually contrived to spend a few minutes in Henry's company, although, again, there was no suggestion of anything improper. Their meetings were very public. And since Henry had a whole host of admirers who followed her almost wherever she went, there seemed nothing particular about Cranshawe's attentions. There was no gossip. Eversleigh did not refer to the matter again, though Henry noticed that he was usually visible whenever she was with his cousin. If he were in another room when Oliver joined her, a sixth sense must have brought him back into the room where they were.

Henry respected her husband. She was even beginning to feel proud to be known as the duchess of such a very handsome and distinguished man. She felt a heightened glow of awareness when in his presence, though she was largely unconscious of the fact. But she was not about to become his slave or his shadow. She liked Oliver Cranshawe and she was not going to spurn him just to cater to the arrogant whims of a man who could not give her a good reason for his demand. She quite deliberately cultivated the friendship.

Henry found herself drawn to Cranshawe's charm and ease of manner. She instinctively relaxed in his company and consequently came to confide in him. She never discussed her husband or their strange relationship, but if she had other worries or concerns, she turned to him. It seemed perfectly natural on the evening after Giles' visit for her to tell Oliver all about it, although she had given only a very edited version to Eversleigh earlier in the day. They were seated in an alcove of a ballroom, in full view of the dancers and of the other guests.

Cranshawe covered her hand with his. "Henry, dear," he said seriously, lowering his voice, though there seemed to be no one nearby intent on eavesdropping, "I have money and I have influence. And both are totally at your command. If there is anything I can do at any time to help you or your brother, I should be more than honored to do so. I can see that you might be frightened to turn to Marius in some circumstances, but never be afraid to come to me. I am your devoted servant."

Henry withdrew her hand and looked uncertainly at her companion. "You are silly when you talk like that," she said, "but I do thank you for your offer of help, Oliver. I do not foresee ever having to call on you, but it is good to know that you are my friend."

Cranshawe always knew how far to carry his sentimental moods. He grinned now. "Allow me to fetch you some lemonade, Henry. Then I must relinquish you to poor Hendricks, who is looking most mournful over there. Do you see him leaning against that pillar? I believe he thinks I am going to steal his dance, the foolish puppy."

"He is really a very sweet boy," Henry said kindly. "But he should spend less time in writing poetry and more in gaining physical exercise. I always tell him so."

As Cranshawe walked away, Henry smiled broadly and with genuine pleasure across the ballroom at her husband, whose eye she caught momentarily. He was talking with a very handsome golden-haired lady. A Mrs. Broughton, she believed. A minute later, when Cranshawe returned with her lemonade, he too remarked on the couple before leaving the field clear to the small group of admirers clustered around Henry.

"I see Marius is dancing," he said conversationally, "and with Suzanne Broughton, too." He managed to make it sound as if there were something almost significant about the fact that the duke was dancing with that particular lady.

Perhaps it was fortunate that Henry was not closer to the dancing pair. They were waltzing, and were thus enabled to carry on a sustained conversation.

"You have become quite the stranger, Marius," Suzanne was saying archly.

He raised his eyebrows and looked down his nose at her. "Ah, but I cannot believe that you have been lonely, Suzanne," he commented.

"I do not languish after any man," she replied haughtily, "but I did believe we had a friendship, Marius."

His eyes narrowed. "We both know what kind of a friendship we had, my dear girl," he said.

"Yes, and it was good, was it not?" she said, smiling at him suggestively.

"Yes, it was good," he agreed.

"It could be so again, Marius," she continued. "I do not believe that little green girl can satisfy your appetites for much longer."

He gazed at her with his half-closed eyes, but said nothing.

Suzanne became uncomfortable. She laughed. "You are not going to tell me, Marius, that she is able to give you all you need between the bed sheets," she goaded.

He continued his silent scrutiny until her gaze shifted to

the couples dancing around them. "You are quite right, of course, dear girl," he said, and she shot him a triumphant glance, "I am not going to tell you."

"One of these days, Marius," she said, a smile on her lips, fury in her low voice, "you are going to want my favors and come begging for them. And I shall laugh in your face."

"That will be very pleasant for you, Suzanne," he agreed meekly.

A few days later, Eversleigh arrived home to discover that his household was sadly changed from the peaceful, orderly days of his bachelorhood. It lacked little more than an hour until dinner; certainly it was well after the usual visiting time. Yet there was noise enough coming from the drawing room to suggest fifty callers. And over it all was the noise of Brutus barking as he stood outside the closed door of the upstairs room, demanding entrance.

Eversleigh, handing his hat and gloves to an impassive-faced footman, glanced up the stairs and looked back inquiringly at his butler.

"I believe her Grace is, er, discussing family matters with her brother, your Grace," that poker-faced individual explained.

Eversleigh nodded, as if the explanation were quite sufficient to account for the commotion. He squared his shoulders and proceeded unhurriedly up the stairs.

"Lie down, Brutus, and take a rest," he ordered languidly. The dog immediately responded by stretching out across the doorway, laying his head on his paws, gazing adoringly up at the duke, and thumping his tail on the carpeted floor.

"You do lack some common sense, don't you, old boy?" the duke continued conversationally. "How am I supposed to enter the room without taking a flying leap over your back? That would not provide a dignified entrance for one of my rank, you know."

Brutus panted with ecstasy at being so noticed by his idol.

When Eversleigh finally opened the door and entered the drawing room, quizzing glass in hand, the commotion instantly ceased. His glass swung over an irate-looking Sir

Peter Tallant, an uncomfortable James Ridley, a weeping Miss Manford, a bright-eyed and defiant set of twins, and a flushed, indignant Henry.

The scene progressed like a well-rehearsed comedy show. The players were frozen for a few seconds as they all turned to view the newcomer. Then all burst to life at the same moment when they saw who it was.

Sir Peter looked smug. "Ah, Eversleigh," he said, "you have returned in good time to help me convince these children of what is proper behavior in London."

"We weren't doing anything wrong," Penelope shrieked.

"We had only gone forward to get a better view," Philip cried.

"Marius, you won't let him split them up and send Phil away, will you?" Henry implored, hurling herself across the room and clinging to her husband's arm.

Miss Manford sniffed rather loudly against her handkerchief.

"Really, your Grace, I must take the blame for the whole episode," Ridley said earnestly and gallantly.

Eversleigh covered his wife's hand with his own as it rested on his arm and fixed a languid glance on his secretary. "That is extraordinarily noble of you, James," he said. "But might I ask for what you are assuming the blame?"

"Your Grace . . ."

"Marius . . ."

Sniff.

"But we didn't . . ."

The duke held up a silencing hand. "I believe only one person in this room answers to the name of James," he pointed out with calm common sense.

"Your Grace," Ridley began, "Miss Manford had agreed to take Miss Penelope and Master Philip to the balloon ascent on Richmond Hill this afternoon. I agreed to accompany them, as this is one of my days off."

"Quite so," Eversleigh agreed, idly fondling Henry's fingers beneath his hand.

"We took the gig, your Grace. But there was such a large crowd of people there that we could not hope to get close. Miss Manford urged her charges to stay close to the gig and not to wander away. We tried to persuade them that when the balloon became inflated and airborne, we would have a splendid view of it."

"But we couldn't see a thing!" Penelope shrieked. "Just bonnets and parasols and carriages and things."

"I believe you," her brother-in-law said unsympathetically. "James?"

"They wandered away, your Grace, and soon we lost them completely. Miss Manford and I searched the area until the last carriage had left and finally returned here in the desperate hope that they would have found their way home."

Miss Manford sniffed again.

"We weren't even lost," Philip chimed in indignantly. "Peter . . ."

"Thank you, dear boy," the duke said. "Perhaps some-one would tell me how you *did* get home. Tallant?"

"I was watching with my wife and her sister, Eversleigh," Sir Peter began, glad of the renewed chance to air his grievance, "when what did I see but my own brother and sister, quite unchaperoned, making spectacles of themselves."

Eversleigh's brows rose in alarm. "I feel for you!" he said.

"Yes, indeed," Sir Peter continued, "they had actually climbed under the cordon and were interfering with the balloon workers."

"We were only asking . . ." Penelope began, but she was quelled by a glance from her older brother.

"I had to face the indignity, Eversleigh, of crawling under the rope myself and, in full view of half the *ton*, gathering these two together and escorting them away. I brought them home immediately."

"But, Marius, he did not give a thought to poor Manny and Mr. Ridley," Henry complained, staring wide-eyed into her husband's face.

Eversleigh squeezed her hand, but continued to look politely at his brother-in-law.

"I had given Miss Manford notice before she came here, Eversleigh," Sir Peter stated, aggrieved. "Now perhaps you will see for yourself that she is totally incapable of controlling the twins and quite incompetent as a governess."

"Perhaps I shall," Eversleigh agreed soothingly.

"It is time Philip was sent away to Eton," Sir Peter continued. "I shall begin to make arrangements immediately. Penelope must have a stricter governess, one who will train her to be a lady. You have only to look at Henrietta to see how incapable Miss Manford is of accomplishing that goal. I shall look to it, Eversleigh."

Eversleigh's fingers had tightened imperceptibly around Henry's. His gaze, under the half-closed lids, sharpened. "Penny," he said pleasantly, "perhaps you would help Miss Manford to her room? I believe a rest before dinner would be in order. James, you will not wish to waste what is left of your day off standing around here. You may take yourself off, dear boy. Phil, you may return those two volumes that are on the mantel to the library. Oh, and wait for me there, will you?"

Within seconds, only three people were left in the room. "Have a seat, Tallant," Eversleigh directed, leading his wife to a sofa and seating himself beside her. He still held her hand on his arm. "Now," he said, fixing his brother-in-law with a sleepy stare, "I believe you owe her Grace an apology, Tallant?"

"What?"

"Forgive me," the duke continued, "perhaps in all the excitement of the last few minutes my hearing became defective. I thought I heard you declare publicly that my wife is not a lady."

Sir Peter's jaw dropped. "Those were not quite my words," he said, "but we all know that Henrietta is not exactly everyone's ideal image of a lady of quality."

"She is mine," Eversleigh replied softly.

Henry stole a startled look at his hard profile. She could hardly believe her ears. All her life she had been labeled a tomboy. Her family had always lamented, if in a loving way, her lack of feminine charms. Could the very correct and sophisticated Duke of Eversleigh be seriously claiming that she was his ideal lady? But of course he was not. He was merely a proud man protecting the honor of his property. She sighed.

"I was not offended, Marius," she said, pulling her hand away from his at last. "In fact, I would hate to be the typical lady. I should have to play the pianoforte and sing and embroider and simper. Ugh!"

"Tallant?" Eversleigh asked, momentarily ignoring his wife.

"Well, of course I am sorry if I hurt anyone's feelings," Sir Peter blustered. "I was merely using a brother's privilege of speaking his mind."

"Ah," said Eversleigh, "was that what you were doing too when you planned Eton for Philip and a new governess for Penelope?"

"I am their legal guardian," Sir Peter said stiffly. "I have a responsibility to them."

"Ah, but it is a responsibility that you largely abdicated to me when we made an agreement prior to my marriage," the duke replied.

"It seems that you did not realize what a burden that task might be," Sir Peter commented.

"Tallant," Eversleigh said, raising his quizzing glass and viewing the other lazily through it, "as I see it, there is room for only one master in my home. It may be unreasonable of me, my dear fellow, but I have always insisted that that master be me. Now, I really cannot have you storm into my house when I am not even present and upset my wife, attempt to dismiss my employees, and try to organize the lives of children whom you gave into my charge. I believe I make myself clear?"

"Am I then to stand idly by while my brother and sister frolic around London without restraint and make perfect asses of themselves?" Sir Peter asked, shaking with anger.

"Ah, but you see, my dear fellow," Eversleigh replied, "they were not without chaperonage, had you not snatched them away. And are children to be labeled asses merely because they behave as children?"

Sir Peter rose to his feet. "I felt rather sorry for you, Eversleigh," he said, "when you paid your addresses to Henrietta without any close acquaintance with her. I thought you would soon discover your mistake. Now I believe you have gained only what you deserve."

"Quite so," Eversleigh agreed amiably. "I believe you might be right, dear fellow."

The "dear fellow" stormed out of the room and down the stairs, ignoring the growls of Brutus, who was still stretched across the doorway of the room.

Henry jumped to her feet and clapped her hands.

"Marius, I could hug you!" she cried, her eyes glowing at him. "I have wanted all my life to hear someone give Peter a set-down like that."

"Could you, my love?" Eversleigh asked, also standing, so that he was very close to her.

Henry stood spellbound, a strange churning feeling low in her stomach. Her eyes locked with her husband's. "Marius," she said at last, almost in a whisper, "are we a terrible burden to you? We always get into such scrapes, you know, and I think Peter was right—I am not really a lady."

"Ah, but you said yourself that you do not really wish to be," he said.

"But I do not want to be an embarrassment to you, Marius," she said wistfully.

"You would have to try very hard to be that, my dear," he said, the familiar gleam in his eyes. He reached up a hand and stroked her cheek lightly with one knuckle.

"Why do you put up with us, Marius?" she asked.

"For the reason I mentioned before our marriage," he replied. "You amuse me." He continued to stroke her cheek.

Henry was confused. She wanted to move away from him; she did not like being within his aura of power and masculinity. And yet she found herself involuntarily leaning her cheek into his knuckle. She wanted him to have no binding claim on her, and yet she felt a sinking of her spirits at his last words. What did she want? She did not know. She only felt overwhelmingly grateful that he had taken her part against her brother and won a victory for her. Yet, even this feeling annoyed her. She did not want to appear weak and in need of protection.

Henry's confusion was suddenly multiplied tenfold when Eversleigh quite unexpectedly drew her into his arms and covered her lips with his own. She was so surprised, in fact, that it was several seconds before she realized that she had put her arms up around his neck and arched her hips and thighs against his. She felt the heat rise in him and the kiss deepen before she began to push furiously at his chest.

"Don't do that!" she demanded breathlessly as they drew apart. "You know I dislike it."

He stood, seemingly relaxed, a laugh in his eyes. "Poor little Henry!" he said. "When will you realize that you are a woman?"

"Oh!" she said crossly. "First my brother says I am not a lady, and now you say I am not a woman."

"And I say that Phil will be reaching the far stages of boredom downstairs in the library with nothing to do but look at books," said Eversleigh. "Come, my love, do not be cross with me. I promise to try to curb my animal instincts."

And he strolled from the room, leaving Henry's mind and body in turmoil.

In the library, Eversleigh was soon offering an indignant Philip a choice: either to spend three days indoors doing extra tasks in the schoolroom, or to receive a thrashing there and then.

"But I did not do anything so very wrong," the boy protested. "Pen and I knew how to get back to Manny and Mr. Ridley. We were never lost. And we were not interfering with those men. We were merely asking some questions. If Peter had not hauled us away, there would have been no problem."

"It is not for any of those things that I propose to punish you," the duke explained, strolling over to his desk and perching on the end of it. "It is your behavior to Miss Manford that I take exception to."

Philip stared, uncomprehending. "Manny?" he said. "She is used to us. We are always playing pranks on her, or we forget and do things without thinking. But she knows that we mean no harm. She don't mind."

"On the contrary, Phil," said Eversleigh, "it seemed to me when I entered the drawing room earlier that she minded a great deal."

"That was only because Peter had been giving her a great scold," Philip explained. "She was not mad at us. And she would not have been so upset if Peter had not kidnapped Pen and me and brought us home so that Manny thought we were lost in good earnest. It was all his fault."

"Was it, dear boy?" the duke asked. "Was not your

disobedience to your governess at the root of the whole matter?"

Philip stared, unable to think of an answer.

"You see, Phil," Eversleigh said, standing and wandering over to the fireplace, where he took up his favorite stance leaning an elbow on the mantel, "ladies in Miss Manford's situation can lead a miserable life. Many people feel that they do not have to be treated with the same courtesy and respect that one would afford to a lady of independent means. A true gentleman will not make the distinction. You frightened the lady this afternoon and caused her to become an object of anger and contempt."

Philip continued to stare. He had turned noticeably paler. "I had not thought of it that way before," he said.

"No," Eversleigh agreed, "I thought you had not." He considered the boy in silence for a while. "Well, Phil, which is it to be?"

Philip straightened his shoulders. "I'll take the thrashing, sir," he said.

Eversleigh did not move. "Good lad!" he said. "If you realize that you deserve it, Phil, it seems that you probably do not need it. You are dismissed."

"Now, sir?" stammered Philip. "D-do you want me to return some other time?"

"Not particularly, dear boy," said Eversleigh. "I find myself tolerably contented without your company. But I will require it if I find you disregarding the feelings of Miss Manford again, Phil. Somehow, though, I do not expect it."

"Thank you, sir," Philip yelled, and he tore through the doorway before his brother-in-law could change his mind.

# CHAPTER

## 7

Henry did not see a great deal of Giles in the few weeks
following his arrival in London. He avoided the round of
social events that she now attended almost with enjoyment.
He did visit her and the twins occasionally, and she sometimes spotted him in Hyde Park during the afternoons, when
the whole fashionable world, it seemed, paraded on
horseback, in carriages, and on foot. He was always with a
group of fashionable young men, some of them outright
dandies. She noticed that Giles, too, now dressed in the
height of fashion. His collar points were often so high that
Henry wondered how he could turn his head or even see
to right or left. His coats were so close-fitting that she
imagined he must have been poured into them. His boots
were so shiny that they must surely be polished with
champagne, an affectation that was current among some of
the young bucks, she had heard.

Henry was amused at her brother's obvious enjoyment
of town life. She had always thought he was like she used
to be, happy only in the country when free of social
restraints.

She became alarmed for him one afternoon, though,
when he visited. The twins were away from home.
Eversleigh had begun to spend more time with them since
their escapade at the balloon launching. On this particular
day, they had gone to the Tower of London to see the gate
leading into the building from the River Thames that
condemned persons used to enter prior to execution. They

also hoped to see the dungeons and the axes used to decapitate condemned nobles.

"There are other things to see there, you know," Eversleigh had suggested in his languid way.

"Such as?" Penelope asked.

"Furniture, jewels, a magnificent view of London from the turrets."

"Ugh! Let us stick with the interesting stuff," Penelope replied.

"Quite so, Penny," he agreed. "An admirable decision."

Henry had reluctantly remained behind because she was expecting callers. The guests left soon after the arrival of Giles.

"You are very quiet, Giles," she remarked when they were alone together.

"Well, I don't know those people," he replied.

"No, it's not that," she said, considering him for a while. "Is town life not agreeing with you?"

He shrugged. "It's well enough."

"What is the matter?"

"Nothing is the matter, Henry," he said impatiently. "Don't fuss so."

"I know you too well, Giles," she protested, refusing to drop the topic. "Is it Peter? Or Marian? Are they giving you a hard time? Why do you not come to live here? Marius would not mind, truly."

"Henry, don't be such a bumble brain!" her brother said lovingly. "Can you seriously imagine me moving in with Eversleigh? Anyway, Peter and Marian are all right. I think Peter is reserving his energies for sending me back to Oxford in the autumn."

"It must be money, then," she decided. "Are your pockets to let, Giles?"

"Nothing to signify," he replied, rising from his chair and pacing restlessly across the room. "You used not to be such a shrew, Henry. You were always a good fellow."

"And you used to confide in me, Giles," she returned tartly. "It is money, is it not? You have been spending on clothes and jewels, like as not, to keep up with your friends. How much do you owe?"

"Nothing that I cannot pay sooner or later," he said sullenly.

"How much, Giles?"

He paused and rocked on his heels. "It is not as simple as clothes, Henry."

She looked sharply at him. "Oh, not gambling, Giles," she cried.

He strode back across the room and sat down opposite her. "I started by playing just for fun and for small stakes," he said. "Then I lost a bit, and I owed money all over the city for boots and clothes and such. I thought if I played for higher stakes, my luck would have to change. I promised myself that I would stop playing for all time if I could just win enough money to cover my debts."

"And you did not?"

"I came close one night," he said ruefully, "but my luck did not hold. I lost all my winnings and more besides. And since then I have got in pretty deep."

"How much do you owe, Giles?"

"Oh, nothing to worry your pretty head over," he said airily. "I shall come about."

"But not by more gambling, Giles?"

"No," he agreed slowly. "I shall have to think of something else."

"But what?"

He hesitated. "I shall have to go to the moneylenders," he said. "With very careful prudence I shall pay it off eventually. At least I shall not have creditors hounding me at every turn."

Henry shot out of her chair. "Moneylenders?" she cried. "I have heard of them, Giles. It is said that once you get into their clutches, you never get free. They charge interest that just builds and builds."

"Well, I have no choice," he said emphatically. "And it is not your worry, Henry. I ought not even to have told you."

"Indeed, I am glad you did," she retorted. "You must promise me not to go to a moneylender, Giles. I shall pay your debt. How much is it?"

He laughed mirthlessly. "I am afraid it is beyond any help you might offer, Henry. But thank you, anyway."

"How much, Giles?"

He stared at her for a moment. "Three thousand," he said.

"Three thousand!" she shrieked. "Giles, have you taken leave of your senses? You must have been in gambling dens every spare moment since you were sent down."

"Don't say anything to Eversleigh or to Peter," Giles said. "I shall work this out somehow, Henry."

"Yes, in debtors' prison!" she replied sharply. "Giles, I shall get the money. And do not worry, I shall not beg it from Marius. He has been extremely generous. I have almost enough. The rest I shall get easily. But you must promise me not to go to a moneylender. Will you, Giles? Please?"

Giles was very doubtful and reluctant. At first he refused to accept help in any form from his sister. But gradually he salvaged his pride by declaring that he would accept the money from her as a loan, to be paid back as quickly as he possibly could. He promised neither to visit a moneylender nor to blow his brains out. He was to return in three days' time to collect the money from his sister.

As soon as he had left, Henry ran up to her room and threw herself onto the bed. She lay staring hopelessly up at the canopy over her head. She had no idea how she was to raise the money to help Giles. She had not lied to him when she had said that Marius was generous. He showered gifts on her and made her a very generous money allowance. But Henry was a spendthrift. She could not have money without spending it. And her main clothing bills went directly to her husband, without touching her purse. She knew without troubling to look that her purse held only a small cluster of loose change, a few guineas at the most. It would not go a long way to paying Giles' debt.

She considered breaking her promise and confiding the problem to Marius. She had no doubt at all that he would immediately, and almost without question, write out a bank draft for the full amount and would not even demand that Giles repay it. But she could not bring herself to do so, for two reasons. She had made a promise to Giles, and according to her code of honor, a promise was totally binding, especially when it had been made to her brother, with whom she had always been very close. Second, she could not bring herself to admit to Marius that yet another member of her family was in a scrape. She craved his good opinion, though why this was so she had not stopped to consider. She could not tell him.

She did think of asking him for the money under some other pretext. But how could she justify asking for three thousand pounds? A new bonnet? New kid gloves? There was no possible way she could do it.

Henry was still searching her mind for a solution an hour later when she heard the voices of the twins in the distance and the barking of Brutus. She sighed and rose to ring for Betty. It was time to dress for dinner. She did not want to be caught lying on her bed in the daytime, something she almost never did. Sometimes Marius wandered into her room from the adjoining dressing room to talk with her for a few minutes.

Henry was still wrestling with her problem the following afternoon when she took her phaeton for a drive in the park. She had stayed at home all morning and had instructed the butler to tell any visitors that she was away from home. But all she had to show for her concentrated thinking was a headache and a cross mood. She decided that she needed some fresh air and light conversation with some of her acquaintances. She felt slightly cheered by the court of young men who were soon riding alongside her, lavishly complimenting her on her new blue bonnet and soliciting her hand for dances at Lady Sefton's ball the following evening. She gave a special smile to Oliver Cranshawe, who was on foot and just bidding farewell to a trio of ladies, who were also out strolling in the park.

"Good afternoon, your Grace," he called, flashing his white smile and bowing gracefully as he swept off his hat. "Your beauty rivals the day, as usual."

"And you speak with a flattering tongue, as usual, sir," she replied. "Come, take a turn in the phaeton with me and cheer me up."

He readily availed himself of the invitation. "And do you need cheering, Henry?" he asked, looking at her closely.

"I have the headache and am feeling blue-deviled," she replied airily.

"I have never known you downhearted," he said quietly, serious suddenly and giving her all his attention.

She smiled. "It is merely a passing mood, sir. Tell me how you enjoyed the opera last evening. I saw you in Lord Cadogan's box."

"Yes, I saw you too, Henry," he replied, "and would have waited on you during one of the intermissions if Marius had left the box. But I know he don't like me. However, I believe you are trying to turn the subject. Will you tell me what has happened to trouble you, my dear? You know me to be your friend, do you not?"

"You are very kind, Oliver, but it is a private matter. And not serious, I assure you."

"Is it Marius?" he asked. "I do not wish to pry, heaven knows, but I cannot believe him to be a suitable husband for one as young and full of life as you, Henry."

"You are being ridiculous," she said. "Of course it is not Marius. He is the best of husbands. But it is something I cannot tell him. Oh, may I tell you about it, Oliver? I think it will help me just to talk it over with someone else. And perhaps you may be able to advise me."

"Be assured that I shall do all in my power," he said, all solicitous concern, and he leaned over and eased the ribbons from her hands so that he was now driving the phaeton. Henry sat back and rested her hands in her lap.

"It is Giles again," she began, and she told him the whole story, as it had happened the previous day. When she had finished, there was silence for a while. She realized that Cranshawe had guided the horses into a path that was not as heavily used as the main one, which was always crowded with horses and vehicles at this hour of the day. She smiled at him in gratitude.

"Is that all?" he asked. "That is the whole matter?" She nodded. "But, my dear Henry, there is no problem at all. I shall give you the money. It is the merest trifle, I assure you."

"Oh, I could not possibly!" she cried. "No, Oliver, I could not be so beholden to you or to any man."

"Nonsense, my dear," he assured her. "We shall call it a loan, though I shall have no real desire to recover the money. You may repay it when and as you wish. It need not weigh upon your mind at all."

Henry hesitated. "It is uncommon generous of you," she said doubtfully, "but it does not seem right, Oliver."

"Henry," he said, drawing the horses to a halt and taking one of her hands in his free one, "I am your husband's cousin and his heir. I am family. And I have a personal devotion to you that I shall not embarrass you by relating now. Please, allow me to help you and your brother. I should consider it a signal honor."

Henry looked steadily into his eyes. "I will accept, Oliver," she said, "but only on condition that the money be considered a loan. I will not accept a gift from you."

"I accept a gift from you in being the recipient of your trust," he said softly, raising the hand he still held to his lips. He lifted the reins and started the horses forward again as they both became aware of a lone rider cantering toward them.

Eversleigh!

"Damn!" Cranshawe swore under his breath. "I shall wait on you tomorrow morning at eleven with the money," he said hurriedly to Henry.

"Ah, my love, I was fearful that you might have had some mishap when you did not return to the main path immediately," Eversleigh said amiably as his horse drew abreast of the phaeton. "Good day, Oliver," he added, nodding briefly in the direction of his heir. "Horses all lame today?"

"Not at all, Marius," Oliver replied hastily. "I considered the day particularly suited to exercise on foot."

"Ah, then it is uncommon civil of you, dear boy, to abandon your exercise in order to keep her Grace company," Eversleigh said, viewing his cousin through his quizzing glass.

"It is always a pleasure to converse with Henry," Cranshawe replied irritably. When the duke made no move either to lower his quizzing glass or to resume his own ride, his heir was forced to turn to Henry. "Thank you for taking me up, cousin," he said. "I must leave you now. I am meeting some friends in under an hour."

"Good day, Oliver," she replied gravely, and watched him jump down and walk away in the direction of the northern gate of the park. She returned her gaze to her husband, who had lowered his quizzing glass.

"Indeed, my love, I feel most vexed that I am not on

foot today. I should enjoy riding up beside you," Eversleigh said languidly. "That is a most fetching bonnet. Is it new?"

"Yes, it is," she replied airily, "and since I *must* wear a bonnet, I determine to buy any that take my fancy."

"Quite so," he agreed. "I believe it was a milliner's bill that almost gave James an apoplexy this morning." Henry dimpled. "But I must say, my love, that this one was worth every penny. There was hardly a male head in the main avenue that did not turn in admiration, or a female one that did not turn in envy."

"You are funning me, Marius," she said, giggling. "But I did not see you."

"No," he agreed dryly, "a mere husband has small chance of making his presence felt in such a crush of admirers."

"Absurd!" she said, laughing, the embarrassment of a few minutes before forgotten. "Are you riding my way, your Grace?"

"No, I am not," he replied. "I have a call that must be made before I return home. I shall see you later, my love."

"Good-bye, Marius," she said, and gave her grays the signal to start.

Eversleigh, watching her go before turning his horse in the opposite direction, had a still, brooding look on his face.

Henry contrived to be alone in the downstairs salon by eleven o'clock the next morning. It had not been easy. Marius had lingered in the office of his secretary until just half an hour before. Henry had considered all manner of ideas for persuading him to leave the house. Fortunately, none was necessary, though she was all but hopping up and down with vexation when he took what seemed a lingering farewell of her in her room.

"You did not ride this morning, my love? Or yesterday morning either?"

"No, I did not feel like the exercise," she replied.

"What, Henry, are you becoming too ladylike for such pursuits?" he asked, eyebrows raised.

"Pooh!" she replied scornfully. "What could be more ladylike than mincing along at a sober trot in a sidesaddle?"

"Ah, I forget," he said gently, "it is neck or nothing for you, is it not, my love?"

She smiled. "I must not keep you, Marius," she said, rising purposefully from the stool before her dressing-table mirror. "You must be anxious to be on your way."

"Must I?" he answered meekly. "I did wish to speak with you, Henry, but it can wait until later if you are in such a dreadful hurry."

"I must check the schoolroom," she declared firmly, "and make sure that Oscar is securely in his cage again. I would not want him escaping anymore."

"No, indeed," he agreed. "I might have trouble finding a chef in England willing to work here if that worthy bird finds his way to the kitchen and asks them all what the stink is."

She giggled. "The poor man was furious, was he not? I must go up, Marius."

"Yes, I see you must," he replied. "And I see that I must be going. I shall talk with you later, my love."

Henry really did go up to the schoolroom, mainly to ensure that Miss Manford and the twins were safely occupied. They were, and Oscar, in disgrace, was reposing fairly quietly beneath his pink blanket.

Cranshawe arrived promptly. Henry was standing tensely, her back to the fireplace, when the butler announced him. He strode across the room to her, looking handsome and purposeful, she noted. He took her cold hand in his and raised it to his lips.

"Good morning, Henry," he greeted her, his charming smile muted by a warm sympathy. "I came as soon as I could, for I knew you would be anxious to be done with this business and to set your brother's mind at ease."

"You are very good, Oliver," she said, turning quite pale. "I shall repay the money as soon as I may. But I do not know how I shall ever repay your kindness."

"Do not give it a moment's thought, my dear," he said with tender solicitation. "Here, take this packet and let us not mention the matter again." He removed a long package from inside his coat and handed it to her.

Henry took it with obvious embarrassment and reluctance.

"Now," he said, clasping his hands behind him and

smiling much more dazzlingly at her, "may I beg the honor of a waltz with you at the Sefton ball tonight, Henry? It will be a feather in my cap to be seen with the loveliest lady there."

"I do not like it when you say silly things like that," she said roundly. "But of course I shall dance with you. The second waltz? Felix Hendricks has already asked me for the first."

"Then I must be contented with the second," he decided, bowing gracefully.

They talked on general matters for several more minutes, but Cranshawe, always sensitive to her feelings, realized that she was uneasy with the package of money still clasped in her hand, and soon took his leave.

"Until this evening," he said, smiling warmly into her eyes and raising her hand to his lips again.

While Henry hastened upstairs to the drawing room to write a brief note to Giles, asking him to call on her during the afternoon, Oliver Cranshawe was on his way to Suzanne Broughton's house. She received him in her dressing room, where her maid was still coaxing her piled-up hair into numerous curls and ringlets.

"You choose strange hours in which to call, Oliver," she remonstrated as he was shown into the room. "Can't you wait until a more civilized time in the afternoon?"

"I thought you would wish to hear this news immediately, Suzanne," he replied, flashing her a wide smile in the mirror. "The butterfly has been netted, I believe."

Her eyes stilled on his reflected image. "Is that so?" she said. "Miriam, you may leave. That will be all for now." She waited until her maid had left the room and closed the door behind her before swiveling on the stool and facing her visitor. "Well, Oliver?"

He smiled and sank gracefully into a chair. "The little duchess is fortunate enough to have a brother who likes to gamble and who does not have the means with which to do it," he began.

She smiled slowly. "Fortunate for whom, Oliver? And you, out of the goodness of your heart, have prevented his ruin, I suppose?"

"Of course." He bowed. "How could I bear to see her

Grace, the freckle-nosed duchess, in distress? You know that I am all heart, Suzanne." He proceeded to tell her all that had transpired between Henry and him in the last day.

Her smile had broadened by the time he finished. "So now you have the silly little chit in your power! What do you mean to do with her, pray?"

He flashed his teeth at her. "It is not for you to know, Suzanne," he said, "but you can rest assured that I shall have some personal amusement while getting my revenge on Eversleigh."

"I almost feel sorry for the girl," Suzanne commented with a trilling laugh.

"Do not," he said. "Believe me, Suzanne, I know how to pleasure a woman. In all likelihood, she will not even realize that she is being deliberately ruined. It would be double revenge, would it not, if the little Henrietta were to fall in love with me in earnest?" There was something cold, almost cruel in the smile with which he regarded Suzanne.

"You are the devil, Oliver!" his companion replied. "I do hope that Marius suffers—before he returns to me. Perhaps I shall reject him. That would be most satisfying." She turned her back to examine herself in the mirror.

Cranshawe rose to his feet. "It would be in your own interest, my dear, to be seen with Marius as often as possible in the near future, especially when his wife is visible."

She smiled. "Poison in the ear, Oliver?"

"You may depend upon it!" he assured her. "In fact, I have already begun."

Henry ended up spending the whole afternoon with Giles. He was overjoyed when she handed him the money with which to pay off his debts, once he had ascertained to his own satisfaction that she had had no trouble raising the money and that she had not had to apply to Eversleigh for it. He swore to her that his gambling days were at an end, that he had finally learned his lesson. As a celebration, brother and sister decided on an excursion to Kew Gardens. They took the twins with them.

As a result, it was late in the day before Eversleigh held

the promised meeting with his wife. She had dressed early for dinner and had come down to join him in the drawing room.

"Some ratafia, my love?" he asked, resting his own glass on the mantel and crossing to the sideboard.

"Ratafia, pooh!" she said. "That is for girls. I shall have some Madeira, please, Marius."

"Yes," he said dryly. "I always forget that it is the greatest insult to treat you like a girl, Henry." He handed her a glass of Madeira.

Henry sipped it and found herself admiring her husband's appearance. He was dressed for Lady Sefton's ball in black satin knee breeches and coat, silver waistcoat, and sparkling white linen, lace covering his hands to the knuckles, his neckcloth arranged in an elaborate shower of folds. A diamond pin in the neckcloth and the inevitable quizzing glass on its black riband were his only adornments. His dark hair was brushed forward into waves around his face. His blue eyes regarded her steadily from beneath lowered lids. Henry started and blushed. She had caught herself out in the act of wondering how her hands and breasts would feel against the linen if she were to step forward and push aside his coat. What an extraordinary thought!

"Will I pass muster, Henry?" he asked, his eyes taking on their amused gleam.

"Oh, assuredly so," she said. "You will be the handsomest man at the ball, as always, Marius."

His eyebrows rose. "Splendid!" he said. "I would respond in kind, my love, if I did not know that you would call me absurd or silly or—what was it that one time?—stupid!"

"Oh!" she retorted. "It is unkind of you to remember that."

"Come and sit down, Henry," Eversleigh said, growing noticeably more serious and directing her to a sofa. He sat beside her. "I wish to talk to you."

"I perceive it is about my being with Oliver in the park yesterday," Henry said tightly, having decided to take the offensive.

He regarded her gravely. "Why have you chosen to disregard my wishes, Henry?" he asked.

"I will not be ruled," she cried passionately. "I know

that when I married you I became your property, Marius. I know that you have all the powers of a husband over me. But you cannot expect me to like it or to give in meekly to a situation of which I do not approve."

"Strong words, my love!" he said calmly. "Have I given you cause to consider me a tyrant? Do I curtail your freedom? Do I beat you?"

"No," she replied, her agitation by no means cooled. "You have been very good to me, except in this one thing. You asked something of me and gave me no reason except that it was your wish. And now you are bringing me to task because I have not obeyed. And I would guess that your next move will be to command me not to be sociable to Oliver and to threaten me with dire consequences if I continue to disobey. Well, I will not do it, Marius." She rose to her feet and glared defiantly down at him. "Oliver has been kind to me, and I like him, and there is nothing improper in our meetings. I shall have to take the consequences of going against your commands. But turn away from his friendship I will not."

"Will you not, my love?" he asked softly. He sat and gazed steadily up at her for a long while until she sat down again, feeling rather foolish at having allowed her temper to flare. Eversleigh continued to sit silently for a few minutes. Finally, he took her hand in one of his and with his other hand stroked along each finger.

"It was, of course, wrong of me to require anything of you without giving a good reason," he said at last. "You must remember, my love, that I am new in the role of husband. Since I lost my parents in a carriage accident when I was sixteen years of age, I have been accustomed to giving orders and to having them unquestioningly obeyed. And then I, er, bumped into you, or was it the other way around?"

Henry said nothing. She kept her eyes on his hand, which held hers, and on his slim, well-manicured fingers playing lightly with hers.

"Will you stay away from Oliver Cranshawe if I can convince you that it is for your own safety?" Eversleigh continued. Henry glanced up into his face, startled. "Believe me, I am not being melodramatic," he assured her.

"I cannot say until I hear what you have to say," Henry

said. "I cannot think that anything you say will convince me. Oliver has proved kind to me."

"You are incurably honest, are you not, Henry?" Eversleigh said, turning her hand and clasping it in his. "I see that I must tell you what I swore not to tell anyone, because I have no proof for my suspicions."

Henry looked inquiringly into his face.

"I have never told you anything of my family, have I, Henry?" he began.

"I assumed you had none," she replied.

"And neither have I—now," he said. "Oliver is my closest relative on my father's side. He is the son of my father's sister. His parents died when he was a child. He spent most of his youthful years with us at Everglades. The three of us were very close—Oliver, my brother, Stephen, and I."

"You have a brother, Marius?"

"Had, my love. We did everything together. We frequently had friendly arguments about the succession. Oliver pretended to be angry because he was third in line to the dukedom, behind me and Stephen—although his mother had been older than my father. At least, it seemed to be a joke, though after the untimely death of Mama and Papa and I succeeded to the title, I often had the uneasy feeling that Oliver was perhaps seriously bitter."

"But that is absurd," Henry said. "He seems not to mind at all."

Eversleigh took her empty glass, crossed to the sideboard, and poured them each a second drink. When he sat down again, it was in a chair a little removed from hers.

"I went to university and then spent several months of each year in London," he continued. "Finally I joined . . . a certain club. You would consider it absurd, my love, and you would be quite right. It was youthful folly. The only condition for membership was that each candidate swear to remain single for the rest of his life."

Henry stared. "Then how came you to marry me?" she asked.

"That is another matter entirely," he replied. "Oliver and Stephen, as young men will, took the matter very seriously when I announced my membership to them. And I remember jokingly pointing out that only Stephen stood between Oliver and an almost-certain future claim to the dukedom. Stephen was only nineteen at the time, but he fancied himself in love with a neighbor's daughter. He seemed in hourly expectation of making a declaration."

He paused and took a long swallow of his drink.

"And?" Henry prompted.

"And he died in a riding accident before he could make that declaration," Eversleigh said harshly. "We were on a hunt. His saddle strap broke when he was jumping a fence. He broke his neck."

Henry found that she was having difficulty breathing. "You suspect that Oliver had something to do with it?" she almost whispered.

"Oh, he was nowhere near when it happened," he said. "The saddle strap was badly worn through."

"It was an accident, then?"

"Stephen was a very keen and careful horseman. He would let no one tend his horse or his gear for him. A knife could have been used carefully enough to give the impression of fraying."

"But you believe Oliver did it?" she asked, wide-eyed.

"I have no proof and I have never confronted him with my suspicions," he said.

"What has all this to do with me, Marius?" she whispered.

"You are my wife," he said. "My sons will be born from your body."

"Oh, no!" she cried, leaping to her feet. "You are wrong, Marius. I know Oliver. He is not like that. He is kind and caring and he is hurt by your coldness to him. You have allowed grief for your brother to poison your mind. It is not true. You must see that."

He looked at her, a twisted smile on his face. "Keep him at a distance, Henry," he said. "Your safety matters to me."

"But you are wrong," she insisted. "Oh, somehow I shall prove it and bring you two together again."

"Then nothing I have said has made any difference?" he asked, his eyelids masking the expression in his eyes.

Henry hesitated. She was suddenly plagued by a thoroughly novel desire to rush across to where he still sat in his chair, and cradle his head against her breast. She had never seen him vulnerable, had never even dreamed that he had any weakness. At the same time, she could not agree to humor him by rejecting Oliver, especially after the transaction of that morning.

"You are wrong," she said, "I know you are. I have promised a dance to your cousin tonight and it would be ill-mannered to refuse him now. I cannot turn aside his friendship, Marius, but I will promise to speak with him only in public places, where there are plenty of onlookers. Will that relieve your mind?"

"You will do what you will, Henry," he said, shrugging, "and I will do what I must. Come, let us go in to dinner. The chef will be resigning in good earnest if we keep him waiting any longer."

He rose from his chair and extended his arm to lead her out.

# CHAPTER

# 8

Penelope was in hiding and seething with a feeling of ill-usage. Philip was out with the duke. He had been taken to see Jackson's boxing saloon and even to watch a sparring bout between Eversleigh and the great man himself. Penelope had not been permitted to go, though she had begged and pleaded and threatened. All that the threats had accomplished was to win her a long, cool stare through her brother-in-law's quizzing glass and a very disdainful comment.

"Really, Penny," Eversleigh had said, "if you must use the language of the stable, I shall have to send you to the stable and have you pitch some manure. However, I fear that you might corrupt my grooms, my dear girl."

So Penelope had been left at home. And to add insult to injury, Miss Manford had come up with the idea that this was the ideal time to continue her charge's embroidery lessons, which had been progressing in a very desultory manner for several weeks.

When Miss Manford left the drawing room to fetch the cloth, needles, and silken thread, Penelope came to a desperate decision. She would not be there when Manny came back! She decided on a ground-floor room as a hiding place because the children rarely had occasion to go down there. She darted out of the room, shutting the door firmly in the face of an indignant Brutus, raced along to the staircase, and peered cautiously down. Luck was with her—there were no footmen in the hallway below.

She tiptoed down the stairs and across to the green salon and quickly let herself inside. She settled herself comfortably on a window seat behind the heavy velvet draperies, clasped her arms around her drawn-up legs, rested her chin on her knees, and began to indulge in her favorite indoor activity, daydreaming.

Poor Miss Manford was left to search the house for her charge. Fortunately for Penelope, she did not think of taking Brutus with her. She did look into the salon but did not search it because it seemed an unlikely place for the girl to have gone. She did knock timidly on James Ridley's office door and ask if he had seen the missing child.

"Don't distress yourself, Eugenia," he said soothingly, "she has probably gone to the kitchen for some food or has played a prank on you and has gone outside for some air."

"Oh, dear, but she is not in the kitchen," wailed Miss Manford, "and she can't have gone outside—she was wearing only slippers and has no bonnet or gloves. Where can the dear child be?"

"Dear child!" scoffed Ridley. "The girl needs a good spanking for upsetting you so. What is she supposed to be doing?"

"We were to embroider," Miss Manford said, "but she does not take to it. I fear very much that I shall never be able to teach her a lady's accomplishments."

"Maybe not," he said, "but I certainly feel that her disappearance has been explained. Depend upon it, she is hiding and will come out when she feels that there is no longer any danger of having to do her lesson."

"Oh, do you really think so, James?" Miss Manford asked, clasping her hands to her bosom. "How comforting you always are! So calm and sensible!"

He smiled. "You go back upstairs and ring for some tea," he suggested, "and don't worry about Miss Penelope anymore." And he patted her lightly on the shoulder as she turned to leave the room.

Penelope was feeling a little bored by the time the salon door was opened and she heard the butler speaking to an unidentified visitor.

"You may wait in here, sir, until her Grace returns," he said. "I shall send some refreshment."

The visitor paced the room after the door had closed. Penelope peered cautiously around the curtains. When she saw that it was Mr. Cranshawe, she drew back into the shadows again and stayed very still. She had met the man only on one occasion when she and Phil had been out walking with Henry and he had stopped to talk, but she did not like him. He had been too friendly, too charming. His smile had been too broad, too practiced. She certainly did not want to be caught in the predicament of having to make polite small talk with him while they waited for Henry to return from her afternoon of visiting.

The wait was not a long one. A few minutes after the butler had brought a tray with decanter and glasses, Penelope heard the door open and a rustle of skirts entering the room.

"Oliver?" Henry said. "I did not expect to see you here."

"My dear cousin," he replied, crossing the room, clasping one of her hands in his and holding it to his heart, "I had to come here. Since we danced at Lady Sefton's ball four nights ago, I have hardly seen you. I have almost felt as if you were avoiding me."

"Don't be silly," she said matter-of-factly, and pulled away her hand. "It seems to me I have seen you each day and that we have talked or greeted each other on each occasion."

"Yes, but always in a crowd of people," he complained. "You know that I feel closer to you than that, Henry."

"You must not say so," she said. "We are friends merely, and I have many friends."

"Oh, come, my dear, we are more than ordinary friends, surely," he cajoled, lowering his voice.

Henry stared. "You have been kind to me," she conceded uncertainly.

"Are you referring to the money you owe me, Henry?" he asked. "I have told you to forget it. Is that what has become between us in the last few days? Are you embarrassed?" He tried to take her hand in his, but she eluded him.

"Oliver," she said, moving behind a chair and placing her hands firmly on the back of it, "I shall repay the money, as I have promised. I am not embarrassed in your presence. I acknowledge you as a friend, but there is no other bond between us."

"Are you afraid?" he asked. "Has Marius threatened you since he came upon us in the park?"

"No, he has not!" she exclaimed firmly. "And, Oliver, I do not like the assumption you seem to be making that we are more than friends."

"You know that I admire you greatly," he said, coming around the chair and seizing her by the shoulders. "I cannot bear to see you with someone like Marius, Henry, who does not appreciate you and who disapproves of you and spies on you."

"He was not spying!" she cried indignantly.

"Have you not noticed, my dear, how he is always there whenever you and I meet? He is jealous. He has always had everything he wanted, Henry. There has never been anything he was denied. I hate to see him use you just as another possession. You deserve more."

"I believe you speak out of turn, sir," Henry said coldly. "It is of my husband and my marriage that you speak. They are not your concern."

"Oh, pardon me," he sighed, sinking into the nearest chair and hiding his face in his hands. "I have been unforgivably familiar. I just cannot bear to see a lovely, innocent little creature like you having to face the humiliation of having her husband flaunt his mistress before her face."

"What?"

He looked up, his face aghast. "Henry? You did not know?" he asked. "Oh, what have I said?"

"You will explain your meaning, sir," she said, her head held high but her face noticeably pale.

He groaned. "My wretched tongue!" he said. "But I may be wrong, Henry. In fact, I am sure I must be. Suzanne Broughton was his mistress before he met you. I am certain it cannot be so now. How could any man leave the embraces of so lovely a bride so soon?"

Henry said nothing. She clung to the back of the chair and stared at Oliver, seeing in her mind Marius dancing with Mrs. Broughton at the Sefton ball and on one or two other occasions, seeing him conversing with her during a soiree a few weeks before, seeing him sitting next to her at a recent dinner, seeing all the mature beauty and lure of the woman. And she had never even suspected. How naïve she had been to assume that Marius was as satisfied by their sexless relationship as she was. And why did it hurt like a dozen sharp knives to think of that woman in his arms, that woman's hands in his hair, her lips on his? Henry's own lips parted in shock. The reason—of course! —was that she wanted Marius herself.

Cranshawe had risen and was looking at her in concern. "The best way to fight back is to show him that you do not care," he was saying. "Let me take you out one evening, Henry. Come to a masquerade with me."

"A masquerade?" she asked, dazed.

"Yes, Henry, a masquerade at the opera house. They are bright, gay entertainments. You would enjoy the evening. Your character cries out for more amusement than you can find in most drawing rooms."

"I do not believe I ought," she said doubtfully. "And I do not really wish to."

"You do not strike me as being the docile type of wife who would sit back and quietly endure her husband's neglect and infidelity," he wheedled.

She looked squarely at him. "Very well," she said impulsively, "I shall come." She did not pause to consider whether she really felt ill-used or neglected. She only felt bruised and bewildered.

He turned on her the full charm of his smile. "You will not regret it," he said. "I shall guarantee you a most entertaining evening, Henry. There is a masquerade on Wednesday night. Will you be free?"

"I shall," she said defiantly. "You will let me know when to expect you." She did not resist when Cranshawe lifted her hand to his lips, gazing into her eyes all the time.

He left immediately and Henry soon followed him out of the room.

Penelope lowered her legs painfully to the floor, one at a time, and flexed her neck and shoulders. As she crossed to the door and peered cautiously out, she could feel the blood hammering in her brain. She hoped that Phil was back already or would be back soon. She had a great deal that she was burning to confide in him. Seeing a footman with his back to her close to the outer door, she darted quickly from the salon and up the stairs.

Miss Manford had no difficulty in persuading Penelope, at least, that it was time for bed that night. Philip, seeing his sister's eagerness to retire to her room, realized that something was brewing and did not employ his usual go-slow tactics.

Half an hour later, Penelope let herself into her brother's room through the connecting door. She crossed to the bed without the aid of a candle, climbed up onto the high mattress, and sat with her legs dangling over the side.

"You aren't sleeping, are you, Phil?" she whispered.

"Of course not, silly," his voice replied scornfully from the mound of pillows that she could see dimly in the darkness. "I knew you were coming."

"Henry is in trouble," she announced dramatically.

The dim shape of Philip was now clearly visible sitting up against the headboard. "Henry? In danger?" he asked excitedly. "I say, Pen. What has happened?"

"The toothpowder genius has some sort of hold over her," Penelope said. "I think she owes him money."

"Mr. Cranshawe?" Philip said. "I always knew there was something sinister about him."

Penelope gave her twin an exhaustive account of what she had heard in the green salon that afternoon.

"I say, Pen," Philip said when she had finished, "you really had an adventure. Are you not glad now that you weren't allowed to come to Jackson's with the duke and me?"

"I don't know about that," she replied, not so easily mollified. "But what are we to do, Phil? I don't believe what he said. I think his Grace really cares for Henry. He would not prefer this Mrs. Broughton. Otherwise, why did he marry Henry?"

"No, I don't believe it either," Philip agreed. "The duke is a great gun. But why would Henry owe old toothpowder money, Pen? And how much? Don't the duke give her enough?"

"I am certain he must," his sister replied. "He gives us lots."

"Do you think she really wanted to go to that masquerade, Pen?"

"I think she was mad at what he said about his Grace," Penelope replied shrewdly. "But, Phil, if she owes him a great deal of money, don't he have some hold on her? Won't she always have to do what he says?"

"It must be a great deal," Philip said excitedly, "and it must have been for something that she could not go to his Grace about. I don't like it, Pen. We have to do something to help."

"But what?"

"I don't know, but we have to try to find out more. And we have to protect Henry at this masquerade. I don't like the sound of that at all."

"You mean we are going to go there, too?" Penelope's eyes were as wide as saucers.

"I mean exactly that!" he said dramatically.

"But how?"

"This is what we have to work on," he replied, and they both lapsed into a thoughtful silence.

Penelope and Philip were not the only ones to sit up late in a darkened bedroom that night. Henry sat propped up against her banked pillows staring into the darkness. She was feeling lost and confused. All her life she had felt in charge of most situations—bold, fearless, and independent. Even when she married Marius, she had felt in command of her fate. She had feared him a little, yes, but Henry was never one to back away from a challenge. She had been exhilarated by it.

Now, suddenly—and she did not know quite how it had happened—she felt vulnerable. She felt guilty about having agreed to go to a masquerade with Oliver. Although she had refused to believe in Marius' suspicions, she had made an effort to cool her friendship with his heir. She certainly had intended to keep her promise to see him only in public. And yet she had agreed to go with him to a place where really respectable people did not go. She had asked Marius once to take her to a masquerade and he had explained that they were rather wild and vulgar affairs, not suitable for a lady of her station.

And now, in the privacy of her own room, Henry had to

admit to herself that she had been cleverly manipulated into accepting the invitation. Oliver had played his cards very well. Had he really let slip the suspicion about Marius and Suzanne Broughton, or had he deliberately divulged the information? His words were very probably true, she thought, but why had he wanted her to know? If he were really the friend he claimed to be, would he not do all in his power to protect her from the knowledge? And why would he wish to take her to a place that was not quite proper? For the first time Henry felt a twinge of uneasiness about Oliver Cranshawe.

She considered sending him a note the following morning to cancel the outing. But she realized with a dim premonition of dread that she could not afford to offend Oliver. He could press for an early repayment of her debt; he could tell Marius the truth. He had it in his power to make life very unpleasant for her. Henry was beginning to wonder if she had been very foolhardy to confide in him and to accept such a large loan from him.

She thought of going to Marius and telling him the whole. It would be wonderful to go now, she thought, into his room and tell him what had happened, to beg him to pay off Oliver Cranshawe for her, to put her head against his chest and close her eyes and relax. Would he put his arms around her and kiss her as he had that day when Peter had been so horrid, that time when she had felt such powerful and frightening sensations pulse downward from her lips to her breasts to her womb and her thighs that she had panicked? It would be such bliss just to go to him and let him take charge of her life. And he would do so, she knew.

Henry had closed her eyes and let her head sink back against the pillows. Suddenly she pulled herself erect again. It was useless and far too feminine to think that way! She did not want to become dependent upon any man. She did not need Marius to get her out of her troubles. She could fight alone. Maybe she was wrong to feel uneasy about Oliver. But, however it was, she would work her own way through this. Besides, she could not confide the whole truth to Marius without betraying Giles, and she had promised him that she would never disclose his indiscretion to Marius, or ask his help.

Henry's eyes hardened and her lips compressed in the darkness as she recalled the new information about her husband that she had learned that afternoon. It hurt more than she would ever admit to know that he had a mistress. And Mrs. Broughton was a formidable rival, Henry concluded. How could she hope to compete against a woman of such poise and elegant beauty, a woman with such an amply proportioned body? She thought of her own slim, boyish figure and small breasts, of her weathered and freckled face, of her short and wayward curls, and for the first time in her life was dissatisfied with her own appearance. How could she ever hope to attract her husband away from his other love? It was ludicrous even to consider Marius really wanting her—Marius, with his very masculine physique and good looks; Marius, at the age of thirty-two, with years of experience with women behind him. He would make love to her within the next few weeks, yes, but what joy or triumph would there be for her when she knew that he would merely be consummating their marriage, merely setting out to ensure himself an heir other than Oliver Cranshawe?

Why had he married her, anyway? There were so many girls of the *ton* more eligible than she. She amused him, he had said on more than one occasion. What sort of reason was that?

Henry turned and thumped a fist angrily into her pillows. "I wish this were your nose, Marius Devron," she said aloud, "and I wish the blood would come gushing out. Everything was fine before those confounded boys thought to wager on my bringing you up to scratch. How I wish they had settled on the chinless one, whatever his name was. I am sure I should be much happier with him!"

The next few days until the Wednesday were unhappy ones for Henry. She had to visit a modiste she did not usually patronize, with only Betty in tow. There she purchased a dark-green domino and mask and hoped either that the dressmaker did not know her identity or that she would find no topic worthy of gossip in the Duchess of Eversleigh's having bought those particular items.

Worse, Henry had to deceive her husband. They had not accepted any particular invitation for Wednesday. She perused the small pile of cards that she had received and set aside as being of no particular importance. Which one would Marius be least likely to want to accept? She settled on a musical evening to be held at the home of Mrs. Augusta Welby, a lady strongly suspected of being a bluestocking. The program seemed particularly promising to Henry. It was proudly billed as a ladies' evening: an unknown but promising lady pianist, lately come from the provinces to take the capital by storm; Lady Pamela Bellamy, one of the year's crop of debutantes, who had generously agreed to contribute a rendering of several English love songs; Signora Ratelli, the Italian soprano who was currently enjoying great success in a tour of England. She was actually known to have sung for Prinny at Carleton House. Henry read no further. She could almost picture Marius holding the invitation at arm's length while he regarded it incredulously through his quizzing glass before languidly ordering poor Mr. Ridley to get rid of it.

After dinner that evening, while riding in the carriage with Eversleigh on the way to the theater to watch the renowned Kean play Lear, Henry told him that she had accepted the invitation. At the same time her heart beat painfully with the necessity of telling the lie.

"Good God, Henry!" he exclaimed, his language unusually strong. "When did you acquire such highbrow tastes?"

"I thought it time to learn about more cultural matters," she answered primly. "You keep reminding me that the Duchess of Eversleigh is expected to behave in a more ladylike manner."

"I believe I was talking about bonnets," he said, giving her a sidelong look. "But an evening of ladies' musical talent, Henry? Is that not going too far?"

"I think not," she replied crossly. "Why should female talent be more to be laughed at than men's?"

"I might have known I could depend upon you to change the focus of the discussion, my love," he remarked indulgently. "Go and enjoy the triumphs of your sex. But you will not expect me to accompany you, will you?"

"I had hoped you would," she replied cunningly, "but I shall not try to insist, of course. I am sure you can find some other way to spend the evening."

"Horton has invited me to play cards that evening," he continued. "It will break my heart to be away from you for a whole evening, of course, my love."

"Absurd!" she said, dimpling. But then she remembered that her part in this conversation was all deception and turned to stare into the darkness outside the carriage window.

By the time Wednesday evening came, Henry was feeling quite wretched. She had spent the afternoon with Marius and the twins at the British Museum, viewing the Elgin Marbles. It had been an absurdly happy-go-lucky outing. The twins were in high spirits, as they usually were before some prank, Henry had noted from past experience. They did not get into trouble, but had merely darted from exhibit to exhibit, exclaiming over everything with loud enthusiasm. Henry had held to her husband's arm and had been almost breathlessly aware of his masculinity. He had used his quizzing glass freely and affected a shocked disapproval of the nakedness of many of the statues. Henry had giggled more than she had since leaving Roedean.

Eversleigh had been invited to Lord Horton's home for dinner before the all-male card party. It was a relief to Henry at least not to have to face him across the dinner table, knowing what she was planning to do that night. It also eased her mind that it was a card party that Marius was attending. It was bound to keep him away from home almost until morning. But her conscience was not eased at all. It was with a heavy heart that she left Manny sewing placidly in the drawing room (the twins had already gone to bed, yawning loudly and claiming to be tired out by their afternoon excursion) and retired to her room to get ready for the masquerade.

Betty helped her into a modest cream-colored silk evening gown. It was high-waisted and fell almost straight to the hemline, an ideal dress to wear beneath the domino. She folded the domino beneath her evening cloak and put the mask into her reticule. She did not wish the servants to know where she was going. They might conceivably leak the information to the duke.

Oliver Cranshawe arrived promptly at nine o'clock. The

butler knocked on Henry's door and informed Betty that he was waiting downstairs in the hallway. Henry left her room, feeling that doomsday had come, and descended the stairs quickly, before she could lose her resolve.

Oliver, she was relieved to see, was also not dressed for a masquerade. He wore a plain black cloak over his blue satin evening clothes.

"Ah, your Grace," he said, bowing over her hand and playing to the audience of two footmen and a butler. "How lovely you look. And how honored I am to conduct you to the concert in place of my cousin."

She smiled bleakly. "Let us not be late, Oliver," she said, and swept out of the house ahead of him.

Upstairs, about one hour later, Philip let himself quietly into his sister's room. He was dressed in plain, almost-ragged breeches and shirt, borrowed from a stableboy who had considered the loan of two outfits well worth the guinea he had received in exchange. A cap was pulled low over Philip's eyes.

"Are you ready, Pen?" he hissed into the darkness.

"I think so," she whispered back anxiously. "Do I look like a boy, Phil? I just hope my hair stays tucked under this cap. I should have it cut short like Henry's."

Philip peered into the darkness. He could see his sister dimly in the light that came through two large windows. "You'll do," he said. "Apart from the hair, you never do look much like a girl, anyway, Pen. You don't stick out in front."

"Good," she said, not one whit offended by this blunt reference to her underdeveloped femininity. "Shall we go?"

They crept stealthily down the servants' staircase and let themselves out a side door, hoping that no one would come along and shoot the bolts across while they were still out. Penelope kept close to her twin as they turned south in the direction of the opera house, whose location they had studied carefully in the last few days.

"I wish we might have brought Brutus," she said. "But I suppose you were right. He would draw attention to us, and Henry and old toothpowder might recognize him if we get close."

"Now, Pen, let's go over again how we are to do this," her brother said.

"I still don't think it fair that you get to do the exciting part," Penelope complained.

"Ah, but you have the most difficult part," Philip replied diplomatically. "You have to do some acting."

They trudged along, going over once more their campaign plan, which had been formulated in many secret meetings over the previous few days.

When they reached the opera house, they stood across the road watching for a while, standing in the shadows of a doorway. Somehow their plan seemed more flimsy now that they could see the actual building and the activity going on before the doorway. There were two doormen on duty, both guarding the entrance against unauthorized persons and helping to open carriage doors and pull down carriage steps. And vehicles drew up with fair frequency.

"You see that pillar to the left of the entry?" Philip asked. "When you see me safely behind that, you wait for the next carriage to come and do your part. All right?"

"All right," she said, but she grabbed his shirt sleeve as he made to leave the doorway. "Phil, be careful," she added.

"Aw, don't start acting like a girl," he replied scornfully. "Just make sure that you wait for me at the corner of the street where we planned."

A few minutes later, Penelope could see that he was safely tucked behind the pillar. And she could see a carriage approaching down the street. With a deep breath and a thumping heart, she sauntered across the road. The doorman who had stepped forward to greet the approaching vehicle made shooing gestures with his hands. The other stayed where he was, hands clasped behind his back.

Penelope waited quietly until a dandified gentleman and a lady displaying an ample amount of bosom had descended from the carriage, and then stepped forward, palms cupped together.

"Spare us a penny, guv'nor," she whined, sidling up to the dandy. "Me mum's sick an' I ain't had nuthin' to eat in two days."

" 'Ere, 'ere," the closest doorman said, "be off with you, little tramp, and leave the quality be."

The lady gathered her skirts around her to avoid the contaminating touch of the beggar, and prepared to move around Penelope. The dandy completely ignored her.

"Just an 'apenny, then, lady," she said shrilly, stepping across the path of the female. "The baby's starvin' and there ain't a crust o' bread in the 'ouse." She sniffed loudly and cuffed her nose noisily.

" 'Ere, I'll get the watch after you," the doorman growled, grabbing Penelope by the collar of her shirt and dragging her backward. The couple who had just alighted attempted again to go around her. In the meantime, another carriage had drawn up and the other doorman had helped two couples down onto the pavement.

Penelope tore herself away from her captor and flung herself screaming to the ground. "Me pa's dead," she shrieked, "an' me mum's dyin'. The young uns is starvin' an' only me to provide for 'em. Have pity, ladies and gents. Have pity."

Everyone's attention was riveted to the ragged little figure rolling its eyes and drumming its heels on the pavement.

" 'Ere, Jake," said the first doorman, " 'elp me clear the beggar away from the entrance."

Jake came forward obligingly, a menacingly burly figure as viewed from Penelope's vantage point on the pavement.

"Poor little soul," said a lady's voice, and Penelope looked up into the heavily painted but kindly face of an overweight lady from the second carriage. "Give him some coins, George. And please let him go in peace," she instructed the disappointed doormen.

Both George and the footmen obeyed, and within moments Penelope was slinking off down the street, a shilling clasped in one hand, while the street behind her was returning to normality. She noticed as she passed the pillar that Philip was no longer behind it.

Philip had taken advantage of the commotion that his sister had created in order to slip through the doorway into the opera house. The ruse had worked even better than he had hoped. But now came the hard part. How was a scruffy urchin to be able to roam around this grand old building, which teemed with richly dressed men and women, without attracting suspicion? He ducked into a dark corner, removed his hat, and took from inside it a cloth apron such as the kitchen boy wore and a white cloth. The apron he tied quickly around his waist; the cloth he clutched in his hand. He smoothed his hair as best he could without either comb or mirror, abandoned the cap, and walked purposefully along the narrow corridor that circled around the auditorium behind the ground-level boxes. He hoped that his air of open confidence would allay suspicion and convince anyone who might wonder that he had been sent about some clean-up job.

Philip's eyes darted sharply over every figure he passed and through every open doorway, in search of the sister he had come to protect. He came upon her finally, quite unexpectedly, in a shadowy doorway in the corridor. It was unmistakably she, even though she was enveloped in a green domino and wore a green mask. Her hood had fallen back and those short, unruly auburn curls could belong to no one but Henry. She was clasped in the close embrace of a black domino and was being very masterfully kissed. But her clenched fists were between her own ribs and his, Philip noticed as he stood still and gaped in shock for a moment.

# CHAPTER

# 9

The Duke of Eversleigh threw his cards into the center of the table, his face impassive, though he had won a considerable amount of money in the first two games of the evening.

Lord Horton threw in his cards, too. "I should know from experience never to play against you, Marius," he sighed. "You're always a lucky devil!"

"We miss you at the club, Eversleigh," Rufus Smythe commented. "Tell us, do you still believe you were wise to choose a bride so carelessly?"

Eversleigh raised his quizzing glass and eyed his questioner slowly, his face still expressionless. "Ah, but I never do anything without care," he answered.

Sir Wilfred Denning smoothed the lace of his cuffs over his well-manicured hands and shuddered delicately. "You certainly chose fast enough, Eversleigh. I am still smarting at the loss of my grays. I see you have given them to her Grace. A nicely ironic touch, that!"

"Indeed you have brought the duchess into fashion, Marius," Horton commented. "She is all the rage, I understand."

"Henry is one of a kind," Eversleigh answered enigmatically.

Rufus Smythe laughed. "I see that even your cousin has taken a fancy to her," he said.

Eversleigh toyed with his quizzing glass again, but did not lift it to his eye.

"I lunched with him at Watier's today," Smythe continued. "It must be pleasant, Eversleigh, to have a relative willing to relieve one of the tedium of accompanying one's wife to all the social functions."

Eversleigh's hand, clasped around the quizzing glass, stilled. The half-closed eyelids hid eyes which had sharpened. "To which event in particular are you referring, Smythe?" he asked with a languidness that was at odds with his alert eyes.

"Oh, he was taking her to something or other tonight, was he not?" said Smythe, gathering the cards together and proceeding to shuffle them.

"Ah, tonight, yes," said Eversleigh, and prepared to play the hand that was dealt him.

At the end of the game, which he again won, Eversleigh rose to his feet in leisurely fashion and brushed an imaginary speck of dust from his coat sleeve. He turned to his host. "This has been pleasant, my dear fellow," he said, "but I have another engagement for tonight that I cannot avoid."

"Marius!" said Horton, also rising to his feet. "The night has scarcely begun. I thought we were to have a fair chance tonight of stripping you of your fortune."

"Ha! See what marriage has done to him?" Denning mocked with his haughty drawl. "He does not even have the stamina to sit up with his friends to play cards."

"Perhaps he has better things to do," said Rufus Smythe, leering.

"I am delighted to have left you with a topic on which to speculate for the next hour, my dear fellows," Eversleigh said, seeming quite unperturbed by the good-natured teasing.

A half-hour later, the Duke of Eversleigh was announced in the music room of Mrs. August Welby's home. That lady was all aflutter. Having a real live duke present at her musical evening, especially such a distinguished one as Eversleigh, was beyond her wildest dreams. Finally she would be a success, counted among the foremost of society's hostesses.

The guests were partaking of tea and pastries when he arrived, the first part of the program having been completed.

The Italian soprano was billed for the second half of the evening. Eversleigh accepted a cup, remained on his feet, and languidly surveyed the gathering.

"Marius," a familar voice said at his elbow, "one does not expect to find you at such events. Have you suddenly acquired culture?"

"Like catching a cold?" Eversleigh returned, turning his lazy, half-closed eyes on Suzanne Broughton.

"That does not answer the question," she said archly, slapping him on the wrist with her fan. "Is Signora Ratelli the attraction? Rumor has it that she is looking for a new protector."

"Hmm," he replied, "I believe I should find it a little disconcerting to share a bed with a partner who has to practice scales."

She laughed. "I miss you, Marius," she said. "Have you not tired of the freckled little chit yet?"

"You mean her Grace?" he asked, eyebrows raised, hand straying to the handle of his quizzing glass. "Good Lord, no!"

He strolled away in the direction of the chairs that had been set out for the audience and suffered through the first aria sung by the Italian. During the first break, before the second selection, he made his excuses and left.

Henry chattered brightly during the carriage ride to the opera house. She felt uneasy with Oliver for the first time and wished there were some way of avoiding the evening's entertainment. But cowardice was not one of Henry's vices. She smiled brightly as Cranshawe handed her from the carriage, her face now covered with the green mask, her figure covered with the matching domino. Her companion looked almost sinister, she thought, dressed all in black.

The atmosphere inside the building was quite different from that in the various ballrooms that Henry had visited. The noise level was noticeably higher. The dancing was considerably less elegant. In fact, the music seemed to provide only an excuse for men and women to touch and ogle one another. Ladies' fashions even among high society favored low necklines and a generous display of bosom.

Yet many of the female dancers here made Henry blush with the obvious vulgarity of their dress.

As Henry preceded Cranshawe to the ground-level box he had reserved, a smiling gallant reached for her hand and tried to pull her onto the dancing floor with a "Dance, m' dear?" as the only introduction. Oliver's black arm encircled her waist and drew her against him. For the moment, Henry was glad of the protection.

Her relief was short-lived. When Oliver drew her onto the floor to waltz, he held her close, with one hand splayed firmly across her back so that her breasts and thighs came continually into contact with his body. When she raised an indignant face to his, she noticed that his eyes glittered strangely behind the black mask.

"Don't hold me so close, Oliver," she ordered crossly. "I shall tread on your feet and hurt you."

He flashed his charming smile. "I should consider it a pleasure to be trodden on by you, Henry," he said. "And I do not believe you are heavy enough to inflict much pain."

"Even so, sir," she persisted, pushing firmly against his shoulder with her left hand, "I wish to have more room."

"For one so young, you are a remarkable tease, Henry," he said, smiling tenderly down on her. "I hold you close merely to protect you from the crowd."

"I don't like it," Henry said bluntly. "I believe most of the people here have had too much to drink!"

Cranshawe threw back his head and laughed. "Henry, I never had you labeled as a prude," he said. "I believe you are cross only because these revelers have a start on you. Let us return to our box and order some refreshments."

Henry followed him, though she resisted all his attempts to ply her with alcohol. She insisted on drinking lemonade. Soon they were joined by two other couples, who appeared to know both her and Cranshawe. The talk became noisy and vulgar. Henry, who could usually hold her own in any conversation, found herself sitting in uncomfortable silence. When one of the men asked her to dance, she found again that she had to constantly fight to maintain a decent distance from him. At the same time she had to keep her head averted to avoid the smell of liquor on his breath.

As soon as she could attract Cranshawe's attention on her return to the box, she asked to be taken home.

"Henry?" he said in surprise. "We have just arrived and have hardly begun to enjoy ourselves yet."

"I shall never begin to enjoy myself here, Oliver," she said. "Take me home, please."

"My dear," he coaxed, "you lack experience. Come, let yourself go and join in the festivities."

"This place is vulgar, and so are the people in it," she said coldly. "I wish to go home."

"I am afraid we must stay longer," Cranshawe replied, his own voice stiffening. "I have instructed my coachman not to return before midnight."

"Then we must take a hackney," Henry said firmly, rising to her feet and grasping her reticule.

"Henry," he said, his tone becoming wheedling, "have I not earned this evening with you? It is true that many people of a lower order are permitted to attend these masquerades, but there are also many people of quality here. Do you not trust me to protect you from insult?"

"I wish to go, Oliver," Henry said, her own tone more reasonable. "I should not have come in the first place. I know that Marius would not like it. And, yes, of course you have earned my gratitude. But I shall repay you in time. Now, will you please hire a hackney?"

"No, I will not." He laughed, grasping her hand and leaning toward her. Come, Henry, let us dance again and forget these maidenly fears. You are not a maiden any longer, you know!"

Henry tossed her head. "If you are not gentleman enough to take me," she said icily, "I shall go alone." And she turned and stalked from the box.

She made it into the corridor that encircled the auditorium of the opera house before Cranshawe caught up with her. He caught her wrist in an iron grip.

"Stop behaving like a spoiled brat, Henry," he commanded in a tone she had never heard from him before. "Come back into the box."

"Let me go immediately," she hissed, "or I shall make a scene."

Cranshawe laughed unpleasantly. "You would not attract much attention here even if you screamed at the top of your lungs. Do you think I am about to let you go now, Henry, when I finally have you to myself?"

"What do you mean?" she demanded, eyes wide with a mixture of indignation and dawning fright.

"I have wanted you for quite some time, my dear," he said, smiling confidently down into her face. "Tonight I intend to have some reward for my care of you."

"You must be mad!" Henry cried, fear forgotten in a terrible burst of anger. "I intend to leave this place right now!"

She turned to leave, but before she could move one step, two hands clamped onto her upper arms. Henry kicked out with one foot; her evening slipper came into sharp contact with Cranshawe's shin and he swore.

"Little minx!" he said between his teeth. "It is going to be a pleasure to teach you some manners. I see that Marius has failed."

"Don't defile my husband's name by mentioning it," Henry raged, struggling against the hands that were like iron bands around her arms. She was rewarded for her pains by being hauled unceremoniously against his body. She managed to get her clenched fists only waist-high before his arms encircled her and precluded all movement. Although she shook her head furiously from side to side, she could not for long avoid his seeking lips. His mouth clamped over hers without any pretense of tenderness. Her own lips were pressed against her teeth until she could feel the soft flesh being cut. Her mind soon became aware of the heat of his body pressed against her own, her breasts crushed against his chest, the breath being forced from her body until she felt she could fight no longer. Her head was falling back; the hood with which she had earlier covered her head slipped off, revealing her unruly auburn curls. Henry felt a rising nausea.

Just when she felt she must faint away for the first time in her life, Henry was suddenly released. Cranshawe muttered an oath and grasped one shin—the same one that Henry had kicked—hopping on the other leg for a moment. Then his attention focused on a young serving boy fleeing along the passageway and he started in pursuit, anxiously patting his pockets to see if anything had been stolen.

Seeing her chance, Henry gathered her domino around

her again, pulled her hood over her head, and fled in the opposite direction. Luck was with her. As she came to the outer doors, deliberately slowing her pace so as not to attract undue attention, a hackney cab was dropping its passengers and making to leave again empty. Henry signaled one of the doormen and he hailed the driver and helped her inside. Ten minutes later, a very relieved Henry was being admitted into her own home by a footman.

She climbed the stairs wearily and entered her own room. She stood with her back against the door for a few moments, eyes closed, waiting for her heart to resume its normal beat. She considered ringing for Betty and for a light for her candle, but rejected both ideas. She wanted only to be alone to consider what had happened.

Henry pushed herself away from the door with a sigh and began to undress herself with the aid of the moonlight filtering through the windows. She pulled on her lawn nightdress and sat down at the dressing table to brush her hair. She sighed again. Marius had been so very right about Oliver. After the experiences of that evening, she now had no doubt that the whole of the story about him was correct. He had befriended her and loaned her a large sum of money only to get her into his power so that he could somehow embarrass his cousin. How far he had intended to go with her that night she was not sure, but she had no doubt that he had intended to ruin her reputation if not her virtue. Had he meant to boast to Marius afterward, or had he intended to drop tidbits of gossip in the right ears so that she would become the talk of the town?

Henry realized suddenly that, although she had escaped from him with no more than a brutal kiss, he could still damage her reputation. She had gone with him to a place where no respectable lady of the *ton* would be seen, and now she understood why. And she had been recognized there by at least the two couples who had shared their box for a while. How naïve she had been!

How would Marius react if he found out? Henry had mental images of his scorn. She could picture him sweeping her from head to toe with his quizzing glass. She imagined him sending her away to one of his more remote estates, perhaps even divorcing her. She would never be able to appear in society again if that happened. Not that she would care, she tried to convince herself. She would persuade Peter to send her back to Roedean and she would spend the rest of her days there, where she had always been happiest.

But she could not fool herself. It was true that she loved Roedean, true that she could live quite happily there without the distractions of high-society life, but she could no longer live happily without Marius. She wanted his good opinion, his friendship, his love. But she had effectively cut herself off from any of these. For one wild moment she considered going to him next morning in his library and confessing the whole. But she knew she could not. She could not bear to think of the look of disappointment or anger that she would bring to his face. And, most of all, she could not break her promise to Giles. Somehow she was going to have to get herself out of this mess.

Henry had been unseeingly regarding her own darkened image in the mirror while the brush moved mechanically through her hair. But suddenly her eyes focused on the faintly moonlit reflection of the wing chair behind her that stood beside the empty fireplace. The brush dropped with a clatter to the dressing-table top, and she spun around on the stool, eyes wide.

"How long have you been sitting there?" she demanded.

Eversleigh considered. "Since about a half-hour before your return, my love," he replied affably.

"What do you want?"

"Partly to know that you are safe," he said. "But I see that you are." He rose leisurely to his feet and proceeded to light the branched candles that stood on the mantelpiece.

"Marius, you are supposed to be playing cards tonight," Henry accused, her voice trembling slightly. "I did not expect you to return much before morning."

"Did you not, my love?" he replied, giving her a long, hard look.

Henry rose to her feet and gave her husband a bright smile. "Well," she said, "now that you know I am safely home, you need not wait up. Good night, Marius."

Eversleigh lowered himself into the wing chair again and looked maddeningly at his ease, clad in a blue velvet dressing gown and slippers. "Did you enjoy your music tonight, my love?" he asked conversationally.

Henry opened her mouth to reply, looked into his half-closed eyes, and shut it again. She looked down at her hands. "You know I was not there, do you not?" she said.

"You did not miss much," he assured her. "Signora Ratelli was somewhat off-key tonight, I believe. Though, of course, I am no connoisseur of music."

Henry did not reply. She continued to stare at her hands.

"Where were you, Henry?" he asked softly.

She looked up at him. "I went to the masquerade at the opera house," she said, and then added with a defiant tilt to her chin, "with Oliver."

"Ah, quite so," he said, still with his maddening air of nonchalance. "And did you enjoy yourself?"

"Yes, I did, very much," she lied.

"You are home early," he observed, "for one who was enjoying herself."

"I was supposed to be at the concert," she replied defiantly. "I did not wish to arouse suspicion by returning home late."

"An admirable forethought," he commented.

Henry could stand his amiability no longer. "Marius," she cried, "if you are angry, say something or do something. Don't play cat and mouse with me!"

"My love," he said, eyebrows raised in surprise, "what should I have to say or do? You have made it abundantly clear in the past that my wishes and my feelings mean nothing to you. All that is left for me to do is to try to ensure your safety."

"Oh, that is not true," she flared. "I do care for your feelings and wishes."

"Do you, my love?" he asked gently. "Forgive me. I must have misinterpreted everything you have said to me and done since our marriage."

Eversleigh rose to his feet and came toward her. Henry stood her ground, though she swallowed nervously.

"Henry," he asked softly, "do you love Oliver Cranshawe?"

Her eyes widened. "No!" she whispered.

"Because if you do, and if he can convince me that

he truly loves you," he continued, "much as I distrust him, I shall release you. We can still have an annulment, you know."

"I do not want an annulment," she said.

"Do you not?" His eyes focused suddenly on her mouth and remained there. He reached out a hand to cup her chin, and with a very gentle thumb drew down her lower lip so that the torn skin where Cranshawe had pressed the flesh against her teeth was visible. He closed her mouth again and kept his thumb lightly on her lips.

"He has been kissing you," he said. It was a statement, not a question.

"Yes."

He looked deeply into her eyes for several uncomfortable moments. "Has he been making love to you, Henry?" he asked gently. "Have you been to bed with him?"

"No," she whispered, her eyes wide with horror. And then the unspeakable happened. His face suddenly blurred before her eyes and she felt hot tears on her cheeks.

His hands warmly framed her face and his thumbs brushed aside the tears. She was still gazing into his eyes.

"Henry," he said softly, "don't cry, my love."

As the first sob shook her, his mouth covered hers, open, warm, moist, and infinitely gentle. He avoided putting pressure on her bruised lips. But his tongue lightly traced them and passed over the cuts inside, soothing and comforting. Henry felt more sobs and more tears coming. There was such a wonderful feeling of safety and rightness about the moment. She, who had always fought against any man's dominance, welcomed now the strong arms that encircled her and the warm, strong body against which she leaned.

Henry was not sure how or when the kiss changed course. She was only hazily aware after a few minutes that her arms were around his neck, one hand thrust into his hair, and that her body was arched tautly into his, eagerly responding to its heat. His tongue was now plunging deeply into her mouth, boldly exploring its surfaces and fencing with her own tongue. One hand was undoing the buttonholes that extended down the front of her nightdress to the navel and was reaching inside to cup first one breast and then the other.

She did not resist when Eversleigh drew the lawn material away from her shoulders and let the nightgown fall into a heap on the floor. She did not struggle when he lifted her and set her down on the cool white sheets of the bed. She watched him wide-eyed as he shrugged out of his own dressing gown and nightshirt. She received his weight on top of her with a sort of wild relief.

And then sensation took control. Marius' taut male body was heavy on her, his hands first on her breasts, coaxing the nipples to an almost-unbearable hardness and then moving up over her shoulders and down her back until he clasped the lower half of her body ever closer to his. His mouth covered hers again and moved down to caress her throat, her shoulders, and finally, her breasts.

Henry felt completely surrounded by the man she loved and wanted, but she still lay with muscles taut, in an agony of unfulfillment. She waited feverishly for she knew not what. And then he was in her, too, the shock and pain completely depriving her of breath for a moment. She was sobbing again without realizing it, holding herself steady against his entry in total disregard of that momentary stab of pain. And then he was moving in her, deeply and surely taking her to that unknown destination.

Henry became vaguely aware that someone in the room was alternately moaning and gasping, and sometimes saying his name. She knew, without shame, that it was her own voice that she heard. She heard him murmuring soothing words against her ear, but could not translate the sounds into any everyday meaning.

And finally it was coming, that total sense of giving and belonging that she had fought against for so long and that she now craved with all her being. The thrust of his body was slowing and her own inner being was opening and relaxing against him, allowing him to penetrate the deepest secrets of her womanhood. She bit down on her lower lip as it happened, stifling a cry of wonder and delight. Her fingernails dug into the strong muscles of his back. He sighed aloud against her face and relaxed all his weight onto her unresisting body. They lay thus for several minutes, united, man and wife.

Finally, Eversleigh withdrew from her and moved to her side. He gathered her damp, relaxed body into his arms and gently kissed first one closed eyelid and then the other.

"Henry," he murmured, "did I hurt you, my love?"

She smiled drowsily into the warmth of his shoulder. No, she answered silently, you did not hurt me at all, my love.

"Did you know that that is what was to happen?" he asked against her ear.

No, her mind replied as she slid happily into a deep sleep.

Eversleigh lay staring upward at the shadows thrown on the bed's canopy by the candles that still burned. One hand absently caressed his wife's shoulder. Her failure to answer either of his questions had halted his own descent into sleep. He deliberately thought back over each moment of their lovemaking, reassessing her reactions. Had he merely assumed that she was responding with a passion to equal his own?

While Henry and Eversleigh were deeply engrossed in their world of passion, a very weary set of twins were creeping through the grounds of the house toward the side entrance that they had left unlocked earlier in the evening. It was with great relief that they discovered that no one had detected the fact that the door was unlocked. Philip pushed the door open slowly, peered cautiously into the gloom to make sure that no one was close by, and beckoned Penelope inside. They tiptoed up the back staircase and stumbled thankfully into Penelope's room, closing the door behind them.

"Whew!" said Penelope, dragging off the boy's cap that she had worn and shaking out her long hair. "I did not really think we should get back safely."

"You did a really good job, Pen," her brother said admiringly. "It's a great pity that it's just not the thing for girls to become actresses."

"Well, I was scared they would grab me up at any moment and turn me over to the watch," Penelope said more practically. "I wish we might have taken Brutus."

"How? With a black mask on? Don't be such a feather-brain, Pen," said Philip. "One look at him by either Henry or the toothpowder and the game would have been up."

"You are sure that Henry got away safely?" Penelope asked.

"If she did not, she does not have as much spirit as she used to have," replied Philip. "I certainly kept old teeth off the trail for a while. Almost got m'self caught, too."

Penelope giggled. "I should like to have seen him when he ran full tilt into the waiter bearing a tray of drinks," she said. "It must have been priceless."

"I did not stay to watch the show," her brother said dryly. "But listen, Pen, I didn't like the way he was manhandling Henry. He was kissing her! You know that even his Grace does not kiss her out in public like that."

"We have to do something about it," said Penelope with a sense of drama that seemed to suit the time and the occasion.

"I don't know what," Philip replied, plucking at his lower lip while his brow furrowed in thought. "Manny keeps us busy most of the day."

"Should we tell her?" Penelope suggested.

Philip considered. "It might help," he admitted. "I don't think Manny will be of any real assistance—she goes off into a flap too easily. But I think she will want to help. At least she might let us keep a closer eye on Henry."

"We'll tell her the whole story at breakfast tomorrow, then," said Penelope, and yawned so loudly that her jaws cracked.

# CHAPTER

## 10

Henry turned over in bed. She was only half-awake, but already the events of the night before had returned to her mind. She snuggled over to the side of the bed where Marius had held her in his arms after their lovemaking, only to find that he was no longer there.

Her eyes opened; she was instantly awake. It was light outside already, although the street sounds suggested that it was still early morning. Marius frequently rose early, she knew, to ride and refresh himself before going to the House for the morning business. She smiled smugly to herself and stretched luxuriously in the warm bed.

So this was what it felt like to be a wife, to be loved! She relived again, moment by moment, the whole of their lovemaking. Why had she always thought of physical contact as something repulsive? Last night had been wonderful. It had not been a case of the male taking and using her and making her feel like a weak woman with no worth beyond her sexual function. He had made her feel a partner in what had happened. She knew, inexperienced as she was, that he had taken the time to give pleasure to her as well as himself. And she knew that she had given him pleasure. There was that moment when he had murmured his release against her face.

If only he had not gone away so early . . . Henry would have liked to do again right then what they had done the night before. She felt a throbbing low in her womb at the very thought. Then she blushed with shame at her own desire. Maybe married people just did not do it that often!

But she was happy! She bounced off the bed, grasped the hangings of her bed in her arms, and pirouetted several times until she became so entangled in the heavy velvet that she had to stop and carefully unwind herself, giggling self-consciously though there was no one there to watch. She rang for Betty.

"I want the blue muslin dress today," she told her maid, and hummed tunelessly to herself as she washed, dressed, and had her hair brushed. "Is his Grace still at home?" she asked.

"I believe so, your Grace," Betty replied. "He was coming through the door as I was coming upstairs."

"Good," said Henry, smiling into the mirror.

She dismissed Betty before going down to the breakfast room. She had some thinking to do. Now everything was changed between her and Marius. They were in love; they were truly man and wife; they could now speak openly and freely to each other. She would go down to breakfast and he would rise from his place and hold out his arms to her. He would kiss her and laugh when she glanced uneasily at the butler, who would probably be there too. They would talk about last night and tell each other how much in love they were. And then she would tell him all about Oliver Cranshawe and her awkward debt to him. She would not mention Giles, of course. She would tell him that she had gambled unwisely at some party and that her debt had embarrassed her. But—yes—she would tell him. He would understand and forgive her in the afterhaze of last night's passion. And then she would be free of Oliver and would be ready to begin living happily ever after.

Henry took a last peek into the mirror, adjusted a few curls around her face, and tripped lightly down the stairs to the breakfast room. Alas, it had two occupants. Mr. Ridley was sitting at the table with Marius. Henry found herself suddenly shy as both men rose from their places and Marius moved around the table to hold her chair for her. She smiled vaguely in the direction of his chin and beamed at Mr. Ridley.

"Good morning, my love," Eversleigh said in his usual

tone of bored irony. "You are remarkably early this morning."

"I plan to go riding after breakfast, while the air is still cool," she replied.

"Ah," was his only comment. And to Henry's chagrin, he turned his attention to Ridley and talked about some speech that he was apparently to give within the next few days. Obviously her entrance had interrupted this business.

"I suppose I must come and examine the morning mail," he said at last. "Is there anything important, James?"

"Some bills and some invitations, your Grace," Ridley replied.

"Ah, but I asked if there was anything important, James," his employer repeated, fixing him with a sleepy stare.

"A letter from Kent and one from your Norfolk estate, your Grace." Ridley said in his long-suffering voice.

"Then I must come," said Eversleigh with a sigh. "Will you excuse us, Henry?"

"Of course," she replied bleakly.

"And would you give me the pleasure of your company in the library before you ride, my love? Say in half an hour?" he asked.

"Yes, Marius," she said, spirits soaring again. After the two men had left, she sat sipping her coffee, living again in her imagination the scene that would soon take place. Only the setting was different—it would be the library rather than the breakfast room. But all the better! The library was more private.

Henry found herself blushing as she tapped on the library door half an hour later and let herself inside. She closed the door and leaned against it. Her eyes shone and her lips were parted eagerly as she looked across at her husband. Disconcertingly, he was sitting formally at his desk, apparently engrossed in the papers that were spread out before him.

"Come and sit down, Henry," he said without looking up.

Henry felt a twinge of unease. His voice was not the voice of last night's lover. She crossed the room and sat uncomfortably on the edge of the chair that was across the desk from him.

Eversleigh carefully put down the quill pen he was

using, pushed together the pile of papers in front of him, and finally looked up at his wife. His eyes were hooded behind half-closed lids.

"I owe you an apology," he said stiffly.

Henry was too shocked to reply. But her hands were suddenly cold. She clasped them together in her lap.

"I made you a promise on our wedding night," Eversleigh continued, "and I broke that promise quite shamefully last night. I had been worried about your safety and wished to punish you, I suppose. I regret the lapse, ma'am, and assure you that it will not happen again."

"But Marius, I didn't . . ." she began.

He held up an imperious hand to silence her. "I told you that you would be expected to perform the duties of a wife as soon as we retire to Kent for the summer," Eversleigh continued. "I find, on reflection, that it is distasteful to force my attentions on an unwilling partner. I wish you to know, Henry, that you may retain my name and my protection for as long as you wish, but you owe me nothing in return. Until you say the word, I shall not touch you again."

"Oh," said Henry, leaping to her feet and putting her hands on her hips, "so I do not measure up to the standard set by Mrs. Broughton, do I?"

Eversleigh's body became completely motionless; his eyes became icy. "Would you care to explain that remark, Henry?" he asked softly.

"You thought I did not know, did you not?" she said, eyes flashing. "You thought me naïve. I am not a child, Marius. I know she is your mistress and has been for a long time. I have seen you with her on several occasions. She is very feminine, with that tiny waist and large bosom."

"Who has told you all this, Henry?" he asked, still in the maddeningly calm and soft voice. "Cranshawe?"

"Oh, I do not need him to point out the obvious to me," Henry said. "I know that, with my figure, I cannot compete." She held her arms out and looked down on her own slim body. "You must have found me very disappointing last night."

"Must I, my love?" he asked, the old gleam showing in his eyes for a moment.

"Yes. And do you know what?" she asked rhetorically.

"I am glad! You know I hate to be touched. When you kiss me, I feel like rushing to the nearest washbasin and plunging in my face. And what you did to me last night was quite repulsive. I think I should run away if I felt that I would have to be subjected to that at your pleasure. Keep your Mrs. Broughton. Perhaps she will help keep your lecherous hands off me!"

Eversleigh put his palms on the desk and rose to his feet, keeping his eyes on her. He came around the desk. For one moment Henry thought he was coming to her and she did not know whether she would spit in his face or ignominiously grab his lapels and soak his neckcloth with her tears. But he walked across the room to pour himself a brandy. He stood silently, with his back to her, while he drank it.

"Am I dismissed, your Grace?" she asked tauntingly.

"No, Henry," he replied, turning to face her. His expression was impassive, almost mocking. "I wished to ask you one more question, though now is perhaps not the best time." He put his empty glass down on the table and walked over to the fireplace. He rested one elbow on the mantel and looked steadily across at her. She was still standing in front of the desk.

"Are you in any kind of trouble, Henry?" he asked.

"Whatever do you mean?" Henry said with an artificial little laugh.

He pondered. "I have a feeling that there is something you will not tell me," he said carefully, "something that worries you."

She laughed again. "What would worry me?" she asked.

He watched her steadily. "I wish you would tell me, if I may help you," he said. "I know you feel bitter toward me this morning. You feel, and rightly so, that I have betrayed you. But believe me, Henry, when I tell you that I have the highest regard for you. And you may trust me, you know."

Henry stared, her mind churning in confusion. Her brain was telling her that here was the perfect opportunity to unburden herself, to get herself out of a fix. Her heart was reminding her that her husband had used her the night before and found her wanting. He cared nothing that he was leaving her emotions bruised and raw this morning. She did not doubt that he would help her. But she would not be beholden to such a man. She would fight her own battles, as she always had. She lifted her chin and looked directly into his eyes.

"What nonsense you speak, Marius!" she said. "May I leave now, please, or it will be too late to ride."

Eversleigh's mouth relaxed into what for him passed for a smile, Henry supposed.

"Run along, my love," he said. "I have taken enough of your time for one morning, it appears."

Henry considered slamming the door behind her when she left, but decided that doing so would be a childish gesture. She closed it quietly and stood outside the library for a few moments, head and heart thumping. What had happened in the last few minutes had been so totally unexpected and so completely agonizing that she did not know quite how to cope at present.

The butler approached her before she moved away. He held a letter on a salver. "This was delivered a few minutes ago, your Grace," he said deferentially. "I was to deliver it into your hands."

"Thank you," she replied absently, taking the letter and climbing the stairs wearily to her room. She sat down in front of the mirror and stared disconsolately at her own image. Strange! She looked the same as she had when she went down to breakfast—how long ago? Was it only little more than an hour ago that she had left this room so full of hope and happiness? She had not dreamed that her newfound love would be so effectively shattered in such a short time. How she hated him! He had spoken to her once about his "animal instincts." And that was all they were. He must have been delighted the night before when she had started to cry and been so vulnerable. He had certainly been very quick to take advantage of the situation. And while she had held him and opened to him and called his name, because he was Marius and the man she loved, he had merely been using her as almost any man would use a woman who was so obviously available. But he certainly did not consider her worth a repeat performance. Henry ground her teeth in mortification. Would she never learn not to trust any man—at least not with her emotions?

She crushed into a wad the letter that she still held in her hand, then realized what she was doing. She smoothed it out again on top of the dressing table and broke the seal. The letter was from Oliver, she saw when she glanced down to the signature. She read:

My dear Henry,

I cannot tell you how deeply I regret my behavior of last evening. I can only plead the effects of overindulgence in wine. You must know that I hold you in deep regard. Surely I have proven my devotion to you. But I do not intend to remind you of any obligation.

Please meet me in the park this morning. I shall ride there until noon. I must speak with you. I should regret having to call at the house, as I know you would be distressed should Marius find me there.

I shall be awaiting the pleasure of your company.

Your obedient servant,
Oliver Cranshawe

Henry crumpled the paper again and threw it to the floor. The rat! Could he seriously believe that she would ever trust him again? After what he had said and done the night before? Was ever a girl so unlucky as to encounter two such unprincipled men on the same night? But she would have to go, Henry realized. The threat in the letter had not been so subtle. She knew that Oliver would come to the house if she refused to meet him elsewhere. She crossed reluctantly to a closet and pulled out her chocolate-brown riding habit and the matching hat with the gold and bronze plumes. At least she would look her best. She was not going to let Oliver Cranshawe know that he had her worried.

Fifteen minutes later, Philip opened the door to Henry's room without knocking.

"She probably left it in here somewhere," he said over his shoulder.

"Unless she took it with her," Penelope added from directly behind him.

"Oh, dear, this does not feel right," Miss Manford wailed

from the rear. "Whatever would we say if your sister unexpectedly returned or if his Grace appeared?"

"You know from what we told you this morning, Manny, that Henry needs help," Philip explained patiently, "and that letter this morning looked suspicious. It did not come by the regular mail."

"It's a good thing we were passing through the hall when it arrived," Penelope added.

"It is probably just an invitiation or a notice from a dressmaker," said Miss Manford.

Brutus, meanwhile, galloped past the arguing trio and began to play with a ball of paper that was lying on the floor.

"Brutus, get away from there. That might be it," yelled Penelope, grabbing his hindquarters and hauling him backward, in vain.

"Woof!" replied the dog, enjoying the game and returning to the paper again.

"Good dog! Give!" Philip ordered, but when Brutus showed no sign of obeying, he grabbed the dog's muzzle and tried to force his jaws apart.

"Oh, bless my soul!" wailed Miss Manford. "We shall all be discovered."

Brutus solved the problem by spotting a slipper across the room. He abandoned the paper for more attractive prey.

Penelope pounced on the letter, which was damp but intact, and smoothed it out on the floor.

Philip knelt beside her to read it. "He's sorry for last night!" he cried indignantly. "After mauling Henry around as if she were a chambermaid."

"Oh, dear," said Miss Manford, "I don't believe you should speak like that, dear boy."

"He is as slippery as a snake," Penelope said, "reminding her that she is in his debt and then saying that he does not wish to mention it."

"Snakes aren't slippery," Philip added irrelevantly, and then jumped into action. "Come on," he said, "we must follow her."

"To the park?" Penelope asked, eyes shining.

"We must make sure that he does not abduct her," Philip said.

"The park is a very public place, dear boy," Miss Manford said. "I do not believe your sister will be in any danger there. But I do believe we should confide in his Grace."

"No!" Philip and Penelope chorused together.

"Then perhaps Sir Peter," their governess suggested.

"Peter!" Philip said scornfully. "He would run straight to his Grace and advise him to beat Henry."

"Mr. Ridley?" Miss Manford suggested hesitantly.

Neither twin answered immediately. "He is so loyal to the duke," Penelope said finally. "He would probably tell. But if worse comes to worst, Manny, and we need a man, we will go to him. But now, let's go!"

The twins collided in the doorway, Miss Manford was almost as eager to leave a room she felt she had no business inside, and Brutus, seeing his audience departing, charged out behind them, a pink slipper still dangling from his mouth.

The Duke of Eversleigh was returning home from a short morning errand. He intended to change out of his riding clothes into an outfit more suitable for lunch at White's on St. James's Street. As his horse was cantering through the park, he became aware of a commotion ahead of him. There seemed to be a great number of persons and a great deal of noise involved. As he drew closer—an interested spectator, but one who intended to keep his distance—he could see that someone was up in a tree, someone else on the ground below stretching up arms, someone lying in a mud puddle while a riderless horse danced skittishly around, someone holding with both hands the lead of a large and loudly barking dog, and someone else on horseback making no attempt to take command of the situation. These appeared to be the main players. There were several bystanders, all on foot, including a constable who was waving a club around but who appeared uncertain on whose head to bring it down.

It was the dog that gave away the identity of the group to the duke. He reined his horse to a walk as he drew closer, and approached the scene with all the nonchalance of one for whom such a scene is a daily occurrence.

"Down, Brutus, old fellow," he commanded in a bored voice, and the huge canine, who had caused much of the commotion, according to the loud opinion of the bystanders, dropped on the spot and panted loudly, adoring eyes raised to its master. Miss Manford was released from the immediate danger of having her arms pulled from their sockets.

"Phil, are you planning to join the rest of us on *terra firma* some time this morning?" Eversleigh continued, raising his quizzing glass and gazing upward at his brother-in-law, who was clinging to a branch of a large oak tree.

"I'm not stuck, sir," Philip hastened to assure Eversleigh. "But that cat is." He pointed to a thin and scraggly little creature clinging pathetically to a branch. "I have to move carefully because the branch gets pretty thin out there. And, Pen, for the dozenth time, move away from there. If I fall, you won't help me at all, but I will flatten you."

"I'm here to catch the kitten," Penelope explained indignantly.

"The little lad will fall for sure," a buxom woman carrying a large, covered basket warned, "and all for a stray cat. Call 'im down, sir."

Eversleigh ignored her. "Move back, Penny, until there is something to catch," he advised. "Go ahead, Phil. The branch is strong enough."

Most eyes were turned on the little drama. Eversleigh withdrew his; he did not feel that his brother-in-law was in any grave danger.

"Having a spot of trouble, Oliver?" he asked affably, swinging his glass in the direction of his cousin, who had already picked himself out of the mud, but who was gazing down at his thoroughly blackened cream buckskins with arms outstretched, not quite knowing how to clean himself up without soiling his hands. He rounded on the duke in fury.

"If you do not keep that dog confined to the house, and if you do not exercise greater control over these totally undisciplined brats," he said, voice shaking, "I shall shoot it."

"Dear me," replied his cousin mildly, "I understand from your choice of pronoun that you mean the dog, not the twins, Oliver?"

Cranshawe glared. "You might make yourself useful and

grab my horse, Marius," he said, "instead of sitting up there striking a pose."

"Ah," Eversleigh said, "I take it you did not dismount voluntarily, then, Oliver?" He obligingly moved off to where Cranshawe's horse was now grazing quietly on the grass, and led him back to his heir, who was disgustedly slapping at his mud-caked breeches.

Eversleigh turned his attention to his wife, who was staring intently into the tree where Philip was now little more than an arm's length from the shivering kitten.

"You are all right, my love?" he asked gently.

She turned a stony expression on him. "And why would I not be?" she asked.

"Ah, quite so," he agreed. "You need not worry, you know. Boys are almost invariably a great deal safer than they appear to be to adult onlookers."

"I know that!" she retorted scornfully, and dismounted suddenly after swinging her leg free of the sidesaddle. "Hang on, Phil!" she yelled. "You can't hold on to the cat and get back from there. I'll climb up and you can hand it to me."

Before the onlookers had a chance to dissuade her, she had swung up to the lower branches, long skirt and all, though she did tug impatiently at the plumed hat and send it to the ground.

" 'Ere, 'ere, lady, that's man's work," the constable remarked ineffectually when she was already well clear of the ground, but everyone ignored him.

When Henry came down again, five minutes later, clutching a mewing kitten in one arm, face smudged with dirt, hemline of her habit hanging down, it was to find Marius directly beneath her, on foot.

"Hand down the kitten, Henry," he ordered, and she obeyed before she had time to think of defiance. He took it and handed it immediately to an eager Penelope. Then he turned back, raised his arms, and grasped his wife by the waist. He swung her down to the ground, so that her body slid down the length of his. She felt physically ill as she glared indignantly up into his gleaming eyes.

"I could have jumped," she said as Philip did just that right behind her.

"I don't doubt it for a moment, my love," Eversleigh agreed soothingly, the gleam in his eyes deepening.

"I must look a fright," she said crossly.

"I think you look rather charming, my love, with a smudge on your nose and a twig in your hair," he commented languidly.

"Oh!" she said. "Well, you should be thankful for the twig, your Grace. At least I am not committing that mortal sin of going hatless again."

"Your Grace!" Penelope was plucking at Eversleigh's sleeve, interrupting an interesting scene. "Please may we keep the kitten? I am sure the little thing is a stray, and Phil and I will look after it. Please!"

"Well," he said, "it would seem hardly charitable to rescue the poor thing from one danger only to let it starve on firm ground. Very well, Penny."

"Oh, thank you, your Grace," Penelope yelled. "I am going to call her Cleopatra."

Eversleigh blinked. "As you will," he said tolerantly, "but I fail to see the connection." He surveyed the thin, ugly ginger kitten through his quizzing glass. "I believe we have provided the city of London with quite enough entertainment for one morning," he continued quietly. "I see that Oliver agrees with me and has taken himself off already. Miss Manford, can you head this menagerie homeward? Phil, you take charge of Brutus, if you please. My love?" He stilled Henry's horse, and when she would have placed her booted foot in his hand so that she might mount, he grasped her by the waist again and lifted her effortlessly to the saddle.

Henry could feel the imprint of his hands all the way home as they rode side by side, making small talk. He made no reference to the fact that she had obviously been with Oliver Cranshawe before the family farce had begun.

The morning's activities were not forgotten by any of the actors in it. Henry spent most of the afternoon in her room, after canceling plans she had made to do a round of visiting. She had a very serious decision to make, and although she knew what that decision would have to be, there still seemed to be a great deal of thinking to do.

She had met Oliver in the park and had talked with him

for five minutes before the arrival of the twins and Miss Manford on the scene. Oliver had taken on the tone of his letter, profoundly apologetic, disclaiming all responsibility for what he had said the night before on the grounds that he had drunk too much. But Henry had lost all faith in his words. He claimed to care for her deeply, to be worried about her marriage to "a man like Marius." He wished to see her again, alone, so that he might redeem himself in her eyes. Henry could see only the truth. Here was a man who hated her husband and who hated her for being the chief threat to his position as Marius' heir. He wished to ruin her so that Marius would divorce her or at the very least send her away. Either would suit Oliver's purposes. In either case, there would be no children to succeed the Duke of Eversleigh. And Henry, with childish naïveté, had played right into his hands. Oh, why had she not seen through the hypocrisy of his charm? Why had she not gone straight to Marius with her worries over Giles?

Henry threw herself facedown across the bed. She racked her brain for some solution to the dilemma, apart from the one that she was trying not to face. She had managed to escape any commitment this morning, thanks to the strange appearance of the twins. And that *was* strange, now that she came to think of it. What were they all doing in the park at that time of the morning? Were they not usually at their classes? However it had happened, she had been very grateful for the distraction. But she did not have any hope that Cranshawe would be put off for long. It was only a matter of time before he again forced her into a clandestine meeting.

Henry considered talking to Giles, but she knew she would not be able to bring herself to destroy his peace of mind. She saw him frequently, and he seemed to be quite happy. He did the social rounds, but it seemed to her that he had learned his lesson. He no longer associated with the crowd of wild dandies that had led him into gambling and irresponsible spending. If he was in debt again, she would be surprised. At least there was no sign from him. He treated her with open affection. Henry had been close to her brother all her life. She would have known if something were troubling him. No, she could not go to him with her dilemma.

There was, in fact, only one way out, Henry admitted to herself with a sigh. She propped her chin on her hands and stared gloomily down at the brocade coverlet of her bed. Somehow, she had to get the money to repay the loan to Cranshawe. Only then would she be free of that horrid man. And there was, alas, only one way to get the money, unless she applied to Marius for it. Since she would rather die than go to him now, she would have to go to a moneylender.

The very thought filled her with terror. She had heard many stories of the fate of young men who were unwise enough to get into the clutches of moneylenders. (It seemed that ladies never went to them.) The story was that once a man borrowed money, he never repaid it. All the money he could scrape together went toward paying off the crippling interest on their loans.

But Henry had to put these stories behind her. She really had no choice, unless she sold or pawned some of her jewels. She had considered doing that, but knew that any valuable item that she possessed would soon be missed. Marius, unlike many husbands, accompanied her to most evening functions. And he always noticed what she wore. He would frequently suggest the jewelry that would best complement her choice of clothes. She knew she would not be able to deceive him. No, she must go to a moneylender. She remembered the name and direction of the one that Giles had been planning to visit. It was ironic that she, who had been so adamant that he not borrow money in this way, was now deciding to do the same thing herself!

Henry scrambled resolutely off the bed. Since there was no alternative and since she had made up her mind, there was nothing to be gained by delay. She would go at once. She assumed that Marius was away from home at this time of day. She was sure that the twins must be in the schoolroom, especially after their escapade of the morning. She could accomplish her errand without anyone knowing.

She searched her closet hastily for the dullest clothing she possessed. Pushed far to one side she found a drab, gray cloak that she had worn for years at Roedean. She could not imagine how it had escaped the purge that Betty had made on her old clothes. She pulled it from its place and chose the plainest bonnet she could find, a brown one that looked quite dreary enough once she had removed the green ribbons that adorned it.

Henry glanced at herself in the mirror before leaving the room. She wrinkled her nose in some disgust at the very unpretty picture that she made, draped entirely in the gray and brown. She pushed an auburn curl farther under the brim of the bonnet, took up her reticule, and resolutely left the room. She descended the back stairs and let herself out of the side door and through a back gate that led to a narrow lane used by tradesmen.

Head bent, Henry hurried along until she came to a roadway. She walked briskly for some distance, mingling with crowds of people who did not afford her hurrying figure a second glance. Only one urchin seemed in any way interested. He appeared to be following her, ducking into doorways and behind other pedestrians to avoid being seen, though she did not look back even once. When she finally hailed a hackney cab and climbed inside, the urchin ran up behind. He clung to a bar at the back when the vehicle moved away.

Henry was wrong. The Duke of Eversleigh was not away from home that afternoon. As she was making her escape from the house, he was closeted with James Ridley in his office. He had been there for some time, going over with his secretary a pile of business papers that had arrived from his estates by the morning mail. Finally he got to his feet, stretched, and walked over to the bookshelves, where he stood leaning his weight on one elbow.

"Ah, do you have my wife's bills here, James?" he asked languidly.

"From this week, your Grace?" Ridley asked, looking up startled.

Eversleigh mused. "Are they all paid, James?"

"Yes, your Grace," Ridley replied. "You have instructed me always to do so."

"Quite so," Eversleigh said, inspecting his fingernails through half-closed lids. "Have any of them been excessively large?"

Ridley thought. "There was a dressmaker's bill for almost three hundred pounds last week," he said uneasily.

The duke looked at him steadily. "Nothing larger?" he asked.

"No, your Grace."

Eversleigh stood, examining his boots.

After a few respectful moments, Ridley returned his attention to the papers spread before him. He looked up again when his employer spoke.

"Have there been any gambling debts, James?"

"You mean by her Grace?" asked Ridley. "No."

"Hmm." The duke was again silent. Then he looked closely at his secretary. "You spend too much time in this office, James," he said kindly. "It is not good for your health, dear boy. Take yourself out and do something for me."

"Your Grace?"

"Find out if my wife owes or has owed a large sum of money to anyone in—ah, let me see—the last month or so."

Ridley looked aghast. "How am I to do that?" he asked.

Eversleigh looked hard at him. "You are an enterprising young man who likes a challenge, James," he said languidly. "I am sure you will find a way."

James Ridley did not reply.

"And James," the duke continued.

"Your Grace?"

"This is to be done discreetly and in the strictest confidence."

"Of course, your Grace."

Eversleigh picked a speck of dust from the sleeve of his coat and pushed himself upright. "I have seen quite enough of these four walls for one day," he said. "I am going to go out in search of some amusement. I suggest you do the same, dear boy."

James Ridley stared in dismay at the employer's back, which retreated unhurriedly through the doorway.

Henry had been wrong about the twins, too. Although Miss Manford and Penelope were indeed in the schoolroom, Phil was not. The three of them had held a conference following their return from the park.

"Well, we certainly did not find out anything new," Philip said. "If it had not been for that stupid cat getting stuck in that tree, we might have got close enough to have heard something useful."

"It is hardly likely, dear," Miss Manford said practically, "since Mr. Cranshawe and your sister were on horseback and moving. They would have seen us for sure if we had tried to get close."

"We could have moved along behind the trees," Philip said, sighing over the lost opportunity.

"Well, I think it all worked well," Penelope said, stroking the back of the cat as it lapped up a saucer of milk. "We certainly saved Henry from whatever the teeth had planned for her. And besides," she added, "if Cleopatra had not got stuck in the tree, we would never have found her."

"Well, I think we had better keep an eye on Henry twenty-four hours a day," said Philip melodramatically. "I don't trust that man."

"I am sure you exaggerate, dear boy," Miss Manford said. "He is a gentleman, after all."

"Manny, do gentlemen kiss ladies in public?" asked Philip scornfully.

Miss Manford declined to answer. She blushed instead.

"I think everything will be well for today," Penelope said, gathering the cat into her lap and continuing to stroke its back. "His Grace is taking her to the opera tonight, is he not?"

"We must watch her until then," Philip insisted. "She went to her room after luncheon."

"We have not had our history lesson today," Miss Manford protested.

"Oh, Manny, I can take the book with me and read while I watch," said Philip. "Are you coming, Pen?"

"Who is to look after Cleopatra?" she asked. "The poor little thing is feeling so strange and Oscar has been so rude to her."

"Well, she does stink a little bit, Pen," her brother said. "I shall go alone, then."

Philip, in the true spirit of the drama of the situation, as he saw it, went first to his room and changed into the urchin's clothes that he had worn the night before, and then tiptoed quietly into the empty room opposite Henry's. He settled himself in a chair from which he could see the handle edge of her door through the door of his room, which he left slightly ajar.

Thus it was that Philip saw Henry slip from the house and was all ready to follow her. He did so without hesitation. It was obvious to him as soon as he saw her unusually drab outfit and as soon as she turned in the direction of the back stairs, that she was on some secret errand. He held her very carefully in sight until she hired a hackney cab. For a moment Philip was alarmed. He thought he would lose her. Fortunately, there was time after Henry got into the carriage and before it moved away for him to run forward and swing himself up behind. The driver did not notice, and none of the passersby seemed to consider his actions strange enough to raise any alarm.

# CHAPTER

## 11

Henry sat in her room later the same afternoon, looking flushed but triumphant. She was at a small escritoire, writing a letter. A small collection of crumpled sheets of paper surrounding her on the floor showed that the words of the letter were not coming easily. This time she seemed satisfied. She signed her name with a flourish, shook the paper in order to dry the ink, and reread what she had written.

Dear Mr. Cranshawe [she had written, having discarded the notion of calling him Oliver],

I am now able to repay my debt to you. I thank you with all my heart for having helped me out of a difficulty. You will find three thousand pounds enclosed in this package.

I remain your grateful friend,

Henrietta Devron

Yes, that was quite enough, she decided. She did not need to say more. There was just the correct combination of gratitude and reserve. She folded the letter, slid it into the package with the bank notes, and tied the bundle securely with ribbon. She rang the bell for Betty.

"Betty," she said when her maid entered the room a few minutes later, "which footman is most reliable to send on a secret and important errand?" Henry did not mince her words. She had learned from experience that Betty was devoted to her and could be trusted to keep her secrets.

Betty did not hesitate. "Robert, your Grace," she said.
"Good. Will you send him to me?" Henry directed.

Within ten minutes Robert had been sent to Oliver
Cranshawe's residence with the package. The footman had
strict instructions to deliver it into the hands of Cranshawe
himself or, failing that, into the hands of his personal
valet. He was not to wait for a reply.

Henry breathed a deep sigh of relief when the deed was
finally done. What a delicious sense of freedom there was
in being out of Oliver's clutches at last. He would probably be furious to see her slip through his fingers, she
thought grimly. But he could hardly refuse the money.
And with that debt repaid, she would no longer be obliged
to jump whenever he snapped his fingers. In fact, she
decided, she would not need even to be civil to the man.
Marius would be pleased to see that their friendship had
finally cooled. Not that she had any interest at all in
pleasing her husband! Her hands curled into fists as she
thought again about her abandonment to his lovemaking
the night before and his cool rejection of the morning.

Henry summoned Betty again and had hot water brought
to her room for a bath. She relaxed in the water while
Betty laid out her turquoise satin and lace evening gown
on the bed behind her. For the moment she felt relaxed.
She could get ready for dinner and the opera almost with a
light heart, though it would be difficult to spend a whole
evening in close contact with Marius. But at least, she
thought with a little smile of genuine amusement, she
would have the satisfaction of knowing that he was not
enjoying himself. Marius and music did not mix happily
together.

Tomorrow she would think about her new problems,
for, truth to tell, she had merely exchanged one nasty
difficulty for another. She tried not to think about her
dealings of earlier that afternoon. She had felt horror
when the hackney cab had turned into narrow, filthy
streets filled with all kinds of offensive rubbish and smells.
Doorways and roadsides had been crowded with untidy
and dirty-looking people and ragged children. When the
carriage had stopped, she had not known what to do for a
few moments. But, remembering that she was Henry
Devron and had never been afraid of anything for long,

she got resolutely out of the carriage with the driver's assistance, instructed him to wait for her, squared her shoulders, and bore down on a small group of women gossiping in a doorway.

They had gawked at the sight of her fine clothes (the gray cloak and brown bonnet had looked drab enough back on Curzon Street, but not here), but had directed her readily enough to the first-floor rooms of the money-lender. She had given them each a shilling for their help and had been followed by openmouthed stares to the dark doorway of her destination.

Henry shuddered now in the bathtub remembering those dark, dirty stairs and the smiling, sinister little man who had opened the door at her knock and bowed her into a dingy room whose door he had proceeded to lock. The interview itself, though, had not proved as difficult as she had expected. The little man had been quite willing to lend her the money, especially when he knew who she was (she had decided not to lie, believing that he would more readily agree to do business with a duchess than he would with a Miss Nobody). Henry had eagerly signed the papers, not at all deterred by the interest rate, which she did not understand. The only nasty moment had come when the moneylender had demanded a pledge of security.

"But I have nothing!" she had protested. "You must trust me."

"But of course I trust you, your Grace," the little man had said, smiling all the while. "Such a charming lady must be honest. But you see, my dear, I do not work for myself. My superior is a hard man, a hard man."

"I do not believe you," Henry had declared hotly and none too wisely.

"Oh, but, dear me, it's a fact," the little man had said, rubbing his hands together, his grin never faltering. "But for such a pretty and grand lady, a mere token. What jewelry do you have, my dear?"

"None!" was Henry's prompt response. "And my purse is almost empty, sir. If I had wealth to leave as security, would I be here borrowing money?"

"Oh, dear me, such a spirited young lady," he had said. "You wear rings, my lady. One of them will serve the purpose. A mere token, you see."

Henry's eyes had widened. "You cannot have either," she said, glancing down at the gold wedding band on her left hand and the sapphire on her right. It was unthinkable to pledge the wedding ring. The other had belonged to her mother and had been left to Henry. Ever since her hands had grown large enough, Henry had worn it. She hardly ever removed it.

In the end she had pledged the sapphire ring. Now she felt sick looking down at her soapy hand and seeing it bare. For her own sake she hated to be without it. Perhaps more important for the present, she was afraid that Marius would miss it and ask her for an explanation. She might as well have pawned more of her jewels for the whole sum, she reflected gloomily.

But she shook off the gloom. She would think of some explanation to give Marius. And tonight she was going to celebrate her freedom from Oliver Cranshawe. Tomorrow she would worry about her new debts.

Miss Manford, in the schoolroom, was showing unaccustomed firmness.

"No, my dears," she was saying, "we cannot handle this matter ourselves. The poor dear duchess must be in terrible trouble if she has resorted to appealing to a moneylender. I have heard that they are dreadful people."

"But we can watch after her, Manny," Philip protested. "As long as one of us stays close, she can be in no danger. I stayed outside that house while Henry was inside. If she had not come out within a few minutes, I planned to stir up those people in the street and wail loudly that my sister had been kidnapped. I would have scared the old money leech."

"I think not, dear boy," Miss Manford said. "Those people would have kept out of trouble, you may depend upon it. No, we must enlist the help of someone who can offer real assistance to dear Hen—I mean, to her Grace."

"Well, she would never have gone there if she felt she could have turned to the duke," said Penelope. "And I cannot understand why. He seems to me to be ever so kind. Brutus, will you stop licking Cleopatra all over? She will take a chill."

It was finally decided that two adults would be consulted.

Miss Manford declared that she would talk to Mr. Ridley the next day; Philip and Penelope were to summon Giles and tell him the story. None of them was willing to seek help from Sir Peter Tallant.

The Duke and Duchess of Eversleigh dined alone that evening and consequently were seated in their private box at the opera a good ten minutes before the performance began. Henry let her eyes rove over the pit, which was already crowded with noisy, exotic-looking dandies. It seemed obvious to her that very few of them had come out of a love of music. They were there to ogle the ladies in the boxes and to preen their male feathers before them. The occupants of the boxes seemed similarly inclined. They were there to see and to be seen. How many of them would remember more than the name of the opera once it was over?

Henry smiled to herself. The opera and its artiste would be the topics of polite conversation the next day. Everyone would be an expert critic. The smile faded when she met the stare of Oliver Cranshawe from across the way. He was sharing a box with Suzanne Broughton and two other couples, Henry noticed at a hasty glance. He smiled and bowed in her direction. Henry inclined her head stiffly in return. He did not at all look like a man who had just lost a war, she mused. She felt Marius beside her bow in the direction of a smiling Mrs. Broughton. Henry, giving no visible sign that she had even noticed the exchange, wished heartily that the woman were within reaching distance so that she could gouge the smile out of her beautiful face with her fingernails.

Eversleigh's hand reached out and took her right one in his. "I have not told you how lovely you look this evening, my love," he said, turning his attention to her. "It is a new gown, is it not?"

"Yes," she said, and for once was lost for words. The blood was hammering in her head as she tried to remove the ringless hand from his grasp without jerking it away and attracting undue attention.

"Where is your ring?" he asked, and Henry let her hand fall limp in his.

"What ring?" she asked, looking up at him and flushing, furious at her own response.

His lazy blue eyes looked into hers and the lids dropped farther over them. "Your mother's sapphire, I mean, Henry," he said softly. "Where is it?"

"Oh, that ring!" she said with false brightness. "I took it off tonight. It did not match my outfit, you see."

She looked down into the pit again and smiled briefly at a gallant who had a quizzing glass directed her way. She could feel her husband's glance boring into her. "A sapphire ring does not suit the turquoise of your dress?" he said. "Henry, my love, you must be color-blind."

She did not reply.

"Have you lost it?" he persisted.

"Oh, no," she said with a trilling laugh that sounded false even to her own ears. "I remember now. I took it to a jeweler's to have the setting checked. It has never been checked, you know, and I have been afraid that the stone might fall out. I should be dreadfully upset, you know, if I lost it. It is the only memento I have of Mama. I hate to be without it for a while, but it seemed—"

"Hush, my love," Eversleigh said gently, clasping more warmly the hand that he still held, "the orchestra is about to begin playing."

Henry felt her heart gradually slowing to a normal beat as she tried to concentrate on the overture that the orchestra was playing. But she was uncomfortably aware for some time that her husband was still looking at her.

The usual court of young men came to pay their respects to Henry during the first intermission. Eversleigh stayed with her until his cousin, Althea Lambert, with an escort, arrived to visit. Then he strolled away, leaving the young people to their own chatter.

Only a few minutes had passed before Oliver Cranshawe appeared in the box. Henry was aghast; she had not thought he would have the nerve. Perhaps he had not yet received her letter and the money, she thought.

"Althea," he drawled after bending low over Henry's hand and kissing it, "how delightful to see you. Er, I do believe Lady Melrose was looking for you a moment ago. Something about a rout, I believe?"

"Oh, that will be her Venetian breakfast," Althea said, brightening visibly. "Yes, indeed, she did suggest that I be a hostess with her daughter. Come, Mr. Rawlings, let us go to her at once."

Mr. Rawlings dutifully led his charge away and Henry was momentarily alone with Cranshawe. The other three men in the box were deep in conversation about a horse race that was to be run the following afternoon.

"Did you receive my package, sir?" Henry asked frostily, deciding that it would be best to go on the attack.

"Yes, indeed, cousin," he said, giving her the full benefit of his most charming smile. "How delightful to know that you have come about so soon."

"Yes, well, I told you I should pay you back as soon as I was able," she said.

"I wonder how you managed quite so soon, though, Henry," he said. "I hope you have not lost your trust in our friendship and put yourself in debt to someone else."

"That is none of your concern, sir," she said spiritedly. "All that concerns you is that you have recovered the full sum that you loaned to me."

His eyebrows rose in surprise. "Oh yes, almost," he said. "I shall not press for the remainder, of course, but then I did assure you that there was no haste for you to repay the principal."

"The remainder?" Henry asked faintly.

He looked puzzled. "But I have lost money while the three thousand was in your possession," he explained. "I must, of course, recover the interest. But I do not wish you to worry your pretty little head over it, Henry. There is no hurry at all. In fact, I should be quite willing to take the loss if you would care to repay me in, er, some other way."

"What do you mean?" she whispered.

He smiled directly into her eyes as he answered. "A night with you, Henry."

Henry's mouth dropped open. "Where?" she asked naïvely.

The smile broadened. "In bed, obviously, my dear."

Henry was saved from the ignominy of being seen to jump to her feet and smack the face of Mr. Cranshawe in that appallingly public setting. As she was about to respond to the impulse, she was aware of Eversleigh stepping back into the box. His eyes found her face immediately and took in its expression. His eyelids drooped over his eyes as he strolled forward.

"Ah, Oliver, dear boy," he said languidly, "you are becoming quite the stranger these days. It seems quite a while since you invited yourself to breakfast last."

"I have the distinct impression that I was not welcome the last time I came, Marius," said Cranshawe, an edge to his voice.

Eversleigh raised his quizzing glass and surveyed his heir unhurriedly through it. "Indeed?" he said. "What can have given you that impression? Ridley was there, was he not? I cannot remember his being rude to you. There was the matter of newspaper being left behind, though, was there not, dear fellow? It is still there for you to claim." He let the glass fall to his chest again.

"You are too kind, cousin," Cranshawe said through his teeth.

"Not at all, not at all, dear fellow," said Eversleigh. "You must give me the honor of your company as well as my wife, you know. In fact, dear boy, I must insist that you announce your visits so that I may not be deprived of the pleasure."

"The second act is about to begin," Cranshawe mumbled, getting to his feet and bowing stiffly. "Your Grace?"

Henry nodded, but she did not look up. The other three gentlemen also crowded around to make their farewells.

As Henry turned her chair to face the stage again, Eversleigh took her hand and laid it on his sleeve.

"I wish to leave," she said, eyes riveted to the stage. "Please take me home, Marius."

"No, my love," he replied gently. "We must be seen to sit here in amicable agreement."

His words hummed in Henry's mind as the music and singing washed over her. What had he meant? Was there already talk about her and Oliver Cranshawe? Was Marius trying to avert it?

The Duke of Eversleigh walked into his secretary's office the next morning before luncheon. He was still clad in riding clothes.

"Ah, James," he said, "how predictable you are, dear fellow. One can always depend upon finding you here."

"Well, you do pay me to work here during the daytime, your Grace," Ridley replied patiently.

"Quite so, dear boy," Eversleigh agreed, "though I seem to remember giving you an assignment yesterday that should have had you up and abroad."

"I have already done my best on that mission," his secretary replied, "and devilish difficult it was too, sir, if you will excuse me for saying so."

"Oh, surely, James," the duke replied, waving a hand airily in his direction. "And what did you discover?"

"I can find no trace of any debt incurred by her Grace that has not been sent here," Ridley said.

Eversleigh regarded him thoughtfully. "Hmm," he said. "Are you sure your information is complete, James?"

Ridley shrugged. "I talked to the persons most likely to know about any gambling debts," he said.

"My wife is missing a ring that she almost never removes from her finger," Eversleigh said almost to himself, strolling over to take up a stand in his favorite spot, one elbow propping him against a bookshelf.

"Pawned perhaps, your Grace?"

"I think not," his employer replied. "I have visited all the most likely jewelers this morning, and none of them knows of it. No, James, I believe it must have been pledged for a large sum."

"Not a moneylender, your Grace?"

"I hope not, dear boy. Perhaps my heir has it. He has her in his power, I am sure."

"You think he has lent her money?" asked Ridley.

"I fear so," the duke replied. "She is frightened, at least, and my wife does not scare easily. I wish I knew why she needed money."

"I—I think I might have the answer," Ridley said, shifting uneasily in his chair.

Eversleigh looked penetratingly at him. "Well, out with it, dear fellow!" he said.

"I discovered that her Grace's brother, Mr. Giles Tallant, had quite large gambling debts a while ago."

"How large?" the duke asked.

"In the region of three thousand pounds, I believe, sir."

Eversleigh whistled. "Rash puppy!" he said. "I doubt if his brother allows him near enough to pay that. And have these debts been paid, James?"

"Yes, your Grace," Ridley replied, "in full."

"Ah," Eversleigh commented, straightening up and tapping his boots with his riding crop. "I believe I shall see if my brother-in-law would like to share luncheon with me at White's. Do take a break soon, James. Too much work cannot be good for the health."

"My midday break is due to begin in a half-hour," Ridley explained to his employer's disappearing back.

Henry spent the morning in her room, breaking with her usual routine of riding early. She felt very close to despair. It seemed that everything was going wrong around her. The new debt to the moneylender looked like an insurmountable problem now in the morning light. Henry did some calculations in her head, and then on paper to make sure that she had not made an error. If she saved most of her allowance each month, she would be able to repay little more than the interest on her loan. There was no way she would ever be free of the whole debt. That meant that she would never recover her ring. Its absence would be a great loss to her. More important, she did not know how she would answer Marius if he asked about it again, and he surely would. Soon he would demand to know the name of the jeweler to whom she had taken the ring to be checked. And then she would be forced into more lies.

She had, in fact, got herself into a terrible mess, and all for nothing, it seemed. Oliver was still insisting that she owed him interest on his loan. He had not said, and she had not asked, how much it was. But she had the distinct impression that the amount was limitless. Even if she went out now and pawned her most precious piece of jewelry and sent the money to Cranshawe, he would claim that it was not enough. And how could she argue? There had been no written agreement.

Henry thought about his words of the night before and clenched her fists. How dare he so openly proposition her? He had looked her right in the eye as he spoke, too, and smiled that charming smile that had so disarmed her when she first met him. Anyone looking across to their box would have assumed that he was paying her some lavish compliment. The rat! Henry considered playing along with his game. What if she agreed to meet him in some private place and set up some devious plan of revenge? She considered how satisfactory it would be to go at him with her fists, to break that handsome, aquiline nose and smash forever that flawless smile. She sighed. How provoking it was to be a woman, to know that there were limits to her strength. She considered using a riding crop as a weapon, but that was too risky. Doubtless the scoundrel was strong enough to wrest it from her grasp. No, the whole scheme was too risky, she decided. Unless she could be sure of overpowering him, she would be in grave danger once he achieved the upper hand. He was already openly set upon ruining not only her reputation, but also her person. She shuddered to think what added indignities he would heap on her if he were also enraged.

What was she to do, then, when she did hear next from Cranshawe? She could not pay him and she would not meet him. The only other alternative seemed to be to make a clean breast of the whole thing to Marius. She found it hard to understand now why she had not just gone to him at the start, or at least as soon as she began to have doubts about Oliver's integrity. It would have been so easy then, and surely she could have thought of some way of keeping Giles' name out of it. However, she had not gone to her husband, and now it was surely impossible to do so. At best, Marius would consider her foolish and stubborn, and he would be right. But he could never respect or love her. At worst, he would refuse to believe that she had not been more involved with Oliver than she had been. He was already suspicious. How could she ever convince him that she had never considered his cousin as more than a casual friend? No, this was a predicament that she would have to get herself out of, though there did not seem to be any way.

But why did she care what Marius thought of her? He did not care about her. He had married her for some reason that she could not comprehend. But obviously all his interest was in that overblown doxy, Mrs. Broughton. Even last night they had not been able to keep their eyes off each other. Henry supposed that he spent much of his days and the evenings when he was not with her at the home of his mistress. Her fingernails dug painfully into her palms as she imagined him doing with the delectable Suzanne what he had done with her two nights before.

Henry could not escape the truth. She loved Marius quite hopelessly. Finally, after believing that no man would ever be worthy of her entire trust and respect, she seemed to have found such a man. And, in addition, he was a man who could make her pulses race and her knees and stomach feel like jelly. Even now Henry yearned to run to him, to curl into his arms and beg him to take her burdens on his own broad and capable shoulders. And one part of her mind was convinced that he would not turn her away, that she could trust him. But how could she believe that when he had turned her away the morning before at a time when she had been glowing with love and vulnerability, and when he kept a mistress with whom he had been involved long before he had met her? Oh, it was all very confusing.

On impulse, Henry leapt to her feet and rang for Betty. She was going to go downstairs for luncheon and then she was going to order her phaeton and grays brought around so that she could go visiting and later drive in the park. She was Henry Devron, and nobody—not Marius, not Oliver—was going to keep her cowering in her bedroom!

Giles Tallant was sitting in the reading room at White's when his brother-in-law strolled in. Although he held a paper in his hands and had his eyes directed at it, it would have been obvious to anyone who cared to observe that he was not, in fact, reading. Truth to tell, his mind was still reeling from what his brother had told him just a few hours before.

Philip had gone himself to Peter's house to consult with Giles. Although his oldest brother was from home already, he was unfortunate enough to run into Marian, who was emerging from the breakfast room. She had quizzed him sharply on the strangeness of his being out alone at a time when any normal and properly reared youngster would be in the schoolroom at his books. Philip had mumbled some excuse about Miss Manford's having postponed lessons

until the afternoon, but was very relieved when the footman had returned to say that Mr. Giles would receive his
brother in his bed chamber.

Giles had been still in bed, nightcap pulled rakishly
over one eyebrow. A cup of chocolate was cooling on the
night table at his side. He woke up in a hurry, though,
when he heard Philip's story. At the first part he bristled
with indignation.

"She borrowed money from Cranshawe?" he said. "The
fellow's nothing but a rake. Don't trust him."

"But why would she, Giles?" asked Philip. "What would
Henry want money for? His Grace buys her all the clothes
and finery she wants, and she don't gamble. She lectures
Pen and me regularly on the sins of playing cards."

"It was all my fault," Giles said gloomily. "I'm the one
who gambled myself into debt. Henry wormed it out of
me. Said she had enough money to pay it off for me. The
little widgeon. And I believed her." He snatched the
nightcap off his auburn curls and slammed it down on the
bed.

"Oh, I say," Philip commented, "you're lucky Papa is
not alive, Giles. You would have got a whipping for sure."

"And would have deserved it, too," Giles admitted.
"And you say Cranshawe has been threatening her? I'll
call him out over this. Hand me my clothes, Phil."

"You haven't heard the worst of it yet," Philip warned.

"Eh?"

"She went to a moneylender yesterday," Philip said. "I
followed her."

"She what?" Giles blanched. "Why would the little
sapskull do a thing like that?"

"Manny and Pen and I guess that things got too hot for
her with the teeth, and she went for the money to pay him
back."

Giles groaned and clutched his head. "Oh, Henry,
Henry!" was all he could say for a while.

"What are we going to do, Giles?" Philip asked. "Pen
and I thought you might have some ideas."

Giles groaned again. "Let me think about it, Phil," he
said. "I'll come up with something." Philip got up to
leave. "But, Phil," he added, catching his brother by the

sleeve, "keep on doing what you have been doing. Keep an eye on Henry, will you?"

Sitting in his chair now at White's, Giles was no nearer finding a solution than he had been while reclining in his bed at home. His first impulse had been to go to Eversleigh right away and confess all. That certainly was what he should have done at the start. He could have asked his brother-in-law for a loan. He did not think the duke would have refused. It would have been humiliating to have to go to him when Eversleigh had already taken on so many of the family burdens with his marriage to Henry. But he deserved the shame; he had behaved with terrible irresponsibility, getting himself sent down from university and then gambling away money that he did not possess.

But how could he go to Eversleigh now? It was Henry's secrets more than his own that he would be revealing. And she must have been more than reluctant to turn to her husband if she had gone to a moneylender rather than appeal to him. Poor Henry! He could not betray her now.

There seemed to be only one other solution. Giles would have to go himself to a moneylender and borrow the money with which his sister could repay both her debt and the interest that would have already accumulated. But it was a mad idea! Not only did he have no prospect of ever being able to repay the debt, but by acting in such a way, he would belittle the sacrifice that Henry had made for his sake.

While he was still wrestling with this problem, Giles was interrupted.

"Ah, here you are, Giles," said the Duke of Eversleigh. "This is the last room in the club I have thought of looking in. Are you acquiring studious habits in your rustication, dear boy?"

"Y—you were looking for me, your Grace?" stammered Giles, lowering his paper and staring aghast into the face of his brother-in-law. This was the last person he wished to see just now.

"I was merely looking for a luncheon companion," Eversleigh explained. "It is tedious to eat alone, you know. Nothing to think about except the food."

"Oh, yes, much obliged to you," Giles lied, getting to his feet and wondering what Eversleigh was up to. He was a very popular figure in the club. He could attract any table companion he cared to choose.

Fifteen minutes later, the two men were cutting into large platters of veal and vegetables.

"So, dear boy," Eversleigh said, abandoning the small talk that had occupied them thus far, "what have you found to amuse you in town?"

"Oh," said Giles evasively, "this and that."

"Ah. Parties?"

"Yes, some."

"The races?"

"Not often, your Grace."

"The muslin company?"

"Er, not too often." Giles was feeling decidedly uncomfortable.

"Cards?"

There was a pause. "Not any longer," Giles said finally.

"Ah," said the duke. "Excellent veal, is it not?"

"Eversleigh, what is the purpose of this interrogation?" Giles asked, putting down his knife and fork with hands that shook slightly and looking defiantly at his companion.

"Interrogation, dear boy?" Eversleigh replied, his sleepy eyes widening for a moment. "But I suppose you are right. Tell me, Giles, has my wife been paying your debts?"

"I . . . She . . ." Giles had paled again.

"You need not be afraid to speak out," Eversleigh said gently. "I wish to protect Henry as much as I assume you do."

"She seems uncommon afraid of you, sir," Giles said doubtfully.

Eversleigh considered. "I think not," he said. "I believe Henry is afraid only of herself. It irks her to know that she is a woman and might at times need to depend on a man."

Giles laughed shakily. "You do know her rather well, your Grace," he said with respect.

Eversleigh regarded his brother-in-law steadily. "Of course," he said. "I happen to love her, you see. Now, tell me what you know, dear boy. I suspect that she has got herself into quite a mess."

Giles judged it expedient to tell Eversleigh everything Philip had told him that morning.

"A moneylender," Eversleigh mused. "Do you happen to know which one?"

"I suspect the one that I planned to go to," Giles guessed. "I believe I mentioned his name to her. Phil would be able to take you to the place."

"I prefer to leave the two amateur Bow Street runners out of this," Eversleigh said dryly. "And quite soon I am going to have to reintroduce those two to the schoolroom."

"What are you planning to do about Henry?" asked Giles.

Eversleigh favored him with a sleepy stare. "Don't worry your head about it, dear fellow," he said. "Your sister will be safe in my care, I assure you."

"Yes, I am sure she will be," Giles agreed. "It was the best day's work Doug Raeburn ever did when he trapped her into that wager."

Eversleigh's eyebrows rose. "Wager?" he repeated.

Giles gave him a long look, then dropped his eyes to his plate. "Oh," he said, "she did not tell you."

"Suppose you tell me, Giles," said Eversleigh, "so that I can know if the incident merely slipped my mind."

"Oh, I say," said Giles, "perhaps she don't want you to know."

The duke continued to stare at him disconcertingly through half-closed lids.

"It was just a piece of nonsense," Giles blurted at last. "Henry did not want to have a Season and she didn't want a husband. Then Doug Raeburn, our neighbor, you know, got her mad and wagered that she could not get an offer by a certain date—I can't remember what—from a man he would name. We decided on you." He laughed in some embarrassment. "She won the wager."

"Yes, indeed," Eversleigh agreed softly, "and a certain high-perch phaeton, I believe? And you were quite right, dear boy. She had not told me."

Giles toyed with his food for several more uncomfortable, silent minutes.

Miss Manford had her promised talk with James Ridley also during the luncheon hour. She was surprised that much of what she had to say was not news to him. She was even more surprised to find that his source of information had been the Duke of Eversleigh himself. Ridley did show concern, though, over the news that Henry had been seen to visit a moneylender in an undesirable area of London.

"The duke feared as much," he observed. "I must tell him, Eugenia, as soon as he returns home."

"Oh, please do not," she pleaded, hands clasped over her bosom. "I fear the dear duchess will be in grave trouble if his Grace learns that she has been that indiscreet. Indeed, James, I should never forgive myself if I were the cause of bringing her into disgrace."

"You do not understand, my dear," her companion replied. "The duke seems genuinely concerned for her welfare. I believe he would be very relieved to know how he may rescue her from her difficulties."

"I don't know, James," Miss Manford said. "I should feel that I had betrayed the children's trust and dear Henry's—I mean, her Grace's—if word should get back to the duke."

"But there is little I can do on my own," Ridley protested.

"Oh, bless my soul," said Miss Manford, "is there nothing, James? You seem to have such strength of character and such practical ability."

"And I am honored that you should turn to me, Eugenia," Ridley replied, laying a comforting hand over hers on the table for a moment. "What I shall do is have someone watch Cranshawe to make sure that he does not bother her Grace unduly. I am afraid there is little I can do to rescue her from the moneylender, since I do not have the funds with which to pay him off."

"Oh, you are a dear," Miss Manford cried, leaping to her feet and gazing admiringly down on her hero. "I must return to the schoolroom. The dear children missed their lessons this morning and I do not wish them to grow up ignoramuses."

# CHAPTER

———— ∽ ————

# 12

Some of Henry's confidence and natural ebullience of spirit had been restored by the time she turned her phaeton into Hyde Park at the fashionable hour of five. She had paid duty calls on several acquaintances and had been made much of by male and female friends alike.

In the park she was soon surrounded by her usual court of young men, who enjoyed her company because they could talk freely in her presence without sending her into a fit of the vapors if they happened to say the wrong word. She also tolerated talk about horses and hunting and boxing. In fact, she was often treated merely as "one of the fellows." Most important, perhaps, was that Henry was a safe companion. She was safely married. They could talk and laugh and flirt with her without their intentions being misconstrued by a watchful parent. Henry was very obviously not even in the market for an affair. Either she had nerves of iron, the young men concluded among themselves, or she was incredibly innocent (they were inclined to favor the former), because even the most blatant sexual innuendo left her unflinching and unblushing. Soon no one even tried to proposition her. She was apparently either very afraid of her husband or else very much in love with him. And not many of her frequent companions could imagine Henry being afraid of any man.

The exception to all these trends was, of course, Oliver Cranshawe. He sensed that he was close to achieving the great goal of his life, and he intended to press his advantage.

He was again on foot, nodding to acquaintances, smiling at them with easy charm. He joined the small crowd of men surrounding Henry's carriage, which she had drawn to a halt.

"Good afternoon, cousin," he called affably. "I see that it is, as usual, well nigh impossible to get close enough to you to pay one's compliments."

Henry smiled. "But you always seem to find a way, do you not, Mr. Cranshawe?" she cooed.

"But, Henry," he continued, sending a sparkling smile in her direction, "you are not going to keep your husband's relative at such a distance, are you, and with a crick in his neck from gazing up at you? I should not refuse the offer of a turn in the park with you."

Henry's animated expression hid the near desperation that she felt as she looked around the group to see if there was any other man not on horseback, with whom she could claim a prior agreement to drive. There was none.

"I am afraid, sir, that I must return home soon," she said, returning her gaze to Cranshawe. "My husband and I have an early engagement this evening."

"Then let me ride with you to the park gates," he said. "I have something I must tell you."

Henry bowed her head in unwilling acquiescence. While Cranshawe climbed into the high seat beside her, she laughingly engaged to dance with two of her eager admirers during the Spencer ball to be held on the evening of the following day.

She expertly turned the grays in the crowded pathway and started them in the direction from which they had come. "To the gateway it is, then, Oliver," she said grimly, staring straight ahead.

"Oh, come now, my dear," he said, "you need not be so stiff in my presence."

"I am not your dear, Oliver," Henry replied firmly. "And I cannot imagine anyone in whose presence I more wish to appear stiff."

He laughed softly. "Do you know, Henry," he said, "when I first set out to befriend you, I thought it would be an utter bore. I was quite wrong. You are most delightful. I admire your spirit more than I can say. I look forward to unusual sport when you finally capitulate to me."

"Unusual sport is right!" she spat out. "You would go away with a few cuts and bruises for your pains, Oliver Cranshawe, if you even tried to behave improperly with me."

He chuckled again. "Soon now, Henry, you will have to admit that you have no choice," he said. "I offer you an easy way out, do I not? One night spent with me, and I shall give you a signed note to say that all your debt has been paid. You will be free, Henry."

"Do you think I would let you so much as touch me?" she hissed. "If you imagine that I would ever give myself to you for even one minute, you must have windmills in your head, Oliver."

He leaned closer to her and lowered his voice, though there was no one within hearing distance. "How do you know that you would not enjoy it, Henry?" he said. "I think your only experience so far has been with Marius, and I have good reason to believe that he would not make much effort to give you pleasure. I, on the other hand, find that I have a genuine desire to find out what sort of passion you are capable of beneath the bedcovers."

Henry jerked on the ribbons and the horses drew to a halt. She turned on her companion, fury sparking from her eyes. "How dare you speak to me so!" she cried. "I am not so much in your debt that I have to listen to such indignities."

"Come away with me, Henry," he said, quite undeterred by her anger. "We will go to France and Italy, and I shall show you what life has to offer a woman of such vitality."

"You can go to the devil, Oliver Cranshawe," she said. Then an arrested look came over her face. "What did you mean," she asked "by saying that you have 'good reason' to believe that Marius is not really interested in me?"

Cranshawe grinned. "I perceive that his opinion matters to you, Henry," he said. "What a shame, my dear. I have it on good authority that Marius married you only as a result of a rather sordid wager."

"What do you mean?" she demanded, chin jutting forward.

"It seems he was beginning to feel the need to find some female to breed," he said, flashing her his most brilliant smile, "to squash my hopes, of course. When he publicly announced that he despised all women and that it mattered not to him which female he chose, one of his cronies wagered that he would not, in fact, choose so carelessly. He was to choose himself a bride and marry her within some indecently short time. He won the wager, of course."

"You are a liar!" Henry cried. "Where did you hear such a stupid story?"

"Almost from the horse's mouth, my dear," Cranshawe replied. "Are you acquainted with Dick Hanley and his bride? They were sharing a box at the opera with Suzanne Broughton last evening. The wager was made at his bachelor party, it seems."

"I do not believe one word of what you have said," Henry replied. "You merely wish to discredit Marius in my eyes so that I will more readily comply with your demands."

Cranshawe laughed. "Henry, I do believe that you love the man," he said. "How very interesting, my dear. I see that we are close to the gates. I shall get down here. You will be hearing from me, Henry. I believe a few days will help you to see matters in a different light. I shall look forward to our eventual encounter. By the way, how do you like the grays?"

Henry stared stonily at him.

He smiled. "Marius did well out of the wager, did he not?" he said. "He had been trying for months to purchase them."

Henry whipped the horses into a trot and turned from the park entrance into the street at a daring pace. I don't believe it, she thought, I won't believe it. But she found it impossible to believe her own denials.

Philip was feeling rebellious. Manny was insisting that Pen and he stay in the schoolroom and do their lessons. The afternoon before she had refused to allow them to follow Henry when she had gone out alone in her phaeton. He had tried to convince her that his sister was in constant danger from the teeth and from the moneylender's spies, but Manny, for once, had remained firm.

"The dear duke put his trust in me at a time when I had

been dismissed," she had said. "I feel it my responsibility to keep watch over you, dear children, and to make sure that you learn your lessons."

"But, Manny," Penelope had complained, "we can catch up with all that horrid work once we know that Henry is safe."

"She will be safe, never fear," Miss Manford had replied firmly. "Philip talked to Mr. Giles this morning and I talked to Mr. Ridley. He assured me that the duke himself is concerned and is doing his best to protect the dear duchess."

"But, Manny—"

"That will be all, dear boy," his governess had interrupted. "For the next hour we will converse only in French."

Penelope had groaned.

Philip, remembering a conversation with Eversleigh and a narrowly averted thrashing, had decided that it would be ungentlemanly to argue further.

"Blood and thunder!" had commented Oscar from the floor of his cage.

Now this morning Philip had escaped for a few minutes on the excuse that he would go to the kitchen for a tray of milk and cakes. He dawdled about the errand, wheedling the cook into letting him sample some jam tarts fresh from the oven, and watching an undergroom polishing the duke's riding boots. It was quite by accident that he arrived in the main hallway with his tray just when a messenger was delivering a small package to the butler and directing that it be placed in the hands of the Duchess of Eversleigh.

By the time Philip arrived in the schoolroom one minute later, milk from three glasses had been sloshed onto the tray and one cake was looking unappetizingly soggy.

"Henry is receiving a secret message again," he announced excitedly almost before he could close the door behind him.

"What is it and who sent it?" Penelope demanded.

"I don't know, but I mean to try to find out," Philip replied.

"I bet Mr. Cranshawe is sending her gifts and trying to charm her," Penelope said.

"More likely that moneylender making demands already," Philip replied.

"It is probably merely some ribbons that she has had delivered," said Miss Manford, "or some small piece of jewelry she has bought."

"Well, when she goes out later today," Philip said firmly, "Pen and I are going to go into her room again and see if we can find what it is."

"Oh, bless my soul," Miss Manford added, hands waving ineffectually in the air, "do you really think you ought, dear boy?"

Henry was out riding when the package arrived. She was in a very black mood. She knew that she ran the risk of meeting Oliver Cranshawe, but she did not care. If she saw him, she would gallop away from him. If he persisted in following her, she would ignore him or use her riding crop on him if she had to. But she had had to get out.

She had made Marius bring her home early from a dinner party the evening before, pleading a headache. And, indeed, it had not been just an excuse. She had ridden home in the carriage beside her husband in unaccustomed silence. He, too, had made no effort to sustain a conversation. But she had had a feeling, as she gazed out of the window into the darkness, that he watched her from beneath half-closed eyelids. He had accompanied her to the door of her bedchamer and kissed her hand as he said goodnight, with something she might have called tenderness had she not known differently. She had not slept before dawn, but had tossed and turned in her bed, in a fever of jumbled thoughts.

Cranshawe was not in the park. A couple of young men who were occasionally part of her court looked as if they were about to join her, but she smiled and waved vaguely at them and spurred Jet into a canter, and they did not follow.

Henry felt wretched in the extreme. Until her conversation with Oliver the day before, she had not known just how deeply in love with Marius she was. The knowledge that he had married her so cynically, with no feeling for her at all, except perhaps contempt, hurt like a knife being slowly turned in her chest. For a while she had tried to convince herself that Cranshawe had been lying, but she did not credit him with enough imagination to invent such an ingenious story. It was undoubtedly true.

It hurt terribly to know that the conditions of her marriage must be widely known. She must be the laughing-stock—the little green country girl who had been picked at random because she was young and likely to be a good breeder. He would have chosen a horse, or even a cow, with more care.

She could not quite understand why, if he had married her only for her reproductive functions, he had not asserted his rights on their wedding night and continually ever since. Probably he had made that wager on impulse and had found himself repulsed when faced with the physical fact of a wife for whom he had no feelings. He had finally taken her, goaded on by anger at her clandestine meeting with his heir. But he had obviously found the experience unpleasant. He seemed to find it preferable to be without an heir of his own issue than to have normal marital relations with his wife.

Henry wanted to hate him. She did hate him! But she could not stop herself from caring. She had grown to enjoy his companionship, to need his attention and approval. She had come to love him and want his caresses. She had given herself to him completely on that one night they had had together, and had believed that for him it had been as earth-shattering an experience as it had been for her. It was painful and humiliating to know that it was anger merely that had provoked him and that all he had been feeling was contempt, or at best only a momentary lust. Henry had never wanted a man, had never wanted caresses or tenderness. She had certainly never wanted the dependency of love. Her fall was, therefore, all the harder. She had no defense against the pain of an emotion that she had never experienced before and that she did not understand.

She did not know what she was going to do. She could not stay with Marius. She would not live with him day by day, aching for every kind word or chance touch. She would not be thus shamed in her own eyes. But what choice had she? She was her husband's property, totally dependent on him for the necessities of life. He had once told her that he would apply for an annulment if she truly

wanted one, if she loved Oliver Cranshawe. Would he still
be willing? Not an annulment, of course. It was too late
for that. But a divorce? It was almost unthinkable. There
were only a few instances of divorce in living memory, and
the divorced woman was ostracized from society for the
rest of her life. Not that that would bother her, Henry
thought. But where would she go? What would she do?
She had had very little money of her own to start with.
That little had all become her husband's when she married.

Henry's thoughts were interrupted at that point when
she noticed that Jet's coat was beginning to lather. She
realized with guilty dismay, that she had been constantly
spurring him on, refusing to walk him for even a short
distance. It was as if she had been trying to outdistance
her own thoughts.

She rode her horse to the stables and satisfied herself
that the head groom himself would immediately rub down
poor Jet. She walked to the main doors and into the hall,
where she paused to remove her riding hat and leather
gloves.

"I have instructions to deliver this package into your
hands at the earliest possible moment, your Grace," the
butler said, bowing stiffly from the waist and holding the
parcel out to her on a salver.

Henry took it with a murmured thanks. Drat the man,
she thought. Could he not leave her alone even for a day?
What now? She went straight to her room and shut the
door firmly behind her.

A couple of minutes later she sat on her bed, feeling the
blood draining from her head. She believed she was about
to faint. In one cold palm, shining accusingly up at her,
lay her sapphire ring. In the other hand she clutched the
short note that had accompanied it, written apparently in
a disguised hand. Another sheet of paper lay in her lap.

Henry closed her eyes and let her head hang downward
until she felt the blood pounding through her temples
again and knew that she would not faint. She put the note
down on the bed beside her for a moment and pushed the
ring back onto the third finger of her right hand. She had
never thought that she would be dismayed to see it again
so soon. She picked up the paper from her lap. Yes, it was
the contract she had signed and left with the moneylender.

She really was free of that debt, then. She laughed shakily, but the sound came out very like a sob.

Henry picked up the note and read it again.

Your Grace [it said],
    Your debt has been paid in full and your ring redeemed. Please do not be afraid. All will be well.
                      [There was no signature.]

Henry closed her eyes again and crumpled the note into a tight wad. It fell to the floor unheeded, to be found later by Philip and Penelope. How had he found out? She had not given him any indication about where she had got the money. And even if he had suspected, how did he know which moneylender? And why had he paid off the debt and sent her the ring and the contract? Did he delight so much in tormenting her?

One thing was clear, at least. If she had not been entirely in Cranshawe's power before, she most certainly was now. She was more in his debt than ever. The money he had paid to redeem her loan amounted to much more than the original three thousand pounds. And, in addition to the money she owed him, he now held even more of her secrets. He could expose, not only Giles' secret and her own indiscretion in turning to him for help instead of to her husband, but also the fact that she had dabbled in the underworld of moneylenders. Her reputation would be ruined beyond repair. Marius would never believe in her essential innocence. Not that his good opinion mattered any longer, of course.

And so Henry's resolve to leave, to disappear somewhere far away from this life that she had ruined so thoroughly, was hardened. If she left Marius, her social standing would be ruined, anyway. Cranshawe would no longer have the power to hurt her. She supposed that he could still hunt her down in order to demand repayment of her debt. It was even conceivable that she would end up in debtors' prison for failure to do so. But she did not believe that he would go that far. He was comfortably rich in his own right, she knew, and she did not think that the money would be an issue with him. It was her ruin and the humiliation of his cousin that were his chief objects. Well, he would have accomplished his goal. She believed that he would leave well enough alone once she had disappeared.

As for Marius, she did not think he would really care if she disappeared. His pride would be hurt, but his consequence was so great that he would live down the scandal with ease. He would probably be relieved to be out of a marriage that he had entered so impetuously. He would be free to return more openly to his mistress.

Henry's only really big problem was the twins and Miss Manford. She did not suppose that Marius would keep them on after she left. It would be quite unreasonable to expect him to do so. The twins, of course, would go back to Peter. They would hate it, and she did not blame them, but at least he was their brother. They would not be turned away. They would not lack for anything, except perhaps for the tolerant understanding and yet firm guidance that Marius had given them. But they would survive. They were tough, as she was.

Manny was not so easily dismissed from her conscience. Henry knew that Peter would not allow her to return to his household. She would have to trust to the compassion of her husband, who had always treated the governess with gentlemanly courtesy. Surely he would help her find another post, or at least provide her with a good reference.

All that needed to be decided now, Henry thought, was where she was to go and what she was to do. It was not an easy problem to solve. What did a destitute ex-duchess do to provide herself with the necessities of life? She supposed that she would have to try to get herself a position as a governess, though she recalled with dismay her lack of accomplishments. The only other possibility was to try to find some old lady or invalid who wanted a companion. She could not quite picture herself wheeling a crotchety old dear around Bath to take the waters, but beggars cannot be choosers, she decided philosophically.

In the meantime, while she was waiting around for a suitable position with which to fill the remainder of her life, Henry decided that she would go to Roedean. No one need know. The staff there had known her all her life. They would certainly not turn her away, and if she asked them particularly, they would keep her presence there secret from Peter. It would just be a temporary arrangement, anyway.

Henry decided to leave very early the following morning, before the servants were up. She did not believe that she would be missed until late in the day. She would take the stagecoach into Sussex so that she could not be easily traced. She would leave a note to be delivered to Marius late in the afternoon. She hated having to delay; it would have suited her better to leave immediately. But common sense told her that it was too late in the day to begin a journey. Anyway, she would be missed within a few hours. She and Marius were due to dine early at home before going to Lord and Lady Spencer's ball. She did not feel in any mood to playact for a whole evening, but she supposed that she would somehow live through the ordeal.

Henry sat down at her escritoire and set herself immediately to the task of writing her farewell letter to Marius. It took her a long time and many aborted attempts, but finally she was reasonably well satisfied with what she had produced.

Dear Marius,

When you read this, I shall be gone. I shall not tell you where I am going, because I do not intend ever to return. Please do not concern yourself over my welfare. I shall contrive somehow to live alone. I wish you may divorce me.

I feel that I should inform you of a large debt that I have incurred, since it is possible that payment will be demanded of you. I borrowed three thousand pounds from Mr. Cranshawe to pay some gaming debts that I was unwise enough to incur. Later, I borrowed money from a usurer to repay your cousin, but he has since repaid that debt for me. Thus, the money I now owe Mr. Cranshawe must be considerably more than the original. I am sincerely sorry that you may become involved in this matter.

Marius, I know that I am in no position to ask a favor of you. But I beg you to do one thing, not for me—I shall never ask anything more of you for myself. Please, your Grace, will you help Manny find a new post? You have been kind to her. I am confident that you will not leave her destitute.

Good-bye, Marius. I truly believe that I am taking the course that will be best for both of us.

Henry signed her name, resisting the temptation to add a brief message of love. He must not know that this separation would be more painful to her than it would be to him. She folded the letter carefully and hid it in the drawer of her jewelry case.

The evening was as painful as Henry had expected it to be. Dinner passed tolerably well, as Manny, Mr. Ridley, and the twins were also present. Conversation was general, and Henry was able to withdraw into herself and take her silent farewell of the table's occupants. Phil and Penny were boisterous and frequently troublesome, but she loved them fiercely. They reminded her so strongly of the golden age of her own life, when she had been at home with Giles and his cronies for friends, when she had not had to worry about society and what it would think of her, when she had had no idea of the existence of love and longing. It would be hard to leave them. She would see them again, no doubt. But it might be years in the future. They might be quite grown-up. They would certainly be changed.

It was hard, too, to know that Manny was facing a difficult time, and that she, Henry, was largely responsible. The governess was more like a family member than a servant. She was a sweet and sensitive person. It would hurt her to be severed from the family she had served for so many years. Henry shuddered inwardly when she recalled that soon she would know what it was like to be in a situation like Manny's, not really belonging anywhere, not secure in any position.

She watched Mr. Ridley as he talked knowledgeably about the growth of factories in the northern towns and about the changes in society that would surely occur before long. He was a dry and sober man, and yet she had developed an affection for him since her marriage. He was undoubtedly a man of integrity and was devoted to his employer. Even him she would miss.

And, inevitably, her attention turned to Marius himself,

looking darkly handsome in dark-gold satin evening clothes with gleaming white linen; his hair, longer than usual, was brushed forward around his face and over his forehead. He made conversation with each of the varied members of his household with a languid grace; yet each one, Henry noticed, was flushed with happiness. Each was made to feel important. What went on in the mind of the man? she wondered. She had been married to him for six weeks already, had spent time with him almost daily ever since, had conversed with him freely, had made love with him on one occasion. Yet she felt that she did not know him at all. So much seemed hidden behind the half-closed eyelids and the disciplined face that almost never smiled or displayed any other emotion, in fact. Reason warned her that he was a man to be despised, yet, intuition told her that he was a man to be trusted and loved. She supposed it did not matter now which part of her brain was correct. After tonight she might never see him again. She would certainly never live with him again as his wife.

They sat side by side in the town carriage on the way to the ball, in silence for a while. Finally Eversleigh took his wife's right hand in his and looked down at her.

"You are very quiet tonight, my love," he commented. "Are you not feeling quite the thing?"

Henry tried to remove her hand. She could not think straight when he touched her. "I am fine," she said. "Just a little tired, perhaps."

"I thought you did not indulge in human frailties like tiredness, Henry," he said.

"Absurd!" she replied.

"I see you have had your ring returned," he commented, fingering the sapphire on her hand. "Do you feel better now that you have it safely back where it belongs?"

Henry swallowed. "I felt that it needed checking," she mumbled.

"Quite so," he agreed, "but now it should be safe for another lifetime." And, to Henry's discomfort, he continued to hold her hand as he lapsed into silence for the rest of the short journey to Lord Spencer's mansion.

Marius danced with her twice, a pleasure that was too much like torture for Henry to enjoy. She danced every other dance, too, and was very thankful that she had the perfect excuse to avoid Cranshawe. Her card was full, she told him quite truthfully when he came to solicit her hand for a waltz. He bowed gracefully and bared his teeth in what might have seemed a charming smile to any onlookers.

"When will you stop fighting me, my dear?" he murmured, for her ears only. "You know that you must give in to me soon. I can wait for a while, my dear, because the prize seems to be worthwhile, but I am not by nature a patient man, you know. Do not try me too far."

It was at that moment that the need for revenge was reborn in Henry's mind. She could not be contented with simply disappearing and leaving him to his triumph. She had to do something to make him feel as trapped and humiliated as he had made her feel. The plan did not develop at all—she was too busy dancing and smiling and conversing. But she would think of something. She was not Henry Devron if she let the rat get away with what he had done to her.

The most painful part of the evening came when Eversleigh and Henry returned home. She was achingly conscious, as he escorted her as usual to the door of her room, that this was the last time she would be with him like this. She hoped, and feared, that he would say a quick good night and leave her. He paused and waited for her to turn and face him. His hands lightly framed her face, his fingertips buried in her curls.

"Henry," he said, "you have not been quite yourself lately, I think. Would you like it if I finished my business here early and we left for Kent later this week instead of waiting for another fortnight?"

Henry felt dangerously close to tears. "I don't know," she said.

"Perhaps we could spend more time together, get to know each other better," he continued softly.

Henry did not reply, only stared at him wide-eyed.

"You need not fear that I shall press my attentions on you," he said with a strange, crooked smile. "Let us just be friends, shall we?"

Henry continued to stare. "I am tired," she said finally.

He dropped his hands immediately. "Of course," he said. "We shall talk tomorrow."

"Marius!" she said, reaching out a hand as he turned away.

"Yes, my love?" He turned to face her again, a look on his face that she had not seen there before. He looked almost hurt.

She smiled bleakly. "I'm sorry," she said, but she did not know for what she was apologizing.

"Good night, Henry," he said.

"Good night, Marius." She had to rush into her room and close the door hastily behind her so that he would not see her face crumple.

# CHAPTER

## 13

The Duke of Eversleigh was from home most of the next day. His wife had not been up when he finished breakfast. So he left without seeing her and was busy until late in the day. Despite the cool reception his suggestion had had from Henry the night before, he pressed on with his plan to finish his business in the city within the next day or two. He felt that she needed to get away from Cranshawe. His own preference was always for the country, especially at this time of year, when the city was hot and dusty. The children, too, he felt, would be happier with more freedom.

Eversleigh was not sure if his marriage could be saved. His wife had obviously accepted his offer only to win that absurdly childish wager. It seemed as if she had regretted her decision ever since. For one night he had hoped that perhaps she was beginning to lose her abhorrence of his touch. But he had rushed his fences and driven her farther away.

Perhaps in Kent he would be able to woo her trust and, eventually, her love. They would be in a quiet, relaxed atmosphere, free from the constant tedium of social activities, free to spend their time doing what they both enjoyed best, riding in the wide open spaces.

So Eversleigh spent the day with his man of business, settling his affairs for the following few months, at least. He went immediately to his room on returning home and summoned his valet to help him get ready for dinner.

"A letter for you, your Grace," that individual said, handing him the folded sheet that Henry had given to Betty's care the night before, "to be delivered to you as soon as you returned home this afternoon."

"Ah!" said Eversleigh. "Why was it not dealt with by Ridley?"

"It is personal, I understand, your Grace," his valet replied. "Her Grace entrusted it to her maid's care."

Eversleigh gave his servant a swift glance and took the letter. When he had finished reading it, he threw it down onto a dressing table and shocked his man by swearing aloud.

"When was this given to you, John?" he asked.

"At noon, your Grace."

"And how long had the maid had it?"

"I did not ask, sir."

"Summon her," Eversleigh ordered, picking up the letter again and pacing the floor as he reread it.

A frightened-looking Betty knocked timidly at the door a couple of minutes later and bobbed a curtsy when she was let inside.

"This letter," Eversleigh said, "when did my wife give it to you?"

"Last night, your Grace."

"And why was it not given to me this morning?"

Betty was twisting her apron around and around one finger. "Her Grace told me I must not give it to John until noon today, your Grace," she explained, "and I was to tell him to hand it to you when you came in."

"I see," he said, terrifying the poor girl further by fixing her with a stare from beneath his heavy lids. "Have you seen my wife today?"

"No, your Grace."

"No?" His eyebrows rose disdainfully. "Is it not part of your normal duties to help her rise in the mornings?"

"Yes, your Grace, but she was gone when I took her chocolate upstairs this morning."

"Indeed?" he said. "And what time was that?"

"Nine o'clock, as usual, your Grace."

"Did it not strike you as strange that she was not there?" he asked.

"Her Grace sometimes rides early, sir," she replied.

"I see. But did it not alarm you when she did not come home, even at luncheon time?"

."Yes, your Grace," she whispered.

"Speak up, girl," he barked. "Did you tell anyone of your fears?"

"I spoke to Miss Manford and the young lady and gentleman," Betty said.

"Ah, the Bow Street runners," Eversleigh commented.

"They helped me search the room, your Grace."

"Indeed? And by what right, may I ask, did you do such a thing?" Eversleigh asked.

"Mr. Ridley suggested that we see if the duchess had taken anything with her, your Grace."

"Ah, the plot thickens," he commented with irony. "And what did you find, Betty?"

"Some clothes and a valise have been taken, your Grace," she replied.

"And anything else? Any jewelry or other valuables?"

"No, nothing, your Grace."

"Little fool!" he exclaimed savagely. "No, not you, girl," he added when an already overwrought Betty burst into tears. "John, send Mr. Ridley to me."

John ushered Betty out of the room ahead of him. Ridley arrived a few minutes later.

"Well, James," Eversleigh said, "what do you know of my wife's disappearance?"

"Nothing, your Grace, except that she has gone," said Ridley, "and has taken a small amount of hand luggage with her. I have checked at the stables. She has taken no horse or carriage."

"So she is still here in London," Eversleigh mused, "or has taken the stage somewhere."

Ridley did not reply.

"How much money had she, James, do you have any idea?" the duke asked.

"She received her allowance three weeks ago, your Grace. The next one is due next week."

Eversleigh slammed the letter down on the dressing table and swore again. "I am a prize fool, do you know that, James?" he asked.

Ridley was wise enough not to offer an opinion.

"I would return that ring and that signed document

anonymously," Eversleigh continued. "I did not wish to give her the humiliation of knowing that I had discovered her secret and paid her debt. And it never for a moment crossed my mind that she would think that rogue cousin of mine was responsible."

"Did she think that, your Grace?"

"Yes, and has confessed all in a farewell letter to me," Eversleigh answered with vicious self-reproach in his voice. "Where would she have gone, James?"

"I have spent all afternoon searching my mind for an answer, your Grace," Ridley said.

"To her brother, do you think?"

"We have checked there, sir."

"Ah. 'We' being you and the Bow Street runners, I presume?"

"The Bow——? Yes, your Grace. Sir Peter and his wife know nothing of her whereabouts. We did not hint that the duchess had disappeared."

"Thank you, James," Eversleigh replied dryly. "I suppose all of London will know of it before the world is much older."

"Not from me, your Grace."

"Hmm. I believe I shall pay a call on my illustrious heir, James."

Ridley coughed. "He is in London, sir, and has not had contact with her Grace today. He lunched at Watier's and visited Tattersall's this afternoon. He is currently at White's, I believe, sir."

Eversleigh gave him an interrogative glance, eyebrows raised.

Ridley coughed again. "I promised Miss Manford a few days ago that I would have him watched, your Grace. I have taken the liberty of engaging the services of one of the younger footmen."

Eversleigh regarded his secretary through his quizzing glass. "I seem to have a houseful of spies," he commented. "We should perhaps hire ourselves out to the government for use against the French. That will be all, James. And, ah," he added as Ridley turned away, "if my household has not collapsed without the services of that footman for a few days, I could probably do without him for a while longer."

Ridley bowed his head. "He shall receive your instructions," he said curtly, and left the room.

Eversleigh rang for his valet again.

"A clean neckcloth, John," he ordered, "and my cane, please. Instruct the cook that I shall not be home for dinner."

Five minutes later, Eversleigh was again leaving the house to begin the tedious task of visiting every stagecoach stop in London in the hope of discovering some clue as to Henry's whereabouts. He tried not to think about where he would begin looking for her in the city itself if he could find no evidence of her having left it.

Henry sat on the stagecoach for much of the day, although she had had a long wait after her dawn departure from home. She had an inside seat, which would have been a blessing on most occasions. But inside a stage, sandwiched between an amply endowed matron and a thin man in dark city clothes, was not the place to be on a sweltering hot day in July, especially when one was wrapped in a heavy gray cloak to camouflage the fine appearance of a peach-colored muslin day dress. Henry was conscious of leaning into the fat lady to her right, while the city man, gazing through the window to his left and apparently lost in thought, leaned into her left side, his thigh pressed knowingly against hers, his upper arm brushing her breast whenever a jolt in the road gave him the excuse to move. And it was a very bumpy ride.

Henry was thankful when they stopped longer than usual at two inns on the way and there was time to get out and stretch. Although she was hungry at both stops—she had had nothing to eat since the supper at last night's ball—she dared not have more than a glass of lemonade each time. After paying for her coach ticket, she had very little money left. And it had to last until she found a position somewhere. She smiled with gratitude, then, when the plump lady nudged her painfully in the ribs and passed her half of a meat pasty. Henry felt she had never tasted anything so good in her life.

The only thing that gave her any comfort at all on the interminably slow journey was the plan that gradually took shape in her mind. She would see Oliver Cranshawe plead and beg and squirm within the next few days. Revenge on him would never begin to make up for the ruin of her marriage and the loss of Marius, but at least it would give her great satisfaction and occupy her thoughts for a few days. She composed in her mind the words she would write to him.

It was late afternoon when Henry finally finished trudging the three miles from the coach stop to Roedean. How dearly familiar the house looked, she thought as she approached the main door. If only the door would open and she could find inside her father and Giles, the twins and Manny. How happy she would be! But perhaps not. Always from now on there would be Marius. His memory would prevent her from being completely happy ever again.

The butler himself answered the door to her knock. He and the housekeeper and a few underservants were the only ones who had been kept on by Sir Peter Tallant on a permanent basis. Other servants would be hired from the village when the family came down for the summer in a few weeks' time.

"Miss Henry!" he exclaimed in surprise, rushing forward to relieve her of the valise that was beginning to feel as if it was loaded with gold bricks. "I mean, your Grace! What brings you into Sussex? If we had known, we could have prepared. And where is your carriage?" He peered beyond her into the empty driveway.

"I came on the stage, Trevors," she replied, "and I wish my stay here to remain a secret. Please, will you promise not to tell anyone?"

"Of course, Miss Henry, if you say so," Trevors assured her. She had always been a favorite with the house staff. She could twist them all around her little finger, her father had been fond of saying.

The saying proved to be still true. While Henry sat in lone state in the dining room partaking of a cold dinner, the housekeeper bustled around upstairs making sure that her bedroom was properly cleaned and aired. All the servants promised that no word of her whereabouts would be given to anyone. They did not ask questions, though they must have wondered what their little girl was doing

at home scarcely six weeks after causing a local sensation
by marrying a duke.

Henry waited until next morning before writing the
letter to Oliver Cranshawe that she had planned the day
before in the stagecoach. But she wanted to make sure
that it went on the day's mail coach so that he would
receive it the next day. She did not wish to be sitting
around waiting forever. She enjoyed writing it a good deal
more than she had enjoyed writing to her husband.

Dear Oliver,

You were quite right, of course. You said that I
should be forced to see things your way soon. I see
clearly that I have no choice but to comply with
your demands for settling my debt. I propose to
accept defeat gracefully. You will find me at Roedean.
Marius believes me to be visiting for a week. So you
see you will be able to claim your night with me
without fear of interruption. If I like what transpires—
and I begin to think that, after all, I may—perhaps I
shall allow you to extend your stay. I shall be awaiting your arrival hourly.

Yours, etc.

The letter was sealed and handed to the butler. He
promised to see that it was taken to the mail coach with
some letters that Sir Peter's bailiff had ready. Neither of
them remembered that the bailiff had arrived at the house
that morning and had not been informed of the secrecy of
Henry's visit. One of his letters was a weekly report of
estate business to Sir Peter Tallant.

Henry's next task was to visit her father's gun room. He
had been an avid hunter and had taught all four of his
children to shoot. It was several years since Henry had
held a gun in her hand; she would need practice, she
knew. She examined them all and noticed that they were
all gleaming. Someone in the household, probably Trevors,
took pride in keeping them in top condition. After much
deliberation, she chose a dueling pistol. It could be held
and fired easily in one hand. It would be easier to hide on
her person than a larger gun would be.

She found ammunition for the gun in a drawer. She
carefully loaded it, scooped up a palmful of extra bullets,

and ran up to her room, the pistol clutched in her other hand. She had noticed the night before that the breeches and shirts she had always worn for riding were still in her closet. She pulled on the breeches now and selected a loose white shirt. She filled her pockets with bullets, carefully pushed the pistol into the waistband of the breeches, beneath the shirt, and strode out to the stables.

She regretted the absence of Jet. She wondered briefly if Marius would keep him or send him back to Roedean. Either way, it would not matter to her. She would not be able to take him where she was going. She chose the only horse from the stables that was likely to be reasonably fast, saddled him, and set out for the lower meadow, which was out of earshot of the house and of the tenants' cottages. It was almost completely surrounded by high hedges, and a fence ran down one side of it, too. Henry had never been able to understand why it was there. Of what possible use could a fence be on one side of a field?

However, it suited her purpose now. She gathered some leafy twigs from the bushes, balanced them one at a time on top of a fence post, and used them for target practice. For an hour Henry shot at the twigs, varying the distance and the angle. Finally she was satisfied that her aim was accurate, even allowing for the pistol's slight kick to the left.

"Now, you may come whenever you wish, Oliver Cranshawe," she muttered with a grim smile as she swung herself up into the saddle again.

The following morning Giles was picking moodily at a plate of eggs and ham, letting the conversation of Peter and Marian wash over his head. He was feeling worried and guilty. He had spent much of the previous day at Eversleigh's house, going over and over again with Manny and the twins and that Ridley fellow the train of events that had led to Henry's disappearance. How could she have been such a little idiot as to have got herself into such trouble, and all for his sake? And where could she have gone? The only apparent possibility was Roedean, and Eversleigh had already had that checked with no luck. Ridley had thought it probable that she had very little money with her, and Betty was willing to swear that she had taken nothing of any value, except the sapphire ring. And Giles was pretty sure that she would never sell that. Even her gold wedding ring had been found in her jewelry case.

There were only two pieces of comfort. One was that Eversleigh had paid off the moneylender; so they at least knew that Henry was in no danger from him. The other was that Ridley's spy had reported that Cranshawe was behaving in no way out of the ordinary. He was still at home or frequenting his usual haunts. He had had no visible contact with Henry.

But those were small comforts. Giles cursed himself now for ever having been weak enough to accept help from his sister. He should have been man enough to go to Peter or Eversleigh and begged a loan. He might have known that Henry did not have that sum on hand, that she would do something silly in order to get it.

The worst aspect of the situation was that one felt so helpless. One did not know where to start looking or where to make inquiries. Giles had made some afternoon calls on mutual acquaintances. But the necessity of making his inquiries in such a roundabout way that no one would suspect the truth was frustrating in the extreme. He longed to grab each person by the throat and demand to know if she were hiding Henry in a closet somewhere. He did not know what he would do today. It seemed fruitless to go back to Eversleigh's, and yet he could not imagine himself staying away from there.

"What the devil is Henrietta doing at Roedean?" Peter was saying.

Giles stared, the words so pertinent to his thoughts that his mind could not grasp the meaning for the moment.

"Henrietta at Roedean?" Marian echoed.

The fact finally registered on Giles' mind that Peter was holding a letter in one hand.

"What is that? Let me see!" he cried, grabbing the sheet of paper from his brother's hand.

"Giles, really," Marian said, shocked.

"Evans says there that she arrived two days ago, alone," Peter explained to his wife.

"How very peculiar!" said Marian. "She had quarreled with Eversleigh, you may depend upon it, my love. I always knew that Henrietta was too undisciplined to cope with marriage to a duke."

"Yes, and he is not the man to help her cool her heels, either," her husband agreed. "I confess myself disappointed in Eversleigh. I had thought him to be made of sterner stuff."

"So she is there, after all," Giles was muttering. "I deserve to have my nose punched for not guessing. Of course, the little numbskull would get the servants on her side."

"This needs to be investigated personally," Sir Peter said decisively, throwing down his napkin beside his empty plate. "I shall see about having the carriage made ready immediately after luncheon. My love, will you have a valise packed for me? I shall be away from home for at least one night, I should think. I shall write to Eversleigh and tell him where he may find his wife."

"If he wants her back," sniffed Marian.

"I shall come with you, Peter," Giles decided impulsively. He abandoned his plate of still-untouched eggs and followed his brother from the room.

Oliver Cranshawe had gone riding before breakfast. He had hoped to see the little duchess in the park. She had been lying low for the past two days—avoiding him, he believed. The silly little chit! Did she think she could avoid him forever? If she did not reappear very soon, he was going to have to pay her a call. And to hell with Marius if he were there too. He could hardly prevent his cousin and heir from entering the house.

Cranshawe was quite determined to press his advantage. He must be very close to winning. And what a victory it would be. Once he had bedded the chit, he would inform Marius of the fact—probably by letter. He would go to France until the worst of his cousin's temper had cooled. Cranshawe did not fool himself into thinking that he would stand a chance in a duel with Eversleigh, even if he had the choice of weapons. But the marriage would be ruined. The duke was too proud a man to take her back after another man had possessed her, especially his heir.

When he returned to his house, Cranshawe thumbed idly through his morning mail before going in to breakfast.

Nothing but a thin trickle of invitations; the Season was coming to an end. There was one letter that had apparently come from out of town. He took it into the dining room with him and set it beside his place on the table while he went to the sideboard to fill his plate with steaming food. He opened the letter after the first pangs of his hunger had been satisfied.

Suddenly Cranshawe's fork clattered to his plate and he leaned back in his chair, a smile spreading slowly across his face.

"So, my dear Henry," he mused aloud, "we have come to the play's last scene. And I predict it will be a lively and a satisfying one. I think you owe me that extra time, my dear, though I shall not be able to avail myself of more than one night. I have never had to wait so long for a woman, but I find that the longer I wait, the greater my appetite."

He proved that one of his appetites, at least, was in no way dulled. He finished his breakfast before ordering that his horse be resaddled immediately and brought to the front of the house, and that his curricle and pair be ready to leave in one hour's time. Before leaving the house, he ordered his valet to pack a bag for him with enough clothes to last him for a couple of days, and a trunk to be taken to Dover the following day in preparation for a trip to the Continent.

Cranshawe rode directly to Suzanne Broughton's house and followed the butler upstairs to that lady's bedchamber. A maid answered the knock on the door and would have barred the way into the room, saying that her mistress was still in bed, but Cranshawe shouldered his way past both the butler and her.

"Why, Oliver, my dear boy," Suzanne said, startled, "to what mad passion do I owe this honor?"

Cranshawe ignored the flimsy and scantily cut nightgown, the long, thick hair that fell around her shoulders, and the seductive smile that spread across her face.

"I don't have much time, Suzanne," he said. "Dismiss the servants, please."

Suzanne waved away the pair, who were still standing in the doorway, and slid lower on her pillows. "Well, Oliver?" she asked.

"I have all but achieved my goal," he began. "The dear duchess has invited me to her brother's house in Sussex. She is alone there. Once this day's work is over, Suzanne, I believe you will find your way quite easily back into Eversleigh's graces. Who knows? Perhaps he will even divorce the little whore and marry you."

She smiled. "And why have you raced over here to tell me this, Oliver?" she asked.

"I want you to drive him mad, my dear," he said. "See him today and tomorrow. Drop hints in his ear, sympathetic hints, of course, that will help you gain your own ends. You must not, of course, tell him where he may find us. But your word in his ear will make my letter the more credible when he does receive it."

"I have always said you are the devil, Oliver," Suzanne commented. "Now I perceive that you are on your way to hell."

"But what a way to go!" He laughed.

"I believe you really fancy the freckle-faced redhead," she said.

"I must confess that I do not expect to find the process of seduction at all unpleasant," he replied.

"Go, you rogue," she directed, "and don't worry. Marius shall be driven mad. So mad, in fact, that he will be forced to seek comfort in my arms."

They both laughed.

Before the luncheon hour, Cranshawe was on his way to Roedean, driving himself in a fast curricle. He stopped only once to change horses and to partake of some refreshments.

Philip was stretched out on his stomach on the schoolroom floor, one hand inside Oscar's cage. He was trying, in vain, to train the parrot to perch on his wrist. Oscar fluttered around inside his cage, flapping his wings and treating the intruding hand to a string of oaths.

"Oh, bless my soul, what are we going to do about that bird?" said Miss Manford, who was busy clearing away books and papers at the end of the morning's lessons. "Do find the pink blanket, Philip."

Cleopatra purred contentedly on Penelope's lap in the

window seat. Her back was being stroked at a very comfortable tempo.

"I wonder where Henry is now," Penelope sighed.

As if in answer to her question, there was a brief tap on the door and James Ridley walked in without invitation, waving an opened letter in his hand.

"Eugenia, children," he said, unusual animation in his voice, "she is safe!"

"Henry?" shrieked three voices in unison.

"Yes," he said, "the duchess is at Roedean. Sir Peter Tallant has just written to inform the duke of the fact."

"Does his Grace know?" Miss Manford asked.

"No, I am afraid not," Ridley answered. "It is almost impossible to know where he might be found. I have sent a messenger to White's, though, on the chance that he will go there for luncheon."

He hurried from the room again, while its three occupants all proceeded to talk at once. Brutus decided to add his voice to the general chorus.

Fifteen minutes later, as Miss Manford and the twins were about to sit down to their midday meal, James Ridley again rushed into the schoolroom, this time without so much as a courtesy knock.

"Bless my soul!" Miss Manford said. "What is it, James?"

"Cranshawe is on his way to Roedean," he announced.

All three gasped and stared at him openmouthed. Then three voices were all clamoring for attention.

"How did he find out?" Philip asked.

"How do you know he is going there?" Penelope asked.

"Oh, the poor dear duchess, will she be safe?" wailed Miss Manford.

"I have not heard from his Grace yet," Ridley said, agitatedly. "It may take hours to find him. And there is not a moment to lose. I shall have to go myself."

"Where?" Miss Manford asked, hands flapping. "To Roedean? Oh, James, do have a care. He may be armed and dangerous. But, yes, of course, you must go. Oh, how brave you are."

"I'm going too," Philip announced.

"And me," said Penelope.

"Oh, really, no children," wailed Miss Manford, "you must stay out of this. But, of course, the dear duchess may need our help and comfort. Oh, dear, I wish I knew what to do."

"It is most courageous of you to be willing to go, my dear Eugenia," said Ridley, "and I really believe it might be for the best. I shall order his Grace's fastest-traveling carriage brought around immediately. I shall pen a swift note to leave for the duke and hope that he returns some time this afternoon."

Twenty minutes later the carriage was on its way, carrying four anxious people, and—inexplicably—three pets. The twins had loudly proclaimed that the latter could not possibly be left behind, and Miss Manford had been too agitated to argue.

Eversleigh had been at White's since midmorning. He had left home early, but he was experiencing the same frustration that Giles had felt. He did not know where else to look for Henry. He had no leads. His evening spent going from one stagecoach stop to another had proved fruitless. It was not that no one had seen Henry. Everyone had seen her. According to many of the people he questioned, she had been driven off in every possible compass direction. Eversleigh had never suspected that so many young Englishwomen had auburn curls and freckles and possessed gray cloaks or green pelisses (the two outdoor garments missing from his wife's wardrobe) and brown bonnets. He had given up his inquiries in despair before midnight.

A few hours later he had hauled his head groom out of bed and sent him galloping to Roedean. It seemed unlikely that Henry would choose such an obvious destination as a hiding place, but it was worth a try. He had been reluctant to go himself, afraid that he would miss some news of her in London. The groom had returned, very tired, before noon with the news that the servants at Roedean had seen and heard nothing of his wife.

The rest of the previous day Eversleigh had spent wandering around to every possible place where she might be, and attempting to behave with his usual air of unhurried boredom while he talked and questioned very discreetly. There had been no news at all of Henry. He had sought out the footman who was spying on Cranshawe, but with no results. There was nothing suspicious about his heir's movements.

Now, today, he did not know what to do with himself. He cantered through the park, led his horse idly down Bond Street, looking with apparent unconcern into each shop and even into Hookam's Library. Eventually he went to his club, acknowledging for the first time the hopelessness of his search. If Henry really wanted to hide from him, she could remain hidden for a lifetime, and there was nothing he could do about it. Eversleigh sat in the reading room at White's Club, staring ahead of him in despair. A few of his acquaintances, passing the open doorway, would have stopped to exchange courtesies, but passed by when they noticed the expression on his face.

A footman found him there eventually and handed him a note. Eversleigh recognized both the handwriting and the perfume clinging to it, and almost threw it from him in disgust. But, in his present mood, almost any activity seemed better than none. He opened Suzanne's letter. She asked him to visit her that afternoon. Again he almost threw the note down, but then his attention was caught by the last sentence: "I wish to talk to you—about your wife, Marius, Do, please, come!"

Mrs. Broughton had no way of knowing the true state of affairs in Eversleigh's home. She hoped that Marius would come later in the afternoon. She had not expected to have him announced and ushered into her drawing room a mere half-hour after she had sent the note (and at the exact moment that James Ridley was dispatching his own messenger to White's). She rose to her feet, smiled warmly, and extended a hand to her visitor.

"Marius," she began, "it has been a long time."

"What do you wish to tell me, Suzanne?" he asked, standing just inside the closed door and looking at her from beneath dropped lids.

"Gracious, Marius, let us not be in such a hurry," she purred. "Come and sit down. I shall ring for some refreshment."

"What do you know of my wife, Suzanne?"

"About your wife?" she repeated, a puzzled frown on her face. "Oh, a mere trifle, Marius. Gossip, no doubt."

"Tell me, Suzanne," he urged softly. He had not moved from his position before the door.

"Sometimes you can be most uncivilized, Marius," she said. Then she gave a low laugh. "But, then, I think that is what I always liked most about you."

Eversleigh's eyes were glinting as he grasped the handle of his quizzing glass. "Your information, Suzanne, please," he said. "We will dispense with the games."

She looked at him coolly and lifted her chin. "You really have lost your head over her, have you not, Marius?" she said coldly. "I suppose I should be glad that she has proved to be such a slut. But I feel only sorry for you. It seems she prefers a younger man, my dear."

"I am sure you will explain yourself," he said, his hand still clasped on the quizzing glass.

"Oh, I hear that Oliver Cranshawe is currently enjoying her favors," she said, sauntering over to a love seat and seating herself gracefully. Her back had scarcely settled against the cushions before two hands closed like steel bands around her upper arms and she was jerked to her feet again.

"Where is she?" Eversleigh asked softly.

"Marius, let me go immediately!" Suzanne ordered, fear flashing in her eyes for one moment.

"Where is she?"

"How would I know that, Marius?" she replied. "Is she not at home?"

"You seem to know that she is not," he said. "You can have got your information only from Cranshawe himself. You will tell me, Suzanne."

"Marius, really," she said, attempting a light laugh. "You are letting yourself become foolish over the little girl. Oliver did not tell me where they were going."

Eversleigh finally released her shoulders. He lifted his hands and encircled her neck with them.

"Suzanne," he said very softly, "you were always a vixen. I am ashamed that I ever responded to your animal appeal. But it would not hurt me in the least to squeeze the breath from your body right now. I shall do so if you will not tell me where I may find my wife." His thumbs increased their pressure ever so slightly on her throat.

Her eyes bulged with terror and she grasped his wrists

and dug in her fingernails. "They are in Sussex, on her brother's estate," she gasped.

Eversleigh's hands immediately left her throat. He turned without a word and strode from the room.

"I hate you, Marius!" she shrieked after him. "I hope you are too late!" She picked up a porcelain figurine from the table beside her and hurled it at his retreating back. It smashed into a thousand pieces against the inside of the closing door.

Eversleigh did not waste time returning home. He already wore riding clothes and had his fastest horse with him. He turned its head immediately for the outskirts of London and the road to Sussex, cursing himself for a fool in not having gone there himself the day before. He, too, made only one stop on the road, but it was a lengthy one. His horse lost a shoe on an open country road and he had to lead it slowly for two miles before he found a forge and a smith, who worked with painstaking care despite the barely leashed energy of the human animal who paced up and down before his smithy in silence.

# CHAPTER

## 14

Henry had found it impossible to settle to any activity all day. She found herself constantly wandering to her room, from the window of which she could see a long distance down the driveway. She hoped he would come today. She dreaded the thought of having to go through all this again tomorrow.

It was late afternoon when she finally spotted a curricle appearing from among the trees far down the driveway. Her heart beating faster, Henry hurried down to the drawing room and sank into a chair facing the door, a book in hand. Several minutes later, Trevors arrived with the announcement that Mr. Oliver Cranshawe wished to wait on her.

"Show him up, Trevors," she said; then, seeing that Cranshawe had followed the butler, she leapt to her feet and smiled a shy welcome.

"Oliver," she said, extending a hand to him, "you came quickly."

"Did you expect differently, my dear?" he replied, smiling dazzlingly into her eyes and taking her hand in both of his. He turned it up as he lowered his head, and kissed the palm.

"Trevors," Henry said to the butler, who was hovering disapprovingly in the background, "I should like a light meal served immediately, please."

"Immediately, Miss Henry?" he asked. "It is not dinnertime yet."

"Nevertheless, I wish it," she replied. "I wish to take my husband's cousin riding while it is still daylight."

The butler bowed stiffly and withdrew.

"Riding, Henry?" Cranshawe queried. "I had other plans in mind, my dear."

Henry glanced at him coyly from beneath her eyelashes. "What, Oliver," she said, "in the house here where I am surrounded by faithful retainers? I know of a very pleasant and very private meadow from which we can count the stars."

He laughed and pulled her roughly into his arms. "To hell with the retainers," he said, "but I do like the idea of finally possessing you under the moon and stars. Where may I go, my dear, to change my clothes and freshen up for you?"

Henry leaned back and looked up into his face. "I have had Giles' room prepared for you," she said. "Come, I shall take you there. I must change, too, into a riding habit." To her immense relief, he released her and stood back to allow her to lead the way.

Less than an hour later, Henry and Cranshawe were on horseback, trotting toward the lower meadow. Henry had selected a russet-colored riding skirt because it had large pockets that hid the bulge of the loaded dueling pistol. But she could feel it bumping against her leg as she rode.

"Is it not as lovely and as secluded as I promised?" she asked gaily as they rode the horses single-file through the gap in the hedge into the daisy-strewn grass of the meadow.

Cranshawe smiled appreciatively at her and followed her lead as she dismounted from her horse and tethered it. "Indeed it is, Henry," he said. "I could hardly have discovered a more charming love nest. Come here."

She laughed. "The other side will be better," she said, "away from the horses and with a more open view of the sky." She picked up her skirts above her ankles and began to run lightly across the grass. Cranshawe followed.

"Oh, what is that?" Henry asked, suddenly stopping in her tracks. She pointed to a piece of paper fluttering against a stone in the middle of the field. "Do go see, Oliver."

"For you, tonight, anything, my dear," he replied, and changed direction to rescue the sheet of paper. He picked it up and read it, his back to Henry as she continued on her way across the field until she came to the fence.

"What is this?" he asked incredulously, turning with the paper in his hand. He found himself looking down the barrel of a pistol held by a very determined-looking Henry.

"Read it more carefully, Oliver," she said coolly. "Perhaps it will make more sense a second time."

"What is going on here, Henry?" he asked, eyeing the gun. "You are not intending to fire that thing, are you?"

"Indeed I am," she replied, "and I would advise you to stay very still if you value your life."

"Little fool!" he exclaimed. "You would not dare. Murder is a hanging offense, you know."

"Oh, but I do not intend to murder you," she said, "as you would know if you had read more carefully the note that you hold. I am going to shoot you in the arm, Oliver. I am a good shot, I assure you. I shall hit the mark if you do not move. If you do move, of course, I might kill you by accident. That would be a pity, would it not?"

"This is madness, Henry," he said impatiently. "You know that sooner or later I shall have my way with you. Why make it harder for yourself? Now give me the gun." He took one purposeful step in her direction.

"Take one more step, Oliver, and I shall shoot you in the leg," Henry said calmly. He noticed that the barrel of the pistol angled downward very slightly. "I do not want to shoot your arm, you see, until you have signed that note."

"You will give me that pistol, Henry, right now," Cranshawe ordered, red with fury, "and be thankful if I end up making love to you tonight instead of thrashing you within an inch of your life, as you deserve." But he did not move.

"Be careful, Oliver," Henry replied, "your charm is slipping. Now, if you look at that note in your hand, you will be able to confirm that it says you were shot in the arm by Henrietta Devron, Duchess of Eversleigh, while you were trespassing on her brother's estate and attempting to seduce her. You will note also that there is a space at the bottom for your signature. If you look on the ground, you will find a container of ink and a pen beside the stone that was holding down the paper. You see, I think of everything. Now, will you please sign it so that we can get the shooting over with?"

"You are mad," he said. "What is the purpose of this, pray?"

Henry smiled grimly. "You see, Oliver," she said, "you will be returning to London with your arm in a sling. You would be the laughingstock for a long time if it became known how you received your injury. I shall have it in my power to prevent or to provoke that ridicule."

"Very neat," he declared, a ghost of his old smile playing about his lips. "Your silence in return for mine, is that it?"

"There is a brain behind the charm, I see," was the answer he received.

"I shall not sign, of course," he said, the smile becoming firmer.

"Then I shall have to put a bullet in your leg," Henry announced coolly. "The left one, I believe, just below the knee." She raised her left hand to steady the wrist of her right.

"All right, you minx, you win this round," Cranshawe said hastily, "but it will go all the worse for you, Henry, when I finally get you within my grasp."

"Perhaps, but you will need two sound arms for that, Oliver," she replied, lowering her left hand again.

Cranshawe searched around on the ground until he found the items she had described. He dipped the quill pen in the container and hastily scratched his name on the paper, using his knee as a desktop.

"Here is your paper," he said, holding it out in her direction. "I am going to turn and leave, Henry. I trust that you have enough gallantry not to shoot a man in the back."

"I shall still be aiming for your right arm between shoulder and elbow, Oliver," she said, quite unperturbed. "Of course, it is always harder to hit a moving target with accuracy. I advise you to stand absolutely still."

Again her left hand rose to steady her wrist. Cranshawe did as she bade him. A cold sweat broke out on his face.

"Don't shoot, your Grace!" a voice yelled frantically from the gap in the hedge. The gun dropped a few inches as Henry, unnerved, glanced across the meadow to see James Ridley rushing in her direction, having dismounted while his horse was still in motion. Oliver Cranshawe moved at the same moment but stopped abruptly again when she brought the gun jerking back into line with his body.

"Don't move!" she directed him coldly. "Mr. Ridley, you are far from home. May I ask what brings you here?"

"We heard this morning that you were here, your Grace," he replied, hurrying closer. "Then we found out that Mr. Cranshawe was on his way here too."

"We?" asked Henry.

Her answer came in the form of a loud bark from the other side of the hedge, followed by voices.

"Where did he disappear?" called a high, piping voice that was unmistakably Penelope's.

"Into the meadow, silly. I hope Trevors was right. He said they came this way. Let's go, Pen." The voice was Philip's.

"Wait for Manny. She's all tired out from running," yelled Penelope.

A few moments later, there was a new invasion of the field. Brutus was in the lead. He rushed first to Henry in an ecstasy of recognition, and then to Cranshawe, who was still stranded, motionless, in the middle of the meadow, his attention fixed on the pistol. Brutus seemed unable to make up his mind if this person was friend or foe. He settled the problem for the time being by flopping to the ground and fixing Cranshawe with an unwavering stare. He panted heavily and occasionally growled.

Philip, Penelope, and an exhausted-looking Miss Manford came next.

"Henry!" Penelope yelled.

"Oh, I say," said Philip, "a gun. Are you going to shoot him, Henry?"

"Oh, bless my soul," Miss Manford gasped, "are you safe, dear girl? Please put down the gun. There is no need to kill Mr. Cranshawe, indeed there is not. Mr. Ridley is here to protect you."

"Come, Henry," Cranshawe coaxed, his voice not quite under control, "you really must do as you are told. There are witnesses now, you know."

"Yes, but friendly witnesses," she replied, "and I have not changed my mind. I want you to sweat and squirm for a while, Oliver. Maybe you will have an inkling of what I have been through in the last weeks. Don't come any closer, please, Mr. Ridley. You will be close to my line of fire if you do."

"Really, your Grace, I sympathize with your feelings," Ridley said calmly. "I know much of what he has made you suffer. But nothing can be gained from bloodshed and violence. Give me the gun." He held out his hand slowly, but he did not move from where he stood, about twenty-five feet from Henry.

"Oh, James, do be careful," Miss Manford wailed.

"She is quite mad, as you see, Ridley," Cranshawe said. He was recovering his poise somewhat. The lengthy delay seemed to be to his advantage. Henry's arm would tire soon.

"Read them that paper," Henry ordered coldly.

"What?"

"The paper that you still hold in your hand—read it!" she repeated.

"Don't be ridiculous, Henry."

"Read it!"

There was a pause of some seconds. Finally Cranshawe lowered his head and began to read.

"Louder!" she directed.

He read what was written on the paper in a loud, clear voice.

"Now, Mr. Ridley, would you take it from Mr. Cranshawe, please? I do not really want to have it spattered with his blood."

Ridley did as he was bid, pleading with Henry all the while. Finally he moved to one side and Cranshawe was again isolated in the middle of the meadow. Philip and Penelope stood at the other side of the field, one of Miss Manford's hands on a shoulder of each. Henry adjusted the pistol so that it was again in line with Cranshaw's right arm. Again she raised her left arm to steady her wrist.

"Drop the gun, Henry!" said a cool, authoritative voice from the gap in the hedge. The words were not shouted, but they accomplished what all the commotion of the previous few minutes had failed to do. The pistol immediately dropped to the ground from nerveless fingers as

Henry turned her head toward her husband. Cranshawe visibly sagged with relief.

"You!" Henry said. "What are you doing here?"

"The same as everyone else, I presume," Eversleigh said, strolling unhurriedly forward, "viewing the beauties of nature." He lifted his quizzing glass to his eye as he gradually approached Cranshawe.

"Oliver!" he said, affecting surprise. "I did not know you were one of nature's devotees."

"I never thought I should be glad to see you, Marius," Cranshawe said, his self-assurance visibly restored. "Your wife was just about to kill me. She should be locked up in a madhouse."

Three voices chorused from the sidelines.

"Don't talk about my sister like that!"

"Don't listen to him, your Grace. He's a black-hearted villain."

"Oh, bless my soul, what an evil man."

Brutus growled threateningly.

"There is a letter here that you should read, your Grace," Ridley said calmly from his place to one side of Henry.

"I heard it, thank you, James," Eversleigh replied. "I think it would be rash of you to thank me for saving your arm, dear boy," he continued, turning his attention and his quizzing glass back to his heir. "I stopped Henry only because I could not possibly deny myself the pleasure of dealing with you myself."

"Oh, no, you don't!" Henry exclaimed, fury animating her again. "Why should men get all the satisfaction of working out their anger? This one is mine!" She strode determinedly toward Cranshawe, and before he could see what was coming and react, she had raised her fist and driven it with all her strength into his face. Her target had been his nose. She missed and connected with one eye instead. Her sapphire ring gashed him just below the eye.

"Little vixen!" Cranshawe gasped, clamping one hand over the wounded side of his face.

There was a chorus of cheers from the background, including some from Miss Manford. Brutus leapt to his feet, barking with excitement.

"Bravo, Henry!" Eversleigh said quietly. "Now stand

aside, my love." He beckoned Ridley to his side, carefully removed his coat, and handed it to his secretary.

"I suggest that you do likewise, Oliver," he said amiably. "I do believe you will be measuring your length on the ground rather soon, and there might be some bloodshed. I would think it a shame to ruin a perfectly good coat, wouldn't you?"

"Yes, this is just the type of situation you like, is it not, Marius?" replied his cousin bitterly. "You can show off your superior physical strength in front of an appreciative audience."

"I know it is not your style, Oliver," Eversleigh replied calmly, unbuttoning the lace cuffs of his shirt and rolling the sleeves back to the elbows. "You prefer to wound your opponents through women and through lies and trickery. Unfortunately, dear fellow, on this occasion you have no choice."

Cranshawe grimly pulled off his coat and tossed it from him. His eye was already beginning to swell, the onlookers noted with satisfaction.

Really, the fight was disappointing when it finally got started, Philip confided to a small audience later. Eversleigh's very first punch—a right jab to the chin—produced a crunching sound and Cranshawe fell backward. He scrambled to his feet again, but spent the rest of the unequal contest defending himself. He did manage to land one lucky punch on Eversleigh's mouth; he even drew blood. But one punch after another of Eversleigh's was a potential leveler.

Cranshawe's weakening guard would drop to protect his ribs and stomach after the breath had been knocked out of his body by a well-placed fist, and then the same fist would punish his face and jaw. When he chose to protect his head, then his body was pummeled. To his credit, he did not go down easily the second time, but in the end he was swaying on his feet, his hands, still held in loose fists, hanging useless at his side.

Eversleigh held his opponent by the right shoulder, while he threw all his weight behind the final punch, a wicked right hook that caught Cranshawe squarely below the chin and snapped his head back. The duke released his hold and watched his cousin crumple to the ground.

There was a curious silence among the onlookers. Even Brutus, standing to one side, was only panting. Henry broke the spell.

"Marius, you are hurt!" she said, her voice shaking uncontrollably, and she rushed to him, hurled herself into his arms, and burst into tears against his shoulder.

One arm came around her. The other hand cupped the back of her head and held it against him. "It's all over now, Henry," he murmured soothingly. "You are safe, my love."

All else was forgotten for a couple of minutes as Henry let herself sag against him, allowing all the firm warmth of him to penetrate her exhausted limbs. She felt the truth of his words. Nothing could ever threaten her again now that Marius was here.

Finally outside noises began to penetrate her consciousness and she pushed herself wearily away, aware again that nothing had changed except that she was free of Oliver Cranshawe and that apparently all the world knew about her indiscretion.

"What the devil is going on here?" a new voice was demanding crossly. "Are you all mad? Am I master here or am I not?"

"I say," said Giles admiringly, "is this your handiwork, your Grace? How splendid!"

"Not entirely," Eversleigh replied modestly. "The eye is Henry's work."

"I say!"

"You should have seen it, Giles," Penelope shrieked. "He must have a broken jaw. I could hear the bone cracking way over there."

"Henrietta, what is going on here?" Peter demanded in fury.

"It is quite a long story," she replied. "Could I tell you at the house, Peter?"

Cranshawe was beginning to stir on the ground. Eversleigh, carefully rebuttoning his cuffs and smoothing the lace over his hands, stood over him until he opened his eyes.

"I shall be returning to London tomorrow, Oliver," he said gently. "When I get there, I would wish you to be gone. I would advise you to remain outside the city for at least one year. If I encounter you within that time, or if after that time you so much as let your eyes alight on my wife, I shall engineer a quarrel in which, for honor's sake, you will be forced to call me out. That will give me the choice of weapons, and I shall choose swords. I trust I make myself clear?"

Cranshawe gingerly fingered a split lip and moaned something unintelligible.

"Quite so, dear boy," his cousin replied, and turned away to put on his coat.

"Are we just going to leave him here, your Grace?" Ridley asked doubtfully.

"This is Sir Peter Tallant's property," Eversleigh pointed out coolly. "If he wishes to extend his hospitality, it is no concern of mine. But I would suggest that Mr. Cranshawe be allowed to recover here in quiet and take himself off to the nearest inn when he feels ready to travel. He may save his pride there, if he wishes, by saying that he has been set upon by highwaymen."

Sir Peter was not eager to offer hospitality to a rake of Cranshawe's reputation. Thus, Eversleigh's advice was followed, and the party returned to the house, Penelope riding with Eversleigh, Philip with Giles, and Miss Manford, blushing and protesting, with Mr. Ridley.

Two hours later, the company dispersed to their several rooms, hastily prepared by the housekeeper. They had partaken of an equally quickly thrown-together meal, and had relived over and over again the events of the previous few days. Finally even the twins had no more to say. Oscar's colorful comments had been cut off by the pink blanket an hour before.

"I wish to talk to Henry alone for a while, Tallant," Eversleigh said, explaining why he was not preparing to leave the drawing room with everyone else.

Henry sat down again, and soon they were alone. She kept her eyes on the carpet beneath her feet.

Eversleigh regarded his wife in silence for a while.

"Well, Henry," he said finally.

She kept her eyes lowered. "It was you who paid the moneylender, was it not?" she said. "And redeemed my ring?"

"Yes, Henry," he admitted, "and I am sorry for the misunderstanding. It did not occur to me that you would think my note came from Cranshawe."

She did not reply.

"Will you come back home with me?" he asked. "Or are you serious in your intention to leave me?"

"I shall stay here, Marius," she said quietly.

"Might I ask why, Henry?" His voice was very gentle.

She hesitated. "I just wish it that way," she said. "I have not been happy."

"I see," he said. "Henry, please do one thing for me. Keep my name and allow me to care for you. I shall not force you to live with me or see me, but please, let me keep you in the sort of life that you are accustomed to. Don't disappear from my life. When you meet the man you will love, I shall divorce you so that you can marry him. And I shall see to it that you are not ostracized from society. I have considerable influence, you know."

"Yes, I know," she said, "but I shall not want to remarry, ever."

"Then remain as my duchess," he said, "wherever you wish to live."

"But you will need to marry again," she said. "You will want a son."

"No," he replied.

They lapsed into silence.

"I shall leave in the morning, early," Eversleigh said at last. "You need not see me again. I shall send Ridley down in a few days to make whatever settlement you decide upon."

"Perhaps," she said dully.

"And do not worry about Miss Manford," he continued. "I shall see her well settled. I believe she would be happier in retirement. I shall have my bailiff find her a suitable cottage on my estate in Kent. She will have a comfortable pension."

"Thank you," she whispered. "You are very kind."

"Come, my love," he said, rising to his feet and extending a hand to her. "I shall see you to your room."

"Thank you," she said.

They walked in silence up the broad staircase of Roedean

and to the door of Henry's room. There Eversleigh took her hand in his, bent, and kissed it.

"Good-bye, Henry," he said. "You are young. You will forget this episode soon and be happy again as you were when I met you. I am sorry that I have saddened you, my love."

He turned and entered his own room, which was directly across from hers. He closed the door softly behind him without looking back.

Henry had been sitting in the window seat of her darkened room for over an hour. She had undressed but had not gone to bed. She knew she would not sleep, and she hated to toss and turn in bed.

How would she bear the pain? It was ten times worse than it had been three days before when she had taken a silent farewell of Marius. There he had not known. He had not been so sweetly and so sadly noble. He had not just fought for her honor. He had acted today as if he really cared.

Was it possible that he did care, just a little bit? He had come tearing down from London on horseback, without any luggage at all—he had had to borrow a nightshirt from Peter. He had punched Oliver far more than was necessary merely to bring him to the ground. He had held her and soothed her afterward as if her safety were really important to him. He had begged her tonight to let him care for her, although her refusal to go home with him had offered him the perfect excuse for washing his hands of her. He had offered her her freedom while disclaiming any wish to be free himself. Could something of their marriage be salvaged? Could she possibly oust Suzanne Broughton from his affections, make him forget how and why he had chosen her as his bride?

Henry leapt to her feet. What was she doing, planning to stay at Roedean, allowing Marius to return to London and his mistress? If she could get up nerve enough this afternoon to almost shoot Oliver Cranshawe and to punch him in the face, did she not have the courage to fight a mere woman for her husband's love?

Before her resolve could cool, Henry quickly let herself out of her room, crossed the hall, and opened the door to her husband's room. She stepped inside and closed the door behind her. She stood with her back against it for a moment, letting her eyes get used to the deeper gloom of this chamber.

Eversleigh was standing at the far side of the room, leaning against the window frame.

"What is it, Henry?" he asked.

"I wish to return to London with you tomorrow," she said.

There was a pause. "And where do you propose to go when you arrive there?" he asked.

She lifted her chin. "Home with you," she said.

He pushed himself away from the window and came toward her. She could see that he wore no shirt, only his breeches. "Why?" he asked.

"To fight for you," she announced defiantly.

He laughed softly as he stopped in front of her. "Absurd child!" he said. "Why do you have to fight for me? Who is threatening me?"

"Suzanne Broughton," she said. "She shall not continue to have you, Marius. This is the end."

"Indeed?" he asked softly. "And who is going to stop her?"

"I am," she said. "You saw this afternoon that I can fight."

"Heaven help Suzanne," Eversleigh muttered fervently. "And what do you propose to do after you have left the lady with a pair of black eyes, Henry?"

"Make you love me," she said.

"And why would you want to force me to do that?" he asked.

"Because you are my husband," she said, "and I will not share you."

"Ah," he said. "And why would you be so selfish, my love?"

"Because I love you!" she hissed at him.

He stood motionless in the darkness. "I see," he said. "And when did you come to this conclusion, Henry?"

"Oh, I'm sure I loved you when I first set eyes on you," she said in a rush. "You are so despicably handsome, you see, and I admired immensely that way you have of reducing people to size with your quizzing glass. And when you

219 THE DOUBLE WAGER

kissed me—twice—I hated it because you made me feel
like jelly inside. Then, when you made love to me that
night, I knew I must love you because, although you still
made me feel like jelly, I knew I did not wish you to stop.
And I was glad afterward that I had not made you go
away."

"Were you, my love?" he said. "Now, how was it that I
touched you? Was it like this?" Both his hands enclosed
her breasts lightly and then then slid under her arms to
pull her gently against him. His lips trailed a line of little
kisses down one side of her face to her earlobe, which he
took between his teeth.

"Yes, like that," she said, "except that you have never
done that to my ear before."

"Perhaps like this, then, my love?" His hands wandered
lower to encircle her waist and then to bring her hips
against him. His mouth moved across her throat, forcing
her head back, and then up to claim her lips,

Henry seemed suddenly to come to her senses. "Don't,"
she said, jerking back.

"Why not?" he murmured, "I thought you liked it,
Henry. Can't you cope with the jelly?"

"No games, Marius," she said severely. "Nothing has
been settled yet."

"What a shame!" he sighed. "Can we not wait and settle
everything tomorrow?"

"No," she said, "I know this is all a game to you."

"You don't like games, my love?" he asked softly, reaching for the buttons on her nightgown. "Let us get serious,
then." One hand reached for her naked breast, and Henry
had to gasp to get herself under control.

"You are not serious, Marius," she scolded. "You are
making mock of me."

"Am I, my love?" he murmured, his mouth against her
throat again. His hands already had her nightgown off her
shoulders and were easing it down her arms. "I thought I
was making love to you."

"Oh," she cried, exasperated, "I'll not stand for this,
Marius!"

"Then you shall just have to lie down for it, my love,"
he said soothingly. "What a good idea." He lifted her into

his arms and deposited her on the bed, where he joined her after removing his breeches.

He lay beside her on the bed and trailed his hand lightly down her naked body. "Now, what was it you liked?" he asked. "Can you remember? Was it this?" He leaned across her and kissed one breast, then the other. He took one tip into his mouth and caressed it with his tongue.

"Oh, stop this instant, Marius," Henry protested. "Oh, this is not fair."

"Maybe not, my love," he soothed, "but it creates wonderful jelly, does it not?"

"Oh!" wailed Henry as he lifted himself from the mattress and lowered his weight on top of her.

"I have just had an inspiration," Eversleigh whispered against her ear. "I think maybe it was this that felt so good."

He parted her legs with his own and entered her deeply. Henry moaned and was lost. Soon her arms and legs were around him, urging him on to the climax that was very close for both of them. They both cried out when it came.

Henry wriggled out of Eversleigh's arms when he moved to her side. She lay on her back, staring up at the canopy above her head. "I shan't let you go back to Mrs. Broughton after this, you know," she said belligerently.

"Shan't you, my love?" he asked sleepily. "And what makes you think that I want to go back to Suzanne?"

"Because she is all woman," Henry said severely, "and I am not. I look like a boy. I don't curve out at the hips and I have small breasts."

He laughed softly. "Naughty, Henry," he said. "You are not supposed to mention bosoms, Giles told you. You might embarrass me."

"Well, it's true, anyway," she grumbled.

"Yes, it is, is it not?" he agreed, surprise in his voice, as he levered himself up onto one elbow. "Look! No curves, no bulges. Strange! You felt very much like a woman to me a few minutes ago." He lay back down and closed his eyes.

"Even so, I shall make you love me," she persisted, hurt. "I shall make you show me how I may entice you and tell me what pleases you."

He opened one eye and regarded her sleepily. "Always

wear your bonnet in public," he said mildly. "May I sleep now, Henry?"

"No!" she said firmly. "First you will promise to give up Mrs. Broughton."

"I promise, I promise," he agreed meekly.

"No, I mean really promise."

"Ah. I really, really promise, then."

"You are being quite absurd," she scolded. "Will you be serious?"

"What, again?" he asked, leering across the bed at her.

Henry slammed over onto her side and lay facing away from him, staring into the darkness. Soon she was aware of the warmth of his body close behind her. An arm encircled her waist.

"Henry," he said softly against her curls, "what a jealous little child you are. I have never loved Suzanne. I have not touched her since the day I met you except to half-throttle her this morning when she would not tell me where you were. Do you not know that I love you more than is good for me?"

"Don't make fun of me!" she snapped.

The arm around her tightened and he rolled her onto her back and into his body. "Silly little freckle-face!" he said. "How could I help loving you? When you first ran head-on into me at that dreary come-out ball, you bowled me off my feet. I was completely enchanted, and have been ever since. Don't you know how you have turned my world upside down? I thought it obvious enough. I have followed you around to every social function of this infernal Season like a lap dog just because I was bursting so with pride to display you as mine."

"What about that wager?" she asked doubtfully.

"Ah, you know about that, do you?" he said. "Well, touché, my love. What about yours?"

"Oh," she said. "Well, that did not make any difference. I loved you regardless."

"And I loved you regardless," he said.

"Really?"

"Really. And I will add this. I believe that was the most fortunate double wager ever made, my love."

"Oh."

"Now, will you let me sleep, Henry?" he asked wearily,

peeking at her through one half-closed eyelid. "I have been living a celibate life for so long—with one memorable exception—that I fear I shall have to take this marriage very gradually again for a while. Advancing age, you know."

"No," she said. "I want to start finding out what pleases you. Is it this?" She leaned across him and blew a light kiss on his neck where it joined his shoulder.

"Minx," he commented. "I should have let you shoot Cranshawe and been hauled off to Newgate."

Iron-hard hands suddenly grasped her hips, and she found herself lifted up and deposited on top of his body.

"This might prove the death of me, my love," he sighed, "but I'll show you."

"Absurd!" she murmured into his ear.

## About the Author

Raised and educated in Wales, **Mary Balogh** now lives in Saskatchewan, Canada, with her husband Robert and her children Jacqueline, Christopher, and Sian. She is a school principal and an English teacher.

## JOIN THE *REGENCY ROMANCE* READERS' PANEL

Help us bring you more of the books you like by filling out this survey and mailing it in today.

1. Book Title: _____

   Book #: _____

2. Using the scale below, how would you rate this book on the following features? Please write in one rating from 0-10 for each feature in the spaces provided.

| POOR | | NOT SO GOOD | | | O.K. | | | GOOD | | EXCELLENT |
|------|---|---|---|---|---|---|---|---|---|---|
| 0 | 1 | 2 | 3 | 4 | 5 | 6 | 7 | 8 | 9 | 10 |

                                                              *RATING*

Overall opinion of book . . . . . . . . . . . . . . . . . . . . . . . . _____
Plot/Story . . . . . . . . . . . . . . . . . . . . . . . . . . . . . . . . . . . _____
Setting/Location . . . . . . . . . . . . . . . . . . . . . . . . . . . . . _____
Writing Style . . . . . . . . . . . . . . . . . . . . . . . . . . . . . . . . . _____
Character Development . . . . . . . . . . . . . . . . . . . . . . . _____
Conclusion/Ending . . . . . . . . . . . . . . . . . . . . . . . . . . . _____
Scene on Front Cover . . . . . . . . . . . . . . . . . . . . . . . . . _____

3. About how many romance books do you buy for yourself each month? _____

4. How would you classify yourself as a reader of Regency romances?
   I am a ( ) light ( ) medium ( ) heavy reader.

5. What is your education?
   ( ) High School (or less) ( ) 4 yrs. college
   ( ) 2 yrs. college ( ) Post Graduate

6. Age _____ 7. Sex: ( ) Male ( ) Female

Please Print Name_____

Address_____

City _____ State _____ Zip _____

Phone # ( )_____

Thank you. Please send to New American Library, Research Dept., 1633 Broadway, New York, NY 10019.